DOUGLAS WATT is a novelist and his his wife Julie and their three children. He won the Hume Brown Senior Prize in Scottish History in 2008 for *The Price of Scotland: Darien, Union and the Wealth of Nations* (2007). *Pilgrim of Slaughter* is the third in his series of ingenious murder mysteries set in 17th-century Scotland featuring lawyers John MacKenzie and David Scougall. The first two in the series were *Death of a Chief* and *Testament of a Witch*.

D1080992

By the same author:

Fiction
Death of a Chief (Luath Press, 2009)
Testament of a Witch, Luath Press (Luath Press, 2011)

History
The Price of Scotland: Darien, Union and the Wealth of Nations (Luath Press, 2007)

Pilgrim of Slaughter

DOUGLAS WATT

Luath Press Limited

EDINBURGH

www.luath.co.uk

First published 2015

ISBN: 978-1-910021-99-6

The paper used in this book is recyclable. It is made from low chlorine pulps
produced in a low energy, low emission manner from renewable forests.

Printed and bound by Bell & Bain Ltd., Glasgow

Typeset in 10.5 point Sabon

To Jamie

The Lord hath made all things for himself:
yea, even the wicked for the day of evil.
Proverbs 16:4

Acknowledgements

A special thanks to my wife Julie for her perceptive comments on an early draft of the text and all her love and support over the years. Thanks also to everyone at Luath Press.

The Main Characters

Davie Scougall, notary public in Edinburgh
John MacKenzie, advocate in Edinburgh, Clerk of the Court of Session
Elizabeth MacKenzie, his daughter
Archibald Stirling, Crown Officer
Sir George MacKenzie of Rosehaugh, Lord Advocate
Kenneth MacKenzie, Earl of Seaforth, chief of the clan MacKenzie
Colonel Ruairidh MacKenzie, brother of Seaforth
Alexander Leslie, Earl of Pittendean
David Leslie, Lord Glenbeath, eldest son of the Earl of Pittendean
Francis Leslie of Thirlsmuir, second son of the Earl of Pittendean
James Douglas, Duke of Kingsfield
Agnes Morrison
George Morrison, merchant
Alexander Stuart, son of the Laird of Mordington
Jean Stuart, his mother
Adam Lawtie, physician in Edinburgh
Peter Guillemot, French refugee, wig maker in Edinburgh
Maggie Lister, brothel madam
Andrew Quinn, perfumer from Dublin
Helen Quinn, his sister
Alexander Baillie of Lammington, laird
James Guthrie, minister
James Cockburn of Grimston, laird
Archibald Craig, Pittendean's writer
Robert Johnston, student at the College of Edinburgh
Isaac Black, doctor
John Graham of Claverhouse, Viscount Dundee

Historical Note
Scotland in 1688

THE SEVENTEENTH CENTURY was a time of bitter religious division across Europe which had its origins in the Reformation of the previous century when the Continent split into Protestants and Catholics.

In Scotland, two rival branches of the Protestant church – Episcopalian and Presbyterian – vied for domination. The Episcopalians, who were in power in 1688, believed in a church run by bishops and held a hierarchical view of society. The Presbyterians were democratic and puritanical in outlook, revering the National Covenant of 1638.

After the Restoration of the monarchy in 1660, Presbyterians refused to accept a church run by bishops and were persecuted by the government in an attempt to force them into conformity. They resorted to worshipping illegally in fields and hillsides at conventicles. Repression precipitated rebellions in 1666 and 1679 which were brutally crushed. Many Prebyterians fled into exile in the Netherlands, while others were packed off to the plantations in the Caribbean as indentured labour.

As a result, Presbyterians and Episcopalians hated each other. They both despised Roman Catholics who they viewed as servants of Satan. The Pope himself was the Whore of Babylon or the Antichrist. France was the major Catholic power in Europe at the time. In 1685 the French King Louis XIV revoked the Edict of Nantes, ending toleration for French Protestants (Huguenots). Thousands fled oversees with many settling in London and some in Edinburgh.

Catholics were a tiny minority in Scotland in 1688, perhaps only a few thousand individulas spread across the country, mainly in Highland clans and noble households. However, the popular perception was that they were becoming much more numerous, a feeling stimulated by high profile conversions among those who sought to curry favour with the King.

King James VII and II inherited the thrones of England, Ireland and Scotland on the death of his brother Charles II in 1685. By the time he became King he was an open Roman Catholic. His reign was a disaster. In the space of a few years he had alienated many of his subjects in the three kingdoms by his policies of extending toleration for Catholics. In Scotland, both Episcopalians and Presbyterians were horrified as the Mass, which they viewed as blasphemous, was celebrated in the centre of Edinburgh, Jesuit priests were established in the city and a Catholic printing press set up at Holyrood Palace. Among extreme Protestants, feelings of paranoia became a hunger for Catholic blood.

On 10 June 1688 the King's second wife, Mary of Modena, who was a Catholic, gave birth to James Francis Edward Stewart. The House of Stewart had a male heir. The King already had two Protestant daughters, Mary and Anne, from his first marriage. Protestants feared that the King's pro-Catholic policy would be extended, perhaps indefinitely. William of Orange, the Dutch Stadtholder, who was married to Mary, and revered as the upholder of Protestant rights in Europe, was encouraged to intervene. It was unclear if he would aim to influence the King by persuading him to change tack, or, as more radical Protestants hoped, seize the Crown for himself and his wife.

Over the autumn of 1688 the atmosphere in Edinburgh became increasingly frenetic as rumours circulated in coffee houses and taverns of an imminent invasion by William in the south of England. The town was already bursting at the seams, swollen by exiles returning from Holland, as well as an influx of radical Protestants from the south-west of Scotland.

The anti-Catholic mob was increasingly active on the High Street, burning effigies of the Pope, smashing windows and terrorising suspected Catholics. Secret Presbyterian associations met across Edinburgh, planning revolution against the King, while politicians schemed, hoping to benefit from any change of regime. The city was a powder-keg ready to explode.

Prologue

May 1688

THE KNIFE'S BLADE shines before me. I test its sharpness against my finger. The crowd on the hillside are shouting, exhorting me to be done with it, to get the job done. The man is still screaming. His white shirt is pulled up to reveal a lean grey belly.

He only knows me by sight. I have watched him many times. I have seen him in the court house where he works as clerk, where he aids those who abuse the Godly. I have watched him in the ale house, laughing, telling jokes to his creatures, while I ponder from my dark corner – that is the man I will kill.

'Get on with it,' one of them grunts. 'Soldiers will be here soon!'

I act for God and His people, the covenanted folk of Scotland, the abused flock, the crushed remnant. I see their faces around me, beckoning me to sacrifice. Some of the blessed are already in Heaven, cut down as they worshipped in the field by Claverhouse, vile servant of James Stewart, called by some King of Scotland, England and Ireland; slaughtered like lambs.

The man stops screaming. Does he sense a conflict within me? Does he not know with whose authority I act? There is no doubt in my soul. I simply savour the moment. I thank Him for the chance to avenge his poor blighted followers.

I look down on the taut belly, choosing a place for my dirk just above the spot where the cord connected him to his mother. This moment is predetermined from the beginning of time. There is nothing that can be done to save him. I plunge the knife into flesh. It slips through easily; penetrates deeply. For an instant there is no reaction from him or those who watch.

The blade is embedded in his body. We are conjoined by metal; the crowd hushed to silence. Then, blood spurts from the wound and screams rise from him and them. I thrust deeper, working up and down with my knife as his cries echo across the hills. The coils of his bowels steam before me; the bloody intestines of a vile sinner who has paid for his treachery.

I slam the blade into the earth between his legs. Forcing my hands into the cavity, I scoop up the viscera, holding them up for all to see. Each man and woman and child standing on the hillside will bear witness. Then, taking the knife again, I cut the ends and raise the guts above my head, dripping blood and excrement over my face. It is as holy water baptising me.

He has lost consciousness. The blood still gushes from the wound onto the grass of the hillside. I take up my knife again. There is still work to be done. There is still butchery in His name and I am a man skilled in the craft. I slash across the chest; place a boot on the body to give purchase; heave the rib cage open. Bones snap and flesh is ripped.

I cradle it in my hands, mesmerised by its pulsing. I slice through the vessels surrounding it. The blood gulps out like water from a pump. I hold it aloft.

Behold my people, behold the heart of Antichrist!

Screams of exaltation echo around the hillside.

I do God's work. I am saved. I am promised everlasting life from the start of the world. I was born to perform this act from the beginning of time. My name is written in the book of life from the foundation of the earth. I was born to kill Satan. I was begot to defeat Antichrist. I am God's agent of transformation.

An Incident on the High Street of Edinburgh

June 1688

EVERYTHING FOR AN afternoon's work was in place: inkhorn, paper, quills, wax. Scougall looked down on the legal instrument he was working on – a conveyance of land from John Nisbet to James Dickson, two of the burgh's merchants. It would be a long afternoon at the desk, but one he relished. There was nothing to disturb him, no awkward conversations with Papists, or painful thoughts about Elizabeth, although he found it impossible to push her completely out of his mind.

If only he could find a wife, the feelings for her might fade, easing the frustrations of body and spirit which he wrestled with day and night. He was ashamed to confess that he was more and more tempted down the path of self-abuse, his mind overwhelmed by illicit images. Such behaviour was postulated a sin of the first rank by some, though others regarded it as only a minor transgression, and a few blades as no sin at all. Major Weir's dalliance with beasts stood as a dreadful warning of the dangers of the unmarried state. He felt his face redden, despite being alone, and he asked God to forgive him such sinful thoughts. What was beyond doubt was that he needed a wife.

A knock at the door roused him from these reflections, and before he could shout 'enter', a young woman stood in front of him, soberly dressed in black cloak and dark gown with a blue bonnet on her head. She smiled warmly. 'Do you not remember me, Davie Scougall?'

He knew her at once. Agnes Morrison was a year or two younger than him, but much improved in looks by the gap of six years since they last met.

'It's been so long, Agnes,' he managed to splutter out. He was not prepared for a conversation with a woman. After a few embarrassing seconds, he offered her a chair beside his desk.

'You've done well for yourself, Davie,' she said in a half mocking tone with a look of mischief on her face. 'This is a far cry from the honest toun. I hear you are now acquainted with the great and good.'

Scougall thought of the Earl of Seaforth, with whom he was forced to dine that night. Surely she did not have this kind of acquaintance in mind. He had travelled far, perhaps too far, from the simple life of his parents in Musselburgh.

'I'm not changed... much,' he said as his face reddened again.

'You've changed, favourably so. You were a boy when I last saw you.' Unused to compliments, he did not know what to say. There was another uncomfortable silence.

'As you have too, Agnes,' he said finally. 'You look very fine,' but he immediately regretted being so forward.

'I come on a business matter.' Her expression became serious. 'Do you remember my brother George?'

Scougall recalled a boisterous youth a few years older than him, something of a bully in the school yard, with a large looming face.

'Your work as writer comes highly recommended. We've a few instruments for you, if you'll take them.'

He had plenty of work to be getting on with, but would happily work late for Agnes. She was changed into a fine-looking woman. 'What's the nature of the business?'

'As you know, we've suffered terribly since father was accused in the Rye House Plot. We fled Scotland like many others and took up residence in the Dutch Republic. Unfortunately he died a few years ago, joining mother in eternal bliss.'

'I'm very sorry to hear of their demise.'

'It's a terrible loss, but we must look to the future. Great change is afoot, Davie. The Indulgences allow us to return home. St Magdalene's Chapel is sold by the Council to our people. We Presbyterians have a place to worship in the heart of Edinburgh. It's like the days of the Covenant again. George and I decided to come back to our native soil. We wish to buy a property in Edinburgh where we can trade from. We need your help to obtain it.'

'I've always wanted to visit Holland,' Scougall mused. 'The

Dutch follow a sound path in religion and a profitable one in commerce.'

'You could not imagine a more magnificent trading metropolis than Amsterdam,' she replied. 'Everything under the sun can be purchased there. The bank is the safest in the world and there's a bourse where shares in companies are bought and sold. The Dutch are Godly also. They're a fine people, led by a noble prince.'

He listened attentively, impressed by the fluent way she spoke, observing her face carefully, drawn more and more into her serious, but lively, brown eyes.

'My brother wants to establish himself as a merchant in Edinburgh. We'll trade with Holland where we have many friends. All is change... all is flux. We must prepare, perhaps, for greater transformations.'

He nodded again. Scotland was an abused nation. The Stewart King James was a servant of Antichrist. But there were hopes of change. 'Do you think William will come?'

'We've seen the preparations with our own eyes; a fleet will sail.' She smiled, before continuing, 'My brother seeks an audience with the magistrates to obtain a licence for a shop. I'm looking forward so much to living in Scotland again. I've missed it, despite the wonders of Holland. I long for strolls by the Firth, watching the waves. Do you remember flying our kites on the sand?'

He could not remember flying a kite with Agnes; perhaps she was speaking in general terms, or thinking about someone else. What he did remember was her sharp tongue. She had teased him about his shyness at school. But he did not care. He was already captivated. God forgive him, he could not stop appraising the way she looked; her shapely figure and smiling face. She may have lacked the polished breeding of Elizabeth, the silks and jewels and perfumes, but she possessed a natural disposition which was equally appealing. He found himself feeling strangely light. He had not felt so happy since thrashing Hector Stoddart at golf on Leith Links.

'So you'll act as writer for us?'

Working for her family would bring him more than a few pounds. Had God sent her just as dejection threatened to cast him downwards into a spiral of sin?

'Yes, Agnes. It would be a great pleasure...'

A thunderous bang, so loud he could remember hearing nothing like it in the whole of his life, shattered the blissful moment, as the whole building shook. The sound was followed by screams outside on the street. He peered through the window, pressing his nose against the glass. There was a man lying only a few yards from the door. Another was being grappled to the ground.

'My God! Someone's been shot. Wait here, Agnes.'

'Don't endanger yourself, Davie.'

He climbed the few steps from his office in the basement of the tenement up onto the High Street. In front of him a young man was being pinned down. To the left, an older figure lay on his back attended by a servant. He knew the victim was James Douglas, Duke of Kingsfield.

'Fetch a doctor!' a voice screamed from the crowd.

The Duke was groaning in agony, the blue silk of his suit stained darkly at the chest. A long periwig had fallen from his head which Scougall picked up. He noticed the name Simon Tippendale on the label, one of London's most famous periwig makers.

'The Duke's shot!' a cry came from an onlooker. 'Papist bastards!' a woman's voice shrieked. A man waved his fist at the young man on the ground, screaming obscenities about the Pope and the Jesuits. 'Run the fuckin Papists oot o toon! This is the murderous rule of Antichrist!' The volume of abuse rose like the stink from a midden. 'The Papists have shot Kingsfield!'

'Whaur's the doctor?' Kingsfield's servant cried. The Duke was lying motionless, his old head resting in the man's hands.

Scougall recognised Adam Lawtie, a physician employed by Crown Officer Stirling, emerge from the throng. Kneeling beside the Duke he sought a pulse. After a minute or so, he shook his head.

Screams exploded from the crowd. 'Papists hae murdered Kingsfield! Papist sodjers will burn the city! Oor King is a Papist Traitor! The King's servant o the Whore of Babylon! The rule of Antichrist has come tae Scotland!'

Scougall had never heard such visceral hatred at close quarters before. From his attire, the man who was being restrained appeared of some means, probably from a landed family. A few yards away a pistol lay on the ground. The feeling of lightness was gone. Kingsfield was assassinated in broad daylight. He was known to be a supporter of the Presbyterians. There would be uproar in Edinburgh that night.

2

News of a Birth

THE MESSENGER STOOD at the doorway allowing his eyes to adjust to the gloom. Having spotted the man he sought at a table towards the back of the coffee house, he squeezed through the crowd, eager to unburden himself of the news.

A thin middle aged man looked up with alert eyes. He put his pipe down carefully on the table.

'Ah, Mr Stark. How are you?'

'I hae news, sir,' Stark spoke breathlessly. 'I've come aw the way frae Lammington today as fast as I could. I kenned you'd want tae be the first tae ken, sir.'

'News?' Lammington repeated. The others at the table stopped talking and looked up at Stark who gathered himself before speaking deliberately in a whisper. 'The King has a son, sir.'

'The King has a son,' Lammington repeated and then with more volume: 'The King has a son. James Stewart has a son.' There was a smile on his face.

One of Lammington's companions, an older man with a gaunt face, rose to his feet and roared. 'Our Papist King has an heir! Antichrist has a son!'

The news spread from table to table, provoking curses, screams, shouts and general discord. No one seemed pleased by the tidings.

'Do you know what the bairn's called, Mr Stark?' asked Lammington.

'I'm telt it's James Francis Edward Stewart.'

'Not another king called James,' said a man in a French accent wearing an enormous wig which dwarfed the other head-pieces around the table.

'Just like the French,' said another. 'Louis, Louis, Louis. James, James, James. It's always the same wi despots.'

'But she wasnae due yet. It's surely an imposter. It's an attempt tae help the King oot of his difficulties,' said the older man.

'Calm yirself, Grimston, be seated,' warned Lammington. 'Let's nae lose our heads. I thank you, for conveying such important tidings punctually, Stark. Here's something for your trouble. Now return hame and tell my wife I'm delayed in Edinburgh for a few mair weeks. There's business tae be done, important business.'

'The King will be strengthened by this, Lammington. He has two daughters and now a son. The succession is secured for a Papist,' said a thin man in an Irish accent.

'It may not be so, Quinn. The birth will nae be celebrated with enthusiasm in England or Scotland.' He took up his pipe again and began puffing slowly, savouring the tobacco. He looked animated by the news. Things were coming to a head at last, he thought. There was much to be done, but they would be ready. 'Don't lose heart, gentlemen. This may be the trigger we look for. It may encourage William tae intervene. We must continue wi our plans.' His voice dropped to a whisper. 'The boys on the street must be a little mair vocal in their condemnation of Antichrist.'

'Where's Johnston?' asked the Frenchman.

There was laughter round the table. 'He's still at the college, Mr Guillemot,'replied Lammington. 'He is very much the scholar, although vehement in his hatred o the Papist. They will be oot on the street when we have more intelligence. Any news of Black?'

'He's been released frae the castle,' announced Grimston.

Lammington stopped smoking and stared intently at the faces round the table. 'We must be ready, gentleman. The news frae London is good. The King is weak. The birth will encourage our brithers in the south. The Prince of Orange will sail soon. A revolution in the government will follow.'

3

A Letter for Rosehaugh

HE SAT AT the ancient desk sipping claret. He had never known before such utter disregard for sound policy. The King was antagonising everyone, even his closest supporters. The political situation was deteriorating at an alarming speed. He wondered if it had been a mistake to return to office as Lord Advocate. He could not resist being at the centre of things one final time. He was not yet ready for retirement to his country estates. But how was he to advise a King who would not listen, who only followed the advice of the fools who had converted to the Catholic religion? He sighed and poured himself another glass. Whatever happened, rebellion was treason. It could only lead to chaos.

He flicked through his correspondence on the desk; the usual communications from the Privy Council, intelligence reports from his agents, countless letters. One caught his eye. The writing was more florid than the rest, as if the writer had taken care with it:

To Sir George MacKenzie of Rosehaugh, Lord Advocate,
the Tolbooth, Edinburgh.

He put the other papers aside, broke the seal and read the following:

> *Scotland: haunt of the profane, den of iniquity, cavern of chaos, cradle of witches. I look down on you from a great height. I watch your black castle against the western sky, your tenements filthy with squalor, your tollbooths, kirks and palaces. I wander your closes, wynds, courts and vennels. Your King is the slave of Satan. Your King is besotted with the Whore of Babylon. Your King welcomes Antichrist to the heart of your realm where the blasphemous Mass is proclaimed.*

Hear the cries of the people. Edinburgh is a city awaiting deliverance, a synagogue of Satan. I hear your calls. I feel your agony and despair.

My children, I will free you from the chains of Antichrist. I will free you from the government of the Godless. I will liberate you from the plague of priests.

The black stone of the castle speaks to me. The stink of the streets speaks to me. Oh city renowned through Europe for nothing.

Until I returned to you, little land, forgotten, until I stirred you with my breath. You were forgotten by the world, small and insignificant, left alone to suffer the reign of Antichrist, abandoned, until I remembered you, until I was called by you, until I returned to wake you from your slumber.

I seek out your labyrinths of debauchery. I seek out your parlours of hypocrisy. I seek out your ministers with hearts of lust. I seek out your abusers, whoremongers, idolaters, warlocks, witches.

I seek out your great men hungry for mammon, lawyers crafty and covetous, doctors cheating the sick of their last pennies, servants despising their masters. I will bring them to account for their sins.

Let the fierce wind blow. Let the mighty wind blow. Let the gale of reformation blow, stirring you from lethargy, awakening you from this quagmire of atrophy. Oh nation burning and suffering in the pit, I will be as a wave among you, a great wave of the ocean, deep-formed within the mighty water. I will wash through you, sweeping your streets clean. I will cleanse you of the stain of Antichrist.

Rise like the sun, burning red. The time is at hand, oh my children.

Rise like a mighty sun. I bring transformation. I bring glorious revolution.

Rosehaugh shook his head in despair. It was the ranting of another fanatic. Scotland had enough of them these days. He folded the letter carefully and rose from his desk. On the way to the large press in the corner he stopped suddenly. There was the pain again, deep inside his stomach. It was becoming more frequent. He wondered how much time he had left. Whatever happened, he would struggle on. He opened a drawer and dropped the letter on top of a pile of other documents. Should he keep them or burn the lot? The mind of man was troubled indeed, angry and troubled.

4

Dinner at The Hawthorns

SCOUGALL'S EYES TOOK in the large collection of plate on MacKenzie's dresser. It was principally made of silver rather than pewter, a collection of bowls, cutlery, jugs and dishes engraved with hunting scenes of stags and hounds, surely worth a small fortune. In the centre was a round silver salver with the clan coat of arms embossed upon it, a mountain engulfed in flames with the legend *Luceo non uro* around it. Scougall translated the words to himself, pondering their meaning – I shine but do not burn. The light of reason rather than the flames of passion – that sounded like MacKenzie's philosophy of life. The plate showed he was a rich man; the pickings of the law were greatest for advocates at the top, but not for notaries like him. He wondered how much capital he could amass by the time he was MacKenzie's age of fifty-six.

They sat in the dining room at the back of the house where two sash windows looked onto the gardens. Water gurgled from a stone fountain in the gloaming. Across the table from Scougall sat Kenneth MacKenzie of Kintail, the Earl of Seaforth. He was only a few years older than him, perhaps in his late twenties, and did not look like a Highland chief, dressed in his blue silk suit and long periwig. His younger brother, Colonel Ruairidh MacKenzie, diagonally opposite, was even more splendidly attired in a scarlet suit, the latest fashion from Paris.

Elizabeth was wearing a vibrant green gown. She had eyes for Ruairidh only, a man who had fought in battlefields across Europe, and, according to his own account, played a vital role in every one. They made a fine pair, Scougall had to admit. Reason told him to lay his feelings for her aside; jealousy was a sin. But he could not help himself. Could it be possible that she would marry a Roman Catholic? He had heard rumours about his conversion but had not told MacKenzie. He wanted to warn her that the souls of her unborn children were endangered. But it was not his place and, after all, it was still possible the marriage might not happen. He felt his face burning red as he picked at his lamb ragout. He could not understand why MacKenzie insisted on torturing him. He had no business dining with Papists.

MacKenzie had set aside the black garb of the law for his best suit. Having drunk a number of glasses of claret, he was in relaxed mood, his conversation darting back and forwards between Gaelic and English, leaving Scougall feeling left out. Despite learning a few words, he understood little of the language of the Highlands. He nodded grimly as if he understood more.

At last MacKenzie addressed Seaforth in English. 'What do you make of the rumours about the Prince of Orange, my Lord?'

'It'll come to nothing, John.' Seaforth spoke in an unusual accent, influenced by the courts of Europe where he had spent much of his life, with little suggestion of a Scots brogue. 'The Stadtholder will not risk invasion,' he continued. 'Getting bogged down in a British war would play into French hands. The people of England and Scotland remain loyal to their King. His policy of toleration looks to a time when all religions are viewed as equal. He wishes men to follow their hearts in religion. Is that not unreasonable?'

'The aim of toleration is a worthy one,' replied MacKenzie, refilling the Earl's glass, 'but the manner of its introduction is unwise. The Indulgences have unsettled the King's supporters in Scotland, stirring up a hornet's nest. '

Scougall stole a look at Elizabeth who was deep in conversation with her fiancé. They had no interest in politics tonight.

'You're too pessimistic,' Seaforth continued. 'The lawyer always sees the bottle half empty. The world is changed. Seaforth is a Privy Councillor.' Scougall found his affectation of referring to himself in the third person annoying. 'He sits with the great men of the realm, administering the kingdom. He's raised to the Order of the Thistle and looked upon as a loyal servant of the King. The MacKenzies have never been so favoured. Tarbat is on the Council; Rosehaugh restored as Lord Advocate; a dozen advocates of our name prosper in Edinburgh, including yourself. We rival the Campbells as the most powerful family in the realm. Atholl is weak. Hamilton broods in London.' He stopped to sip his wine and emphasise what followed. 'A dukedom is talked of at court. Can you imagine it – the Dukedom of Ross restored, or the Dukedom of Seaforth established! What honour for the clan! What riches it may provide!'

MacKenzie nodded, but his expression had lost its playfulness. He reflected that aristocrats were always puffed up with their own importance, obsessed with obtaining honours at any cost. 'I believe the King's policies are foolish, my lord. Our country has no appetite for the Roman religion. The establishment of Jesuits in Edinburgh inflames the fanatics.'

'The fanatics are diminished since Renwick's execution. Those of a reasonable disposition may worship in private chapels. They've no need to scurry off to the hills.'

'What say you as a man who favours Presbytery, Davie?' asked MacKenzie.

Scougall had said little during the meal. He had to be careful what he said. Upsetting an earl would be a mistake, even a Papist one. 'The King's Indulgence has allowed many to worship in the manner they wish, though not all,' he said quietly. 'The situation has eased for Presbyterians who return from exile. They can listen to sermons in St Magdalene's Chapel. Only those who keep to the fields are persecuted.'

'There, John. Sensible words from your man. Toleration's at the heart of the King's policies. All should worship as they wish. I would've thought that you, as a man of reason, a devotee of the philosophy of the ancients, would support such a position.'

'I believe the King's policies aim to promote Papists rather than introduce toleration. King James is a follower of the French way of absolute rule. Toleration is a fine ideal, one which I believe in passionately. But much depends on the way it's introduced. The hearts and minds of the people must be changed before it's hoisted upon them. There's one clear lesson from history – the Scots despise having their religion tampered with by a distant king. On the death of his brother three years ago, King James had Scotland at his feet despite being a Papist. Recall the joyous celebrations on his succession. He's now hated by half the people in England and Scotland. Never was so much thrown away at so little cost.'

'What's he done to deserve his people's scorn?' Seaforth asked sharply.

MacKenzie could not stop himself. 'The people despise the appointment of Papists to the army and government. They scream of arbitrary rule by indulgence rather than parliament. They fear a standing army with Papist officers, while the Navy is neglected.

Trouble is brewing across these Kingdoms. The King would be well advised to halt his policies immediately.'

As he had done on countless occasions in the law courts, MacKenzie conquered his rising anger. His earnest expression melted into a smile. He did not want to push Seaforth too far. He was his chief, after all, and that still meant something, although not as much as it used to. He raised his glass. 'It may all come to nothing, my lord. Men's minds turn to other matters. The Prince of Orange cast his eyes back to war in Europe. Let's hope he does not sail for these shores.'

'I'll raise a glass to that,' said Seaforth.

Scougall could not bring himself to make the toast. He raised his glass obediently, but under his breath prayed for a fair wind to deliver William.

'Let me propose another,' said MacKenzie, moving the conversation away from politics. Tapping his glass with a spoon, he waited for Elizabeth and Ruairidh to finish their intimate conversation.

'Welcome to The Hawthorns. Let's hope a settlement will be reached soon!'

Scougall reluctantly toasted the couple who continued to have eyes only for each other. Visions of their wedding night flashed through his mind – Elizabeth's body the property of a Papist! He felt a deep desire to be away from The Hawthorns. He did not belong in such company. He yearned for the golf course away from troubling thoughts of politics and women.

5

A Mother's Despair

THE VIEW FROM her chamber always comforted her, the gardens in the foreground, the rolling hills beyond. Whatever happened in life, whatever trouble, whatever good or ill, the hills were there for her; the hills where she had played as a girl. She had watched them change with the seasons all her life.

She remembered hearing the news of her father's death when she was a child. He was slain in the battle of Philiphaugh, fighting with the great Montrose. She had idolised the Marquis as a girl. Many of his men viewed him like a God who was invincible in battle until the grim struggle on the banks of the Ettrick and Yarrow ended his remarkable series of victories.

Before the battle, the army had quartered on her family estates. Indeed, Montrose spent the night in their house, the small tower built by her ancestors, sleeping for a couple of hours in the blue chamber where his portrait now took pride of place – a copy of a painting by a Dutch artist showing him in black armour. His words to her were etched on her memory, 'Your father's a loyal man, Jean. He serves me and his King'; as was the recollection of his cheek on hers as he kissed her farewell.

She had wished with all her heart that she could have married him, even though he was already wed, and some said he had no time for the caresses of women. She had wished it so much that the remembrance of her passion brought a flush to her cheeks. She would have done anything to change things. Montrose was noble and gentle, despite being a man of war, while she was married to a brute. She had learned there was nothing noble about her husband on her wedding night. At least he spent most of his time fighting in Flanders. She had prayed many times, God forgive her, that a Papist bullet would find his gullet.

She tried to direct her thoughts down other routes, avoiding the pain of the present. But she could not do so for long. Her son's portrait was also on the chamber wall, painted when he was sixteen. Pain crushed her, taking the strength from her legs. She dropped to her knees, letting out a deep moan as she fought back tears. How could he have done this to her?

He was unlike the other children of the parish, shy and thoughtful, book-loving, eschewing violent games, avoiding the hunt. She had doted on him too much, spoiling him. He was the focus of all her love, for there were no other children despite her husband's loveless efforts. Her womb remained barren to spite him.

The news of his conversion was like a knife in her heart. She perceived in an instant what trouble it would bring. Others were doing likewise, even some of the great men in the land, like Perth and Melfort, turning to Rome to seek favour with the King. But however much she rationalised it, telling herself that he might be rewarded at court in London, or find a position as a man of business for one of the Papist lords, the thought that her only son was a follower of Rome disturbed her to the core of her being.

When her husband found out, he had beaten the boy senseless. She had feared for his life, so violent was the attack. He had accepted the blows almost with pleasure and she was forced to throw herself between them to stop his kicks. The boy spent a week in bed recovering and while he lay in his chamber, she had tried all means of persuasion, offering him travel in Europe, the chance to remain at court in London, even though they could not afford it, the opportunity to follow any profession he desired, if he would abandon the Whore of Babylon. Her husband left for his regiment saying he wanted no more to do with him. He was no longer his son.

She had asked the minister to talk with Alexander in an attempt to turn him from his folly, but all persuasion pushed him further into the arms of Antichrist. She wondered what sins she had committed to have been given such a husband and such a son. But she could think of none, other than a little vanity as a young woman which was entirely crushed out of her, for she now cared nothing for her own fate.

She had pleaded with him, begged him on knees; prostrated herself before him, saying she would do anything if he would change his mind, if he would reject the priests who were practising in Scotland, if he would return to the fold of the Protestant church.

But he only smiled at her. He could not change his mind. He was happy for the first time in his life, content with himself at last. All he asked was that she accept his decision.

Then he was gone, she knew not where. Perhaps he was off to live with friends in Edinburgh or London or in overseas lands. She was left with nothing but the small estates which she managed for her husband who cared little for land or tenants.

The hills were her only consolation. Their bleak beauty reflected her own despair.

For months she heard nothing and she wondered if she would ever see him again. Then, a few days ago, a letter arrived. It was a strange epistle, asserting his love for her, but passionately proclaiming that he sought to serve God; that he must do a great deed to further the cause of the true religion. She was not to worry, all would be well in the end.

She felt a great weight of foreboding as she read it, for she sensed in his words the certainty of the fanatic. God knew what he would do. He was lost to her. She had no one left in the world. But she was still a mother. She must travel to Edinburgh where the letter was posted. She would bring him all she had left: love and tenderness. She would try one last time to persuade him.

6

The Music of the Virginal

MACKENZIE RECALLED HIS wife's proficiency on the instrument. She would play in the evenings, while he read beside her. They were blissful times. It felt like someone else's life. But he sat in the same chair in the same room. Where was it she had gone?

Looking up now and again from his Cicero, he had believed he was the luckiest man alive. Watching her belly swell week after week, their contentment in the life they had made together. But if there was one law in which he believed, it was that everything changes; good times lead on to bad, and sure enough, his fortune deserted him.

She had gone into labour at four o'clock in the afternoon. It was their first child and a very long one. He waited in the library beneath for hour after hour, listening intently. Finally there was the noise of a child, then a dreadful silence. The expression on the midwife's face still haunted him twenty years later. Her forlorn expression greeted him when he woke each morning; her words were implanted in his memory. 'I'm sorry, sir.'

Before that day, he had lived a blessed life. But the years since were a long road of despair. Sometimes, life was unbearable, so great was the pain of loss. His desire for self-destruction was almost overpowering. Somehow he had not succumbed to the darkness. He went on like a clock or a machine. The dullness of the law was an antidote to the agony. He looked after his daughter, watching her grow into a beautiful young woman. The years passed – nineteen since his wife had died.

Where was it she had gone? Was she still somewhere? Was her essence preserved somewhere – in heaven? If there was a heaven, she would surely be waiting for him. But how could there be one? He saw in his mind's eye the black fleck of a bird far away against a sky drained of colour, circling, waiting to come nearer.

He watched his daughter, Elizabeth, her straight back and nimble hands on the virginal. He felt unsettled. It was not the talk of rebellion, of replacing one king with another. He faced a personal decision of crucial importance for her happiness. She would leave The Hawthorns with her husband and become the lady of Brahan Castle. She had been the lodestone of his life, the one thing that could draw him out of the pit. Who would do so when she was gone? The thought of her departure was a physical pain. There was something else. He had begun to feel uneasy about Seaforth's brother Ruairidh. There were rumours in town which had brought turbulence to his mind. According to gossip, he was not only a Papist but active in the promotion of the religion. The moment he heard this he knew it was true, although he had been assured by Seaforth that his brother passed as an Episcopalian and thought little about religion. If that had been the case, he would have signed the papers on his desk with no concern. But the marriage of Elizabeth to a Catholic was another matter. It would have serious ramifications. His first instinct was to call it off and face the wrath of his chief, but upsetting Seaforth was problematic; he was still a powerful figure in the Highlands, and highly favoured by the King because of their shared religion. There was also Elizabeth to consider. She was set on the match. The dashing young soldier had swept her off her feet. He would have to tread carefully.

She had stopped playing. 'You look worried, father.'

'These are dangerous times, my dear. Edinburgh's full of rumours. The Prince of Orange has prepared a fleet. A new regime might bring about a change of church government.'

'You'd still have your clients. They might need you all the more. You're not a Papist.'

'I'm no Papist. But I'm no supporter of Presbytery. There are always winners and losers at such times. I might be ousted as Clerk of the Session. If Presbytery is restored, Episcopalians will not be looked on favourably, that's the nature of politics.'

She seemed little concerned about the point he was making.

'The Earl of Seaforth might find himself under suspicion,' he continued. 'It might prove difficult for Ruairidh.'

The mention of Ruairidh's name roused her interest. She turned to face him. 'He's a soldier, father. He would still find service in the army.'

'But with whose army?'

'What do you mean?'

'If he was thought to incline towards Rome, he might not be able to serve in an English or Scottish regiment.'

'He's no Papist.'

'Do you know that for certain?' He could not put it off any longer, he had to tell her; she would hear it from her friends. 'There's talk... there's talk in town... there's talk in town that he's converted.'

'What talk!' she snapped. 'He cares nothing for religion.'

'Life might be difficult with such a husband, my dear.'

'Are you saying I should not marry him?' There was anger and fear in her voice.

'Of course not.' He rose from his chair and walked over to her. It was difficult to be honest with the ones you loved. He spoke gently, placing his hand on her shoulder. 'We must be careful, that's all. We need to delve more deeply into the matter.'

'I care not if he's a Papist, Presbyter or Mohammedan!' she screamed.

He gave her his hand but she did not take it. Rising abruptly, she swept past him out of the room.

He sighed, regretting his lack of tact. But there was no polite way of dealing with the issue. The marriage was a political event which would have repercussions for them all. He could not give his blessing if Ruairidh was a Papist. He would never have begun negotiations if he had known. A few legal loopholes could delay the process, of course. It was hardly time for a wedding with the mood darkening on the streets.

He looked out of the window. The sun was dropping behind the garden wall. Birds were circling ominously in the sky, probably crows. There was the familiar feeling of something stirring within him; of a black knot coalescing in the pit of his stomach. He closed his eyes. He felt tightness in his temples, a hint of pain. He saw the bird transforming from speck to creature, filling his mind.

He took his seat again, rubbing his brows, breathing deeply. His melancholy was returning, attacking him just when he needed a clear mind. He must talk to Ruairidh soon, but he would proceed carefully. His opposition must not drive them to elope. He could not bear the pain of losing her entirely. As he watched the sun dip below the wall, he knew that he would prefer she converted to Rome than lose her altogether.

7

Dr Black Secures a Loan

LAMMINGTON DREW ON his pipe, inhaling deeply, watching him approach up the slope. He must be careful to conceal his contempt for him. He could not understand why he was so revered in William's court, while hundreds of loyal Presbyterians were overlooked. But the meeting was not about politics. It was about money. Love of money is the root of all evil. But he did not love money; he was no sinner. Money was power. Money was always in demand. Money was capital. If Black wanted a loan he would price it like any other, work out the likelihood of repayment. A memory of impoverished exile in the slums of Groningen flashed through his mind. Picking the wrong side could be costly, but this time he was on the right one, God had assured him.

Black walked deliberately, placing his boots down carefully on each step, his cane supporting him.

'Good morning, Lammington.'

He was out of breath after the climb. It was just as he liked it. He observed him carefully from head to toe, weighing him up, not as a man, but as an asset. His wig was expensive, as was the dark coat, the breeches and boots – all spoke of quality. He did not practice his craft of medicine but travelled back and forth relentlessly between The Hague and Edinburgh, between The Hague and London. He must have a pension from someone. He must have another source of income.

'It's a fine day, sir,' said Lammington. 'The view of Edinburgh is particularly fine frae Calton Hill. I prefer to do business here rather than the coffee house or tavern. No one can overhear us.'

'I'll get straight to the point,' began Black. 'Things are at a crucial juncture. My time in the castle is testament to that. I'm owed money by a number of rascals who are slow in payment, so I must raise something myself. I've heard you can provide funds at a reasonable interest rate as we share the same political viewpoint.'

Lammington smiled urbanely. 'I'm aye happy doing business with fellow Presbyterians, but I must ask a few questions first. I'm nae an advocate or writer. I don't lend by bond. I don't demand guarantors, witnesses or documents signed and sealed. I deal only by word of mouth and handshake. I must receive payment on the allotted dates.'

'I understand. Your business is not held back by administration.'

'You must answer me honestly, Dr Black. If I find out otherwise I'll demand immediate return of the funds advanced.'

'Ask anything of me. I'm an honest man with friends in high places, the highest, as you know. I've kissed the hand of the Prince of Orange countless times.'

'How much do you want tae borrow?' asked Lammington.

'£500.'

'Scots or sterling?'

'Sterling, sir. My bawbess will not be accepted in Amsterdam or Groningen.'

'What assets do you hae as security?'

Black smiled. 'I'm my best asset, sir. As you know, I've the ear of William. I've a small property in The Hague given to me by the Stadtholder providing an income of about £100 per annum. I also have significant sums lent out to a number of men of quality.'

'Would I ken any of these... men of quality?'

Black was annoyed by the question. He did not like begging from the likes of Lammington. He was nothing more than a bonnet laird from the Borders, while he was the grandson of the Earl of Tullochbrae. But he needed money or he might be imprisoned again. He could not risk being locked up at such a vital time. He had to be at the centre of things.

'I'm owed substantial sums by the Earl of Argyll, Lord Tarbat and Viscount Grindlay.'

Lammington raised his eyebrows. 'I believe they are nae reliable in their repayments. Let me see... I'm willing to lend the sum of £500, a very substantial one, at an annual rent of £120.'

'That's a high rate indeed, sir.'

'Take it or leave it, Dr Black. That's my only offer. If you decide tae tak it I'll tell you my terms.'

Black tapped his stick on the ground. He felt dejected for a moment. He, the personal friend of Carstares, was reduced to borrowing from scum like Lammington. But he would not dress as a pauper. He must have money for wine, women and the table.

'I'll take it, Lammington. I've no choice.'

'I'll provide the sum on the fourth day of August at eleven o'clock in St Giles Kirk. Thereafter you must pay me £10 on the same day each month. If you're late with ony payment the annual rent doubles the following month. If you're late again, I'll be forced tae recover the original sum... by ony means.' Lammington looked straight into his eyes. Black saw for the first time his craft. 'And there's one final condition,' Lammington smiled.

'What's that, sir?'

'In the association you will side with me rather than Thirlsmuir or Grimston.'

'I could not agree to such a thing... politically I must remain a free agent. I'll not become the creature of any faction!'

'Then you'll have nae money, sir.'

Black realised he had no choice. No one else in the city would lend him a penny. He was trapped, ensnared by an upstart moneylender. But when William came he would be rewarded handsomely. He would repay the debt and avenge himself on this petty usurer.

8

Confession of an Assassin

SCOUGALL SAT IN the Flanders Coffee House reading the latest pamphlet. There were rumours that the King was to bring Irish troops to pacify Scotland and that William sought to reform the government rather than seeking the crown. If King James did not come to an accommodation, he would take the throne with his wife, Mary, James's daughter. The people in London did not view an invasion as a Norman Conquest by another William, but as deliverance from the Papist yoke. On the King's Birthday no guns were fired from the Tower of London. Indeed, the sun was eclipsed at its rising, the signal of the victory of William the Conqueror against Harold at the Battle of Hastings. This was held as a good omen and there was expectation among the people of the arrival of William's fleet in a matter of days.

He finished his coffee, left the sheet on the table and made his way to MacKenzie's lodgings in Libberton's Wynd, an apartment of rooms on the third floor of a tenement just off the High Street.

MacKenzie was working in his study. 'I need to visit a client, Davie. Alexander Stuart, son of the Laird of Mordington.'

'The assassin, sir?' Scougall was shocked to hear the name of Kingsfield's killer.

'I've overseen the family's affairs for years. His mother is travelling to Edinburgh from the family estates. His father is a soldier on the Continent. I need to see him this morning, but first let's breakfast.'

The Tolbooth was an ancient stone conglomeration on the High Street beside St Giles Kirk, a couple of minutes' walk away. The city councillors met behind its ancient walls, while prisoners languished in its dark cells. They were shown into a stinking windowless chamber lit by a couple of candles where a young man sat at a stained table. He was a few years younger than Scougall, perhaps in his early twenties, dressed in a finely cut but filthy suit. He wore no periwig, so his thin face, bulging blue eyes and shock of fair hair were visible in the flickering candlelight.

MacKenzie asked Scougall to record Stuart's words in shorthand.

'Tell us what happened on the sixteenth of October, Alexander?' he asked.

The young man spoke slowly without emotion. 'At thirty minutes after ten I rose from my seat in the Royal Coffee House. I walked up the High Street and waited at the entrance of Foster's Wynd. I cocked my pistol in the shadows, keeping it hidden in my jacket. I had to wait about ten minutes before I saw him walking towards me with his servants. I sauntered down the street, cradling the gun under my coat. When he was about five steps away, I removed it and fired at his heart. God's work is done, I said to myself.'

Scougall was disturbed by the cool manner in which he confessed.

'I provided Mr Stirling with the same statement,' Stuart continued. 'I don't know why my mother has asked you to act on my behalf. I've made my confession. Kingsfield deserved to be slain. Now I must die.'

'There are a few legal matters to tidy up,' MacKenzie began in a perfunctory tone as he observed him carefully. 'Why did you do it?' he asked calmly.

'The Duke opposed the King's policy of toleration. He was an enemy of the true Catholic Church. I acted with authority.'

'Whose authority?'

'With the highest authority.'

'God told you to kill Kingsfield in cold blood?'

'Our King seeks toleration for all his subjects. Kingsfield stood against this. He sought our continued persecution.'

'Your mother will be here soon, Alexander. She travels north,' MacKenzie added.

Scougall wondered what agony she must be experiencing, what disgrace – the conversion of a son to Rome was humiliation for a devoutly Protestant family. Stuart's father fought against the Papist on the Continent.

'We'll have to send word to your father. It'll be terrible news for him,' said MacKenzie.

His mention roused Stuart from his lethargy. 'Do you mean my conversion to the true faith or the slaying of Kingsfield?' There was a bitter smile on his face.

'It'll be terrible news to learn his only son's to be executed for murder.'

'My father cares nothing for me. He hates me and I despise him.' There was finally emotion in his voice. 'He's an emissary of the Devil, the darkest rogue. He's abused us all his days. Now I have revenge!'

'You committed murder to spite your father?' asked MacKenzie.

'I sought to serve God and the true Church. My father is irrelevant.'

'What did you mean by him abusing you?'

'I don't have to answer your questions. I've nothing more to say on the matter. I killed Kingsfield. There are a score of witnesses to the slaughter.'

'How did you know when and where to find him?' asked Scougall.

'I was told by God.'

'Someone must have told you.'

'I was told by God.'

MacKenzie shook his head. 'We'll see to your affairs as your mother requests, pay your debts and collect all that's due from your debtors. Is there anything else you want from us?'

Stuart looked down at his hands, gazing at a ring, turning it gently round a skeletal finger. MacKenzie's eyes were drawn to the large blue gemstone.

'There's one thing. I want my final words printed so all may hear the truth.'

'That will cause trouble, Alexander. It'll draw attention to the Papists in town when it's best they lie low,' said MacKenzie firmly, annoyed by the arrogance of the young fool.

'We've no wish to lie low, sir. We've been silent too long, accepting persecution. We've put up with the rule of a corrupt church without fighting against it.'

'You think nothing of your mother, boy?' There was a flash of anger in MacKenzie's voice. 'She's your flesh and blood. She'll be left alone with your father... when you are... gone.'

This last word seemed to make Stuart pause for reflection. 'It can't be helped. She'll join me, in time. But I must serve God first. My dying words will be published. I must speak directly to the people of Scotland; tell them they can worship in the way they wish, celebrate the Mass without disturbance or threat of arrest; raise their children in the faith. I believe she'll understand in the end.'

'As your legal adviser, I recommend strongly that you don't have any statement printed. If you're inclined, make a confession to your friends in a private letter which may be published at a later date. Write to your mother proclaiming your love for her. Don't have your dying words printed. Only the mob will take sustenance from them. For your mother's sake…'

'I serve God, not my mother,' Stuart said resignedly.

MacKenzie rose from his chair, glowering down at him. 'Do you understand nothing, boy! You'll be tortured by the council! You'll be forced to tell them everything in the end!'

'God will protect me. I don't fear torture.'

'If you don't give the names of those who helped you, they'll put you to the Boot or Screw. There's nothing I can do to stop it. Rosehaugh will argue that the security of the realm is threatened. The government will want the names of all the conspirators.'

'There are none. There was no conspiracy. I was told by God what I should do.'

It had not occurred to Scougall that Stuart would be tortured. The devices were appalling: the Screw ripped out fingernails; the Boot crushed the leg to pulp. Few did not talk under such agonising assault. He wanted to feel pity for him for the pain he was to suffer. But his arrogance was palpable. He cared nothing for Kingsfield's kin. He cared nothing for his own mother. He was a foolish Papist who plotted against the Protestant religion. If he was not killed, he would murder again. Papists would destroy everything created since the Reformation.

'For the last time, I ask you not to publish anything.' The anger was gone from MacKenzie's voice.

'I insist upon it, sir. As my man of business, you'll attend to it or I'll employ another.' Now Stuart's eyes flashed with anger.

'You imbecile – you ignorant fool – you've had all the benefits of the laird's life, but you've chosen the path of the knave. You're nothing but a puppet whose strings are pulled by others.' Then MacKenzie switched to Gaelic: '*Amadan na mì-thoirt, bhiodh meas duine ghlic air nam biodh e'na thosd.* The poor fool would pass for a wise man if he held his tongue.' The words calmed him, his anger melting to sympathy. 'I'm sorry for you, Alexander. I'm truly sorry for you. There's nothing more I can do.'

9

An Opportunity for Davie Scougall

SCOUGALL WAS DELIGHTED to find a note from Agnes when he got back to the office, informing him that her brother George wanted to meet him that afternoon. He sent a message back saying that it was convenient and spent the rest of the morning nervously working on his instruments, although he found it difficult to concentrate. From the time he had left her on the High Street after the killing of Kingsfield, he had thought of little else. Elizabeth was now a distant star, flickering on the edge of his vision, but out of reach. Another brighter one had appeared in the sky.

He was not used to entertaining guests so he prepared his office carefully, placing two chairs near his desk, one borrowed from Robbie Dundas who rented the chamber next door. He gave the floor a more vigorous sweep than usual, left the door open to air the room and bought some refreshments in the Luckenbooths. He was not sure if they would take a glass of wine, not knowing how pious they were, but he did not want to seem inhospitable, so he left a bottle in the press where he could retrieve it easily if required. He also purchased a few pies which he left on a tray.

He spent the rest of the morning gazing out of the window. The city was getting busier every day. Folk were arriving from all corners of the kingdom or returning from Holland with rumours of invasion. Everyone had a different view on the timing and size of William's armada, about what it would mean for Scotland, for Presbytery and the King. The rabble on the street was inflamed by a myriad of grievances, which now included the slaying of Kingsfield. There were sightings of more Papists, including Irish soldiers and Jesuits, although he had seen no evidence of any, only hundreds of Presbyterians flocking to the city, hoping to hasten the return of a Godly settlement to the church. Students from the College, artisans, apprentices, merchants and writers, were out on the street every night to the beat of the drum, usually after a few pints of ale. They marched up and down, chanting and cursing as they decried the Papist. He supported the cause, but did not approve of such conduct, especially the swearing. Nonetheless, it felt like a storm was brewing. He could hardly believe Jesuits celebrated the Mass in the very heart of Scotland. How could the King allow such a thing? He was a disciple of the Whore of Babylon himself. Scotland had a Papist king. It was just as Shaftesbury had warned during the exclusion business.

Scougall came from a long line of Presbyterians, loyal followers of the Covenant who believed Scotland was a covenanted nation, with a special relationship to God, like the Jews. Episcopalians like MacKenzie and Stirling supported bishops in a Protestant Church. To Scougall, an episcopal structure was only a step away from Popery. He wondered how his friendship with them would be viewed if there was a change of government or if he was suspected of half-hearted support of Presbytery. And then there was Elizabeth. Marrying into a Papist family at such a time was a terrible mistake, even if her future husband was the brother of a chief.

The appearance of Agnes through the door abruptly ended his reflections. Behind her was the tall figure of her brother, George Morrison. As he rose, Scougall knocked over his inkhorn, spilling the dark liquid onto a letter as he blurted out a greeting. He hated himself for being such a clumsy oaf. He was trying above all to impress them.

'You've not changed much, Davie Scougall! Always colliding with something!' Morrison shook his hand enthusiastically. Scougall recalled the youth who had bullied him in Musselburgh school yard.

He was about to reply that he was a notary public who had golfed with a viscount, when he saw Agnes's smiling face and joined in their laughter. Returning the inkhorn to an upright position, he mopped up the ink with a rag.

'I've not spilled ink in many years! And on a letter to the Earl of Strathmore!'

'You've moved up in the world, Davie! It's been too long.' Morrison gave him a slap on the shoulder. Scougall recalled a dead arm from the same hand in the far off days of childhood. He put it to the back of his mind. All children were cruel in some manner.

'I'm honoured to welcome you. Please be seated.'

Scougall stole a quick look at Agnes. His first impressions had not been wrong. She was bonnie indeed.

'Can you believe we've been away for six years,' said Morrison, taking a seat. 'My deepest regret is that my parents didn't live to see their native land again. But it's so good to be back in Edinburgh. I think Agnes has told you of our fortunes.'

'It's justice to see those forced into exile returning home,' said Scougall.

'They were difficult years. But I didn't waste my time. I studied the Dutch merchants carefully in Amsterdam. It's time to apply what I've learned in Scotland. Our land's been held back too long.' Morrison lowered his voice to a whisper as if there might be someone else in the room to overhear. 'The Stewart Kings have enslaved us. But we'll apply ourselves whatever happens. There's nothing stopping us, only our caution. We'll have companies in Scotland too!'

Scougall wondered why he kept saying 'we'. 'Companies?' he repeated.

'I want to establish a company of merchants in this city like the Dutch and English. The Dutch East India Company sends ships to the Indies each year which return with holds full of spices. The profits are huge for those who invest their money. That's what we can do here, Davie. I see from your face you're perplexed. I run ahead of myself. Let me explain. First, I'll apply our capital to the purchase of a shop, for which we require your services as writer. Once I'm settled as merchant, we'll launch a company by selling shares. Think of it – two Musselburgh lads rising together. In time the venture might encompass the globe.' He let out a bellowing laugh before his face adopted a serious demeanour. 'Money will beget money and trade will beget trade to the end of time, as I've been told by the great William Paterson.'

'How am I to be employed?' Scougall was surprised but delighted by what he was saying. He had never heard of Paterson.

'I want you to be my man of business; my right hand man responsible for the legal side of our endeavour. That is, if you want to.'

'Man of business,' Scougall repeated, parrot-like. The phrase had a certain ring to it – certainly more exalted than notary public. Morrison's words had kindled something in him which he had not known existed. He had ambition, after all, although most believed he had none. Known as dull Davie Scougall, he was reliable with the pen, and a good swinger of a golf club, but often dismissed as a man of few words. He could not rouse a congregation like a minister or plead for a client in court like an advocate. But perhaps he could rise? Was it not time to diversify his interests from the law? The thought of being stuck in a tiny office for the next forty years suddenly appeared tiresome compared to the vista of global trade. He had never left Scotland, but now he might travel to London or Amsterdam, perhaps even America or the Indies. In time he might become David Scougall, Esquire, ultimately Sir David Scougall. The flame of ambition burned stronger as he turned to look at Agnes's smiling face. The prospect of marriage to her would be the icing on the cake, like a hole in one at the seventh on Leith Links.

10

A Customer for Maggie Lister

SHE CAREFULLY RUBBED each coin between thumb and forefinger, admiring each: a rix dollar, pound, bawbee, shilling, penny; each accounted for, each marking a triumph.

God kenned she had worked haird, hairder than maist, surviving six doses o the pox, two stillborn bairns, beatings frae countless men. She would keep working till she had enough, then she was aff, awa frae aabody who kenned Maggie Lister, Madam Lister, the hoor. It was aw about money aifter all. Naething else mattered in the scheme o things, awthing was valued in siller.

What did they ken about her life, the wee scabs that shouted at her on the street? When she got hold of ane she wisnae feart tae clout them haird, batter them wi her stick. The wee shites! What did they ken about her, born in this god-fearing city o hypocrites fifty years afore, illegitimate, a bastard bairn, unwanted by her faither, a gentleman, so her mither telt her; her bonnie mither a servant tae a merchant, poor but honest, guid like, no a hoor like her dochter. But her bonnie mither was deed o plague when she was ten and she was left with naebody. The merchant was nae a bad creature, but he fell on haird times himself and could nae langer afford tae keep her. She was left tae fend for herself with no kin an only a few rags tae her name. She tried tae work honourably, but there was nane for her. It was the time when the ministers had power over aw, a dark time of fear. She was starving, living in a wee hovel with ither bairns frae the streets, poor orphaned bairns like herself. It was only poor orphaned bairns o merchants who were taken in at Heriot's Hospital, nae scum like her. She spent time in the poorhoose but she hated it and ran awa.

Then one nicht a gentleman stopped her in a wynd, offering a shilling. She still minded the coin shining in her hand and what it offered – food and warmth for a few days, a pint o ale; a pie or two.

She did what he asked, for the coin was already in her pocket.

He took her tae a dark corner of a stinking close, felt her breasts, undid his belt and telt her tae gae doon and suck. She did as he asked, trying nae to retch before the seed came ontae her hands like a dug's slaverings.

Men were just like dugs, guid fir naething dugs, willing tae rut onytime with onything. Aw men were the same, lords and ministers, lawyers and lairds, mindless dugs worth naething in the scheme of things.

She learned what it took to get the work over quickly, just a few words would dae, a few words were aw it took whispered in their lugs, a few words and they were puppies, most of them. A few were bastards who would beat ye fir taking their enjoyment too quick, or just wanted tae kick a woman cause they hated aw that lived on the earth, bleak men with nae an ounce of gentleness in them. But God had given her strength in her airms and legs. She kenned the wynds and vennels like the lines on her hands. She could disappear intae a darkness of secret ways.

Ten years she'd worked the streets as hoor, then in the bawdy hoose o Jean Gangie and when Jean was in her coffin she claimed the howff as her ain and it became Maggie Lister's. She stopped serving the dugs and looked aifter her own lasses, counting the pennies they earned and taking her cut. She knew maist o the men in toon who hungered for a hoor. Why did God make Man such a shallow creature, and poor woman, receptacle of his sin, if it was sin at all?

A bell rang above her head. She went through in her mind who she had tae offer. Jenny was nae weel; Jessie six months wi child. Perhaps the new lass would dae, she was a bit strange looking, with an uncanny face, but she had spirit. It would be something new for a regular. They aw liked fresh meat now and again.

A series of faces flashed through her mind as she descended the steep spiral staircase – some of the lasses she had kenned over the years, a long list of deed girls by beatings, births and pox. How could God allow it all? She didna ken.

Having looked through a tiny hole in the door, she pulled back two bolts and heaved it open. She was always canny about who she let in, years of experience had taught her maist of the danger signs.

He staggered in slightly drunk, smiling at her. 'What do you have for a poor man on this summer's night, my dear? I'm inflamed with passion. My soul's burning for it.' She looked down at his stick; the exotic carving on the handle drawing her attention.

A passion in his soul! She shook her head. 'Come away in, sir.' She led him up the stairs. 'Have a seat in the howff. I'll pour you a glass. Let me hae a wee word with the new girl, a sonsie lass.'

'I'm honoured,' he slurred.

'A refugee frae the persecution in France, sir. You'll be the first to hae her in the kingdom of Scotland.'

11

Application of the Boot

STUART WAS SLUMPED on a chair at the side of the room, a metal contraption round his left calf and foot. A group of serious looking men sat at a large table watching him.

'I'll ask you one more time,' Rosehaugh spoke calmly from his seat. 'Who told you to murder Kingsfield?' He knew that in a few minutes the pathetic creature would reveal everything.

Stuart bowed his head and began to pray hoarsely in Latin. One of the councillors, a small man with sharp effeminate features, rose to his feet abruptly. A large sword hung at his side and two long pistols were suspended in holsters from his belt. 'Apply it now. Let's get it over with.'

'Thank you, my lord Claverhouse. I'm conducting proceedings as Advocate,' replied Rosehaugh curtly. He found the little soldier disagreeable, although for some reason the King held him in high regard. His majesty was not a good judge of character.

Claverhouse took his seat, muttering under his breath.

Soldiers were always impatient, thought Rosehaugh. He nodded to the hangman who turned a wooden peg at the side of the Boot. A high pitched howl echoed round the chamber. Some of the councillors looked away. A number had not attended, providing a series of feeble excuses: business, illness, toothache. The weak did not have the stomach for statecraft. The Boot was a brutal, ugly business. But it was effective. Torture could only be justified under extreme circumstances. The security of the state was threatened by fanatics like Stuart. He had tortured Presbyterians and now he would torture Papists. He nodded again to the hangman.

The peg was turned another notch, accompanied by horrific screams. Beneath the contraption, blood oozed onto the floor under the mangled leg; bone, muscle and vessels God had created, torn and ripped asunder. Stuart would never walk again. But he would have little need of his legs. He would be carried to his execution. A cry of despair echoed round the chamber. The peg was turned again – another howl, piercing, horrific, hellish.

'I'll tell all!' gasped Stuart. 'I'll tell all… please, cease!'

The boy had lasted barely a minute. Rosehaugh turned to Claverhouse. 'You see, there was no rush.' The Presbyterians held out much longer. They were harder, tougher men, unlike this spoilt fool who had fled to Rome after a disagreement with his father. 'Remove the Boot,' he ordered.

The executioner kneeled on the floor. He unscrewed half the implement, revealing a bloody mush of flesh. A surgeon was summoned to tend the wound.

'Talk, now, Mr Stuart. Tell us all you know or the cobbler will put the Boot on you again. Give him some water, Scag.'

Stuart raised his head and spoke in a weak voice. 'I belong to the Congregation of Christ, a Catholic Brotherhood which meets for prayer.'

'Who belongs to this group?'

'There are only a few of us in the city.'

'Who?'

'Father Innes and Father Pryde.'

'Two Papist priests. Who else?'

Stuart bowed his head and began to chant in Latin.

'Who else?'

Rosehaugh nodded to Scag. He began to replace the Boot.

'I've sworn not to reveal anything!' cried Stuart.

'You'll tell us all those associated with the brotherhood.'

Rosehaugh nodded. Awful cries echoed round the room.

'Leave it on this time in case he changes his mind. Who else?'

'Seaforth's brother, Ruairidh MacKenzie was the only other,' Stuart gasped.

Rosehaugh was not expecting to hear his own surname. But the expression on his face barely changed; his eyebrows rose slightly. 'You're sure Seaforth's brother attended the conventicle?'

'I am, sir. Please cease.'

'Has Seaforth attended your soirées?'

'He hasn't, sir.'

'Where did you meet?'

'Different places each time.'

'Who gave you orders to kill Kingsfield?'

'I swear no man ordered me. I was told by God. It came to me in prayer.'

'Apply the Boot again, Mr Scag.'

'I swear. I swear. God alone spoke to me!'

12

A Secret Association

SCOUGALL FOLLOWED MORRISON'S hulking frame through the tenements on the north side of the Lawn Market, a warren of dark passageways where some of the poorest inhabitants of the city lived. It was an area he ususally avoided. But if he was to rise in the world, if he was to make something of himself, he would have to be more vocal in his support of the Presbyterian cause. This was not a time to be half-hearted. If he wanted a chance with Agnes, he must keep on amicable terms with her brother. For these reasons he had agreed to attend. Presbyterians were meeting in secret cells across the city. He felt a twinge of guilt. MacKenzie's last words before leaving for The Hawthorns were that he should remain at home that night. The city was still in dark spirits after the shooting of Kingsfield.

They entered a tenement, climbed a spiral staircase to the third floor, and proceeded down a series of passageways to a door guarded by two heavily armed men. Morrison whispered something to one which Scougall could not hear. The guard nodded to the other and the door was opened, allowing them into a dingy candlelit room, a windowless chamber hung with faded hangings where a group of men sat round a table, deep in discussion. One of them was hunched over a book, keeping minutes with a long quill. On the table were bottles of claret, glasses and piles of documents.

The conversation stopped when they entered. Scougall sat beside Morrison, feeling very out of sorts. He did not like being the focus of attention.

'May I introduce, David Scougall, notary public, an old acquaintance from Musselburgh,' said Morrison.

'You're very welcome, Davie Scougall.' A thin well-dressed man spoke in a friendly manner, then took a deep draw on his pipe.

'We must delve a little deeper into your history, sir. We must be very careful at this juncture,' said an older figure with a gaunt lined face.

'Of course, that's only natural,' Scougall murmured. No one ever asked anything about him, unless it was how many words he could write in an hour, or how many shots he took on the golf course. He did not like the thought of folk asking about him.

'We're told you are a good Presbyterian; your family hold firmly to the principles of the Covenant, but… ' the first man hesitated.

Scougall felt like he was on trial. But the stakes were high. It was only natural they would want to find out as much as possible about him.

'We've heard you're on close terms with the Clerk of Session, MacKenzie. He's no friend of Presbytery.'

A wave of anxiety swept through Scougall as he looked round the circle of faces. He was not cut out for such things. He had no appetite for politics. He knew nothing of its ways. But he felt he had to say something. 'I work for him as writer, sir. He's an honourable man. Because of his upbringing in the Highlands he tends towards Episcopacy. He cannot help it. I don't share his views on religion.' He was being fair, but he did not like talking about MacKenzie behind his back.

A man dressed in a gold-fringed jacket and luxurious wig spoke in a refined voice. 'We must all have dealings with some who are tainted with the stain of Antichrist.'

The first man emptied his pipe on the floor and began to pack it with fresh tobacco: 'If you say he's honourable, we'll take you at your word. You're clearly your ain man.'

'Spies will be killed!' The other older man interjected, his passion roused. 'Traitors will be slain.'

'I'm no spy!'

'I can vouch for the character of Mr Scougall,' interjected Morrison.

'The future of the kingdom and the cause of Presbytery are at stake. The Papist must be defeated!'

'Thank you, Grimston,' the first man said firmly to the older one. 'Before we attend tae business, let me introduce our little gathering,' he continued urbanely, puffing on his pipe. 'I must emphasise that everything we speak of tonight must be kept secret.'

Scougall nodded, attempting to make his expression as grave as possible, but feeling angry with himself for agreeing to attend. He hoped it might be worth it in the end – the hand of Agnes and a new life were at stake. Nonetheless, he could not get away from the fact he was being disloyal to MacKenzie.

'I'm Alexander Baillie of Lammington,' said the man with the pipe. 'I'm recently returned frae exile like Mr Morrison. Here's Francis Leslie of Thirlsmuir.'

Lammington gestured towards the finely dressed man in the gold-trimmed jacket who nodded courteously. Scougall knew he was the younger son of the Earl of Pittendean, one of the most powerful nobles in the realm. Thirlsmuir's presence in the dark chamber was highly significant, indicating his father's loyalty to the cause. It was much debated in the coffee houses whether Pittendean was committed to the King or sided with the Presbyterians. The presence of his son among the association suggested he was a supporter of the opposition. It also raised the stakes. Scougall realised he was not among a group of minor plotters.

'Mr Peter Guillemot, Huguenot merchant, now resident in Edinburgh.'

The small man sitting opposite Scougall wearing an extravagantly large hair-piece and dressed in a green silk suit gave him a polite smile and spoke in a thick French accent: 'I've fled persecution in my own land, sir. I stand shoulder to shoulder with the Protestants of Scotland.'

The French Protestants had been persecuted since the tyrannical King Louis revoked the Edict of Nantes three years before. Scougall wondered what tragedy had brought Guillemot to Edinburgh.

'James Guthrie, minister,' continued Lammington.

'I've returned frae Holland also, sir,' said an old clergyman dressed in black robes with a weather-worn face and long grey whiskers descending to his chin. A small white wig perched on his head. 'Our time comes,' he continued emphatically. 'The kirk will be returned tae the true path; reformation completed; Scotland proclaimed a Covenanted nation again. The Papists vanquished frae our land!'

Scougall knew Guthrie was a devoted Covenanter who had fought at the battle of Bothwell Brig and was out with Argyll in the rebellion of 1685.

'James Cockburn of Grimston.' The older man who had already spoken nodded seriously. Scougall guessed that he hailed from the eastern part of the Lothians where the surname was common among devout Presbyterian circles.

'Welcome, sir. I hope you'll nae be tempted by the emissaries of Antichrist,' said Grimston, articulating each syllable in a slow annoying manner.

'Andrew Quinn, merchant of Dublin, now shopkeeper in Edinburgh.' Scougall observed a strange looking man with a rough complexion bowing his head. In Ireland the poor Protestants also feared for their lives.

'Archibald Craig, writer, and Robert Johnston, student.' Craig was a year or two older than Scougall with an oppressive double chin. His small fat hands were wrapped around a quill which he was tapping on the table. Johnston was little more than a boy. Twelve or thirteen years old, a thin spotty youth, smirking in the company of adults.

'Finally, Dr Isaac Black.'

'You do us great service by attending, sir. I'm sure you'll provide much that's useful.' Black's voice had little hint of a Scottish brogue.

Scougall was baffled, but nodded, wondering what on earth he could offer that was of any use. Silence followed as they waited for him to say something. Morrison at last gave him a gentle nudge. Scougall coughed nervously, looked down at his hands, desperately racking his brains. Finally he spoke hoarsely, 'I'll do anything I can to further the cause of Presbytery.' Thankfully there were murmurs of agreement.

'Dr Black had just begun tae tell us the latest news,' said Lammington.

'I've joyous tidings, indeed, gentlemen,' said Black excitedly. 'The Prince's fleet will sail soon. The deliverer will be on English soil in a few days if the wind is a fair one. We must do all we can to make Edinburgh as conducive as possible. The corrupt government here will crumble with a little encouragement. But we need more arms. Please give as much as you can tonight. It's vitally important the cause is funded generously.'

The thought of handing over money was another shock for Scougall. Saving, rather than spending, was his natural predilection. It gave him pleasure to know he had a little put aside for a dreich day. He was not a miser, just careful with his pennies. He did not like to hand over hard-earned cash to any cause. But everyone was rummaging in their pockets. Morrison put a few pounds down on the table. Craig took it, counting the coins carefully with his little hands before noting the contribution in his book. Generosity was to me a matter of public register, monetary evidence of loyalty. Scougall withdrew what was in his pocket. It was only two pounds but departing with it was painful.

'Is there anything from Cathcart?' Thirlsmuir asked.

'There's intelligence of a Papist meeting tonight,' replied Craig.

'We must flush the vermin oot!' exclaimed Grimston.

'We'll give them a wee surprise, gentlemen,' said Lammington puffing on his pipe and smiling. 'Is everything ready, Mr Johnston?'

'The boys are waiting ootside, sir.' Johnston spoke with a surprisingly deep voice despite his youthful appearance.

There was a knock on the door and one of the guards entered ponderously. He handed Thirlsmuir a note.

'I must leave, gentlemen. Something... has arisen,' he said taking his hat from the table. As he departed Scougall caught sight of a boy in the corridor, an urchin's disfigured face in the shadows. He noticed Thirlsmuir had crushed the note into a ball and left it on the table beside Craig's elbow. The fat clerk knocked it onto the floor without noticing. It lay in the dirt beside Guillemot's foot.

'The only other business is the date of our next meeting,' said Lammington.

'We'll meet in seven days' time. William will have landed by then,' said Black. 'You'll be informed of the location in the usual way.'

'Now the stout youth of Edinburgh will fight the Whore on the street,' added Lammington.

There were nods of agreement and a few claps. Scougall was glad it was over. Thankfully, no other request was made of him.

Descending a different staircase, they emerged on the other side of the tenement where a small crowd was gathered in a vennel; about fifty young men and boys, an assortment of students, artisans and apprentices, many holding torches. They stood in silence, waiting.

A strange object lay on the ground beside them, one of the most bizarre things Scougall had ever seen. As his eyes adjusted to the torchlight, he saw that it was a crudely crafted effigy about five feet in height, covered in wax, a grotesque sculpture resembling a witch. However, the shape of the hat or mitre and the long crozier, showed that it was a representation of the Whore of Babylon, the Pope, leader of the Papists in Rome. It rested on a wooden platform attached to poles.

When all the members of the association had appeared, Johnston thrust a torch into the kindling around it. Shouts rose from the crowd, echoing round the narrow lane. A drumbeat within the throng, reverberating in the enclosed space of the vennel, created a deafening sound. As the flames rose, the Whore began to melt. Obscenities were launched at it: 'Fuck the Pope. Fuck the Papist scum.'

'Where are they bound?' Scougall asked Morrison nervously in a whisper.

'They hunt Papists, Davie!' There was glee on his face.

Another cheer rose when the platform was hoisted onto the shoulders of four youths who staggered down the vennel towards the Lawn Market; the burning Whore swaying alarmingly above them, molten wax dripping onto their shoulders.

Scougall joined Morrison at the back of the procession as more cries resounded from above. Dozens of heads were sticking out of the windows of the tenements, calling on God to crush the Papists.

Morrison joined in the chants while Scougall remained silent. Most of the crowd were little older than Johnston. As they continued down the lane, Morrison became increasingly vocal in his cries, thrusting his fist up towards the sky in defiance: 'Fuck the Pope, fuck the Whore, fuck the King!'

A minute later, they spilled out onto the High Street, where they were engulfed by a larger crowd waiting in the Lawn Market, increasing the numbers to a few hundred. Shouts of anger rose into the blackness as other drums joined in.

Scougall noticed most of the association slipping away into the night. They were not to be active on the street. Dr Black remained beside them observing the scene with relish.

'There's peculiar appeal in a rabble, even for an educated man.' He was breathing heavily, but looked elated by the spectacle. 'We must drive home our advantage, gentlemen. The Papists cannot compete with us on the street. They've influence in the noble's house or secret brotherhood but we stand with the people of Scotland. Soon we'll be strong enough to take the palace.'

Scougall noticed the handle of his stick was ornately carved into the head of a creature which resembled an elephant.

Black dropped his voice to a whisper. 'Thirlsmuir believes he has precedence as the son of an earl, while Grimston thinks he should lead because of his long dedication to the cause. Lammington claims he's the natural leader. I, however, have the ear of Carstares who is intimate with Bentinck. It is well known that Bentinck is William's favourite courtier. So the chain leads from me to the Prince. A golden thread, indeed! I'm a man of special influence. You'd do well to follow me in the association.' He gave them an inscrutable wink, turned on his heels, which were high, and with a sly smile bade them goodnight.

Scougall watched him walk up the High Street, his cane tapping on the cobbles, his long wig swaying from side to side against the back of his coat. There was something of the dandy about him. He would not have looked out of place in the streets of London or Paris.

'He wants our support,' said Morrison. 'Two votes could be valuable. Our company can benefit. Come, let's observe the spectacle,' he beckoned enthusiastically, his florid features beaming. Scougall thought that he would have been less keen to have dealings with him if it was not for the fair features of his sister.

'This might be fun!' Morrison shouted above the din, but Scougall was thinking about the execution of a witch he had witnessed on the Castle Hill the year before, the awful sight of the burning body blazing against the darkness, the reek of roasting flesh on the cold wind. He reflected on the similarities with the present rabble and had an overwhelming desire to be off to his lodgings. But to appear a fool before Morrison was out of the question.

'I suppose I could postpone my return for half an hour.'

Bonfires, which were burning every fifty yards, transformed the High Street into a blazing tunnel. The mob was turning its attention to the tenements on each side which rose as high as seven or eight storeys. Word was spread that candles were to be lit in windows as a sign of support for the Presbyterian cause. Stones were hurled at black rectangles which were not illuminated, where Papist supporters were suspected of living. Scougall wondered what happened to folk who were away from town. Having their windows smashed was hardly just. There were cheers as each was successfully hit, the young urchins enjoying the licence to test the accuracy of their arms. Morrison picked up a stone and hurled it, adding a profanity about the Pope. He was delighted by the whole business, as if it were fine entertainment.

What remained of the Whore was dumped in the Lawn Market.

A long orange banner was unfurled and proudly held aloft, its colour articulating support for the Dutch Prince as they called on William to deliver the nation from a Papist King. More drummers joined the throng, intensifying the rhythmic cries. A woman with a basket handed out oranges which were grabbed greedily. Scougall took one of the rare fruits. It was a clever way of buying support for the cause. He wondered who was funding the distribution of such a rare commodity.

Morrison nudged him. 'Papists are in the Canongate.'

The rabble marched defiantly down the High Street past St Giles Kirk and the Tolbooth where Stuart was incarcerated. They would show no mercy if they got hold of him. Scougall nervously cast an eye at his office to the left, praying his windows would not be smashed. The last thing he wanted was a glazier's bill. He offered a short prayer to God to preserve his panes.

They surged through the Nether Bow Port into the Canongate, officially a separate jurisdiction from Edinburgh, although cheek by jowl with it. In this part of the city the houses were not as tall as the soaring tenements towards the castle. Nobles and well-to-do merchants lived in three- and four-storey dwellings with fine gardens to the rear. Halfway down, near the Canongate Tolbooth, they surrounded the entrance of a dark wynd.

There was so much screaming it was difficult to know what was happening. At last, after a few minutes of mayhem, Craig and Johnston emerged from the vennel. 'Two got away! But we have one!' Craig shouted.

A figure was dragged out of the darkness dressed in the attire of a priest.

'Found in the heart of reformed Scotland. The Papists plan the destruction of the city!' someone screamed.

The priest spoke in an English voice: 'I plan nothing... I only serve God and Lord Melfort.'

The mention of the despised aristocrat, a recent convert to the Church of Rome, incensed the mob's fury. The man's hands were bound behind his back as violent screams enveloped him.

'Burn him alive! String him up! Rip his fuckin bowels oot! Take his black heart!'

The priest was on his knees on the cobbles, begging for his life as two large figures appeared beside him. Scougall recognised the guards from the association. He was lifted by his oxters and taken up the High Street screaming. Scougall recalled the slaughter of Protestants in Ireland and France, how the Huguenots suffered under the persecutions of King Louis. But he was troubled by such a blatant example of summary justice. The priest was possibly dragged off to be killed in a dark corner. He believed in the law set down by God and proclaimed in His Book, in particular, Thou Shalt Not Kill. The rabble was taking His precepts into its own hands. He could hear MacKenzie's voice in his head – *We don't know anything about this man. He should be defended in court of law. He must be allowed to make a defence. The mob should not rule above the law.*

'What will happen to him?' he asked Morrison.

'I wouldn't like to be in his shoes, Davie. God knows what awaits the poor fellow. We'll hear tomorrow when the clamour abates. The King's foolish to allow priests succour in Scotland. Does he not understand how deeply the people despise them?'

Scougall recalled how Morrison's family had suffered, spending years in exile for opposing the Stewart Kings.

'We should retire for the night. Perhaps you might take victuals in our lodgings tomorrow? Agnes will prepare something. We can discuss business rather than politics. We mustn't lose sight of the fact this is just a means to an end. The men we met tonight have money. We must persuade them to invest it in our company.'

Scougall was uplifted by the prospect of seeing her again. The mob's anger, so intense a few minutes before, had dissipated, the bonfires already extinguished by buckets of water set beside them before they were lit. Everything had been planned to perfection. All was quiet on the High Street as he walked back to his lodgings.

13

Proclamation of a Papist

It was a fine day, although a cold breeze lent sharpness to the sun's warmth. Scougall felt ill at ease after attending the club the previous night. He had not summoned up the courage to tell MacKenzie about it. He felt it was not the right time yet.

As they stood at the Mercat Cross on the High Street among another throng, a boy darting through the crowd handing out sheets of paper caught his attention. He looked on his face as he took one, recognising the child who had delivered the note at the association. In the light of day he saw the deformity was only a harelip which had been exaggerated in the half-light outside the door. He was small, dirty and barefoot; a poor miserable bairn.

MacKenzie was perturbed by the latest news. It was said the Prince of Orange had landed at Torbay in the south of England with a fleet of seven hundred ships. He had passed through the Channel with a favourable wind, unmolested by the King's navy. The court in London was in consternation but there was universal rejoicing among the people. Some said that William was already at Exeter.

MacKenzie looked down at the title – *The Last Proclamation of a Wronged Man of the True Faith of Scotland* by Alexander Stuart. The fool had not given up his attempt to have his last words published. He shook his head and cursed in Gaelic.

I Alexander Stuart, son of David Stuart of Mordington, make the following proclamation before entering everlasting glory.

'An abused creature rebelling against his father, country and religion; only through betrayal could he achieve revenge,' sighed MacKenzie.

Scougall read it quickly, appalled by the views espoused, in particular Stuart's call for the people of Scotland to reject the reformed faith and convert to the Catholic religion. He shuddered at the growing power of Antichrist within the realm. Only a few hundred yards from where they stood, the Mass was openly proclaimed, although it was contrary to the laws of Scotland. Children were educated by Jesuits, servants of the Devil. King James had turned against his own people, favouring those who converted to the faith of Satan.

'*Na earb thu fhèin ri gràisg.* Don't trust the mob, Davie. This poor creature's death should not be entertainment for the masses. God help us! The rabble believes in nothing but annihilation.'

Scougall nodded vacantly, dreading MacKenzie's anger when he revealed where he had been the night before.

'I've told Elizabeth she's not to come to town until the situation is calmer. You should write to your parents. Tell them to stay in Musselburgh until the frenzy abates. I've heard all kinds of rumours from London.'

'My mother never comes to town, sir. She's rarely left Musselburgh in her life, although my father travels here each week. I'll write to him, counselling caution, although he'll have to conduct his business. People will want fresh herring whatever the political climate.'

Hundreds were packed into the High Street beside St Giles Kirk, all eyes fixed on the low door of the Tolbooth. After the Tron Kirk bell sounded eleven times, a figure emerged. The public hangman was followed by a stretcher carried by two men.

It was only fifty yards to the Cross, the centre of the burgh, the focal point of Scotland, where a gibbet was erected. Soldiers held back the crowd, making a pathway for the hangman. Scougall would have preferred to have been further back but MacKenzie was to act as a witness for Stuart's mother. He felt his pulse racing. His eyes darted round the crowd nervously, looking for familiar faces. Stirling was directly across the street chatting to Rosehaugh beside other lawyers and councillors. Then his heart stopped – he spotted Lammington and Grimston.

Stuart was lifted off the stretcher by the hangman. Skeletally thin, he was dressed in a white Holland shirt and dark breeches, his hair hanging lankly on his shoulders. In agonising pain from his leg wound, he was forced to kneel before a wooden block a few yards in front of them. The volume of abuse from the crowd increased another notch, the screams piercing, the anger unrestrained.

Stuart's right arm was held down on the block. Scougall was so close he could delineate the pale blue veins. He was not prepared for what happened next. Without ceremony the hangman swung his axe. It had come from nowhere, but he must have been carrying it all along. There was a whistle as the weapon swiped the air, followed by a dull thud as it embedded in the block. Stuart's hand dropped to the ground like a glove falling from a table. Blood spurted from the wound. His screams accompanied the roars of the crowd as he stared at the stump, holding it up to his face, observing the protruding white bone in horror.

Scougall looked down at his shoes as nausea swept through him. He feared he was going to be sick. The hand lay discarded like a leather purse a few yards away. It was the hand of the assassin of Kingsfield. Murder begot murder.

The traitor was hoisted onto the gibbet, his wrist-stump still dripping blood and his screams relentless. Another man moved forward, an official of some kind, carrying a scarlet cushion. On it rested a pistol. The hangman picked up the weapon and placed it round Stuart's neck. It was the gun he had used to kill Kingsfield.

Within seconds Stuart was swaying in his death throes. The abuse seemed to know no end. The curses were unrelenting. The hatred was as bitter as bile as the body jerked through its final agonies. Scougall could not look. But the image was implanted on his memory for ever.

At last Stuart hung at rest, his head at a slight angle, blood still dripping from the stump onto the cobbles. Scougall tried to stop himself, summoning up all his powers of self-restraint, but there was nothing he could do. He bent over and vomited. All he could think of was what Lammington or Grimston might think if they saw him boaking beside MacKenzie.

'It's over, Davie.'

Scougall stared at the hand in the dirt, observing the fingers that had pulled the trigger on the day Agnes returned to his life. Then he was conscious of someone towering over him. Was he to be punished for vomiting? But the executioner had seen it all before. Perhaps there was nothing on earth that could shock him. He picked up the hand. 'They want it nailed tae the West Port as a warning tae others,' he muttered under his breath.

14

A Note from Rosehaugh

IN AN INTENSELY bad mood, Archibald Stirling made his way up the High Street. Rosehaugh's short note had come as a shock, interrupting his work. He was adding the finishing touches to a chapter of his history which considered the thorny issue of the Rebellion in the 1630s. There were surely parallels with the present situation. The Whigs were grown in confidence since the Indulgences. Edinburgh was full of schemers multiplying by the day, fanatics plotting armed insurrection.

As he made his way down the steep slope of the Bow, he had to admit that the King's policies were causing the government problems. Even he, a loyal supporter of the House of Stewart, had grave misgivings about them. But the King ruled by God's authority. It was the fault of foolish advisers like Perth and his brother Melfort who sought to feather their own nests.

The last thing he needed was a murder, especially after the killing of Kingsfield. He gained no pleasure from the investigation of such cases. Rosehaugh's note was curt. A body had been found in a storeroom in Niven's Wynd off the Cowgate. *I advise you to visit the scene at once. We do not want any more trouble in the city at this time.*

He turned left into the Cowgate, passing St Magdalene's Chapel on the right which the Presbyterians had recently purchased from the council. Allowing them to gather legally in the middle of the city was another piece of folly. It let them gain in strength each day that passed, like a tumour on the nation. He heard the singing of a psalm inside unaccompanied by musical instrument. They were such grim creatures. He thought of Davie Scougall, MacKenzie's writer. Perhaps they were not all bad. Scougall was a cautious Presbyterian, not an earnest one. It was the earnest ones that were trouble. Earnestness in most things spelt trouble.

Stirling noticed the town guards holding back a few late revellers around the entrance of a vennel about fifty yards down the Cowgate on the left. This was not the kind of attention they wanted. News of a murder spread like wildfire in this congested city. He nodded at Meikle, one of his men, and entered the dark passageway between the tenements. About thirty yards down, two guards stood beside a door with torches.

A meaty aroma struck him as soon as he entered, so powerful it almost made him retch. He raised the torch to reveal a cavernous chamber, clearly used as a kitchen at some stage in its history, now a storeroom for merchandise.

Walking slowly down a gap between the shelves, he held his handkerchief over his nose. At the far end of the room was an indistinct shape. As he came closer, he saw it was a large stone fireplace. He halted, standing about five yards away. The smell was overpowering. He knew it was burnt human flesh. Something was suspended from the spit. The realisation that this was a body had stopped him in his tracks.

'When was it found?' he snapped at Meikle who was a couple of paces behind him. Smoke was still rising from the body.

'At nine o'clock by the merchant who rents the chamber – Mr Peter Guillemot. The flames were already oot when he found him.'

Stirling walked towards the fireplace. Most of the body was burned black, resembling a carcass of beef. The thought made him gag. Because of the victim's height, the head and feet were untouched by the flames. He observed a fine pair of leather shoes, the buckles shining in the torchlight. This was clearly a gentleman. A man of substance. A wave of despair washed through him. The death might have wider political repercussions. He raised the torch to reveal the face and was struck by a bolt of recognition. It was Francis Scott of Thirlsmuir, the younger son of the Earl of Pittendean. The manner of his death was obscene. It was bad enough to kill, but to inflict such outrage on a body. Thirlsmuir was perhaps burned alive, although his face looked peaceful. Perhaps he was killed first, or made unconscious. Rumours circulated that his father tended towards Presbytery rather than bishop. The murder of his son would cause uproar in the city.

'Summon Lawtie,' he barked at Meikle. He wanted medical opinion quickly.

Stirling had an overwhelming desire to quit the chamber at once, to be away from the odour. He recalled the execution of witches and warlocks and other poor souls, strangled then burned to nothing. But revulsion gave way to purpose. He would soon face Rosehaugh's questions. He must make a rudimentary examination, retain as much as he could for his report.

He went back to the body. There was an expensive periwig and fine necktie. The suit was burned through. He decided to let Lawtie deal with the rest; that was what the grasping little doctor was paid for. He turned to take in the room, a rectangle, possibly twenty yards by ten, full of shelving and crammed with boxes. He would have one of his men go through them later. There was another door on the east wall. It creaked open. But when he held up his torch he saw the exit was bricked off.

The only piece of furniture was a small table to the left of the fireplace. Something rested on it – a sheet of paper. It was a letter. Lifting it carefully, he was surprised to see it addressed to Rosehaugh.

Stirling was now in darkly bad mood, knowing he would have to return to the office despite the late hour. He thought of his hero, Montrose, a man who had witnessed carnage on many occasions at the battles of Auldearn, Inverlochy and Philiphaugh. But this was not a time of war. It was an autumn evening in the city of Edinburgh.

He retraced his steps to the Tolbooth and in his office began to pen a brief report. His thoughts soon wandered onto the roots of the disloyalty to King Charles in the 1630s, a subject which he had spent hours thinking about over the years, central as it was to his history of the Great Rebellion. How did a kingdom at peace with itself under a wise king fall into bloody civil war? His face bore a lost expression as his mind sifted through a myriad of visions conjured from books, letters and manuscripts he had read over the years. The theme of disloyalty led him back to the present. The Presbyterians, the same group of fools who precipitated the troubles in the 1630s, were returning from exile in increasing numbers.

Those who plotted to remove the King by violence acted against the order established by God. Such action could only disturb the social hierarchy and turn the world upside down – war, disease and death the only possible outcomes. Stitch by stitch the finely woven fabric of the kingdom was being unpicked. The employment of Jesuits in the Abbey Church at Holyrood was an outrage! By God, he was no Covenanter, but he was a sound Protestant. The agents of the Papacy in the very heart of Edinburgh! It was monumental idiocy, indescribable folly, inflaming the passions of the people. No one could have predicted what signing the Covenant would bring – a King executed by his own people in 1649. A knock at the door pulled his mind back to the present case.

Meikle deposited a sealed letter on his desk.

'What news in town?' asked Stirling.

'Aw is quiet, sir. Though the Presbyterians blame the Papists for the murder.'

Stirling checked the clock. He was due to meet Rosehaugh in five minutes. The Advocate unsettled him – such devotion to work and single-minded commitment to politics. He could not abide such enthusiasm. The pleasures of the private life were everything to him. He desired above all to retire and devote himself to his studies. But he still needed a year or two's earnings to make his retirement as comfortable as his wife demanded.

He waited for Meikle to leave before taking up the report. The second paragraph made him gasp out loud:

'The right hand of the victim is missing, removed by a sharp implement applied through the bones of the wrist'.

How could he have missed it! He read the entire paper again, making sure he had every detail committed to memory. Thank God it had arrived before he met Rosehaugh. His anger would have known no bounds if he had not been told about the missing hand. In Lawtie's view, death was caused by a blow to the back of the head where the skull was smashed. The victim's hand was sliced off afterwards with immense blood loss. The corpse was then strung up on the spit and the fire lit. The details would inflame the passion of the people. They could not be made public. But the town guards showed no discretion. Their tongues wagged like dogs' tails.

Gathering his documents, he left his office, and walked twenty paces down a corridor to a door. Rosehaugh sat behind a large darkly stained desk, a small man engulfed by a large wig. The familiar feeling of despair washed through Stirling as he observed the portraits of previous Lord Advocates looking down at him accusingly from the walls. How unfit he was for public life. Why was he not born into the ranks of the gentry or nobility instead of having to earn a living by following a profession? At least he had not seen much of Rosehaugh since his return as Advocate in February.

'You're late, Mr Stirling.'

'I'm sorry, sir. Lawtie's report just arrived.'

Stirling passed it across the desk. 'And this letter was found beside the body. It's addressed to you, sir.'

'For me?' Rosehaugh looked surprised for once.

'I found it on a table beside the fireplace.'

Placing the letter on the desk, Rosehaugh read the doctor's report with no sign of emotion or surprise at the gruesome details of the killing. Perhaps he had heard them already from one of his spies. He turned his attention to the letter.

An elegant hand had written his name – Sir George MacKenzie of Rosehaugh. He broke the seal and unfolded it.

'What do you make of this, Mr Stirling?'

Stirling took it from him.

The time is at hand, oh Lord. I am your servant. I bow before you in this city beholden to priests which is become the seat of Satan.

Oh Lord, the time of transformation is near. It is as a great wheel which cannot be stopped.

Haunted by them, I follow in their footsteps. I am one with them. I pass through closes. I stand in squares and courts as they seek abatement. Vile sinners, I will follow them through the darkest night. I catch them in the moment of destruction, dark, pure and brilliant. I watch them suffer. I share their agony. I feel their torment. I must smite those who disobey you.

Nations drink of the wine of the wrath of her fornication. I follow men of God, priests, clergy, prelates, bishops, all who seek eradication in lust.

Now I walk with him to the house of the whore, to the palace of Jezebel. I pass with him to her fragrant chamber. I lie in her filthy bed. I inhale the sickly odour of her sheets. I feel her cold embrace.

She was Babylon the Great, the mother of harlots and abominations of the earth. Upon her forehead was a name written.

Oh land of the hypocrite. I will end your suffering. I will snuff it out. I will close the cycle of despair. I will smite them. I will bring them to fruition. I will usher them towards finitude. I will make them as nothing. I will break them with the hammer of righteousness.

Join with me. I am the harbinger. I am the messenger. I am the agent.

'The ravings of a madman,' replied Stirling, 'perhaps one of the Presbyterian persuasion who are now numerous in the city.'

'A man who believes he can hasten rebellion against the King. Or is this just a front for Presbyterians, a way of fomenting revolt, encouraging blood-lust and whipping up the mob.' Rosehaugh looked troubled. Stirling had not seen him like this before. 'This letter must remain secret, Mr Stirling. Don't speak of it to any of your men. Are we the only ones who know of its existence?'

'That's correct, sir. I've shown it to no others.'

Rosehaugh rose from his desk and walked to the press in the corner. He opened a drawer and withdrew another letter which he handed to Stirling. 'I received it three days ago. I believe it's written in the same hand.'

'The writer has a powerful turn of phrase. He sounds like a deranged minister or field preacher,' said Stirling.

'The political situation is serious, Mr Stirling. An arrest will help to defuse the tension. Put all your other business aside. Have all your men focus on this case. I regret that political affairs take up most of my time at the moment, but keep me informed of any developments, day or night. Discuss the details with our mutual friend John MacKenzie. His counsel may prove useful and he can be trusted, unlike your men who gabber like fish wives. Now, you must excuse me. I need to inform the privy councillors of events.'

15

Dissection of a Frog

TAKING A SCALPEL, he carefully cut through the abdomen, peeling back the skin and tissue on each side to reveal the heart, lungs and intestines. The tiny heart was truly miraculous. He thought of the human one, large and ponderous. What was it that connected the frog and man? What was it that made them different? Could a frog be evil like a man? The face came back to him, smothering him, brutal lust in his stinking breath. A poor orphaned bairn should not be abused by his own teacher. But he would have revenge.

There was a knock at the door. Placing a linen sheet over the dissection, he took a dirk from his belt. He must be careful. He had been warned that his life could be in danger.

Opening the door slowly, he peered into the shadows. It was the boy with the harelip from Niven's Wynd. 'I hae something for you, Mr Johnston.' He held a sack in his hand.

'What is it?'

'Rats, sir.'

'I wanted a dog or a cat and you bring me a rat, Troon.'

'I'm sorry, sir. It was aw I could find.'

'Let me see.'

Troon came into the chamber closing the door behind him. He tipped the contents onto the floor. The cadavers of three black rats fell onto the wooden boards. Johnston took out his dirk. Piercing one in the back, he lifted it up to observe the long tail closely.

'I wanted a cat or a dog... but these'll do. Take this.' He gave the boy a coin. 'Next time I want something bigger, understand.'

Troon nodded fearfully.

Without warning, Johnston raised the knife to the boy's throat, resting the point of the blade on his larynx.

'Please, sir. I'll get ye a dug next time.'

'Have you ever seen a man's body cut open, Troon? Have you

ever seen a heart or a brain? Have you ever seen a human being eviscerated?'

'I've not, sir.' He was terrified.

'I've seen it done. I've watched surgeons in the college. I'll do it... myself... sometime.' He moved the blade down to the boy's chest before letting it fall, smiling. 'Don't worry yourself. These'll do for now. I expect better next time, mind. You'll be on the street when I call?'

'Yes, sir.'

'That's all for now.'

Troon was out of the door in an instant. Johnston laughed at his fear. In his mind he saw himself cudgelling the boy over the head and dragging him back into the room. He would never be missed, not even by his own mother. He saw the boy's body lying on the floor. He saw himself remove the clothing. He watched himself cutting open the stomach with his knife... it was only a dream or a vision. Or was it the future that he beheld? His pulse was racing. There was much to do first.

He scooped up each rat with a wooden spade and put them back in the sack. He wondered how much bigger was a rat's heart than a frog's and how much larger was the human heart.

16

A New Case for MacKenzie

SCOUGALL WAS READING aloud from a pamphlet in MacKenzie's study in Libberton's Wynd. 'The Queen is preparing to go to Portsmouth for her safety... Lord de la Mare has appeared for the Prince of Orange in Cheshire... the nobility meet in Yorkshire to decide their position... the Archbishop, bishops and peers in London address His Majesty for a parliament... a mob has demolished a Popish Chapel and pulled down the Nunnery at St John's... On the street it is said that Holyrood Palace will be next, sir.'

'I hope it'll not come to that, Davie.'

Meg's old face appeared at the door. She said something in Gaelic and a few moments later Stirling entered in an agitated state.

'I'm sorry to disturb you, but the situation is grave, gentlemen,' he uttered breathlessly.

'What on earth is it, Archibald? Calm yourself, man.'

'There's terrible news.' He waited until Meg had closed the door. 'Thirlsmuir is murdered!'

Scougall's hand tightened on the pamphlet. He was about to say something, but decided to hold his tongue.

'Ah, Davie. I didn't see you there,' said Stirling.

'Take a seat, Archibald. Tell us what's happened,' said MacKenzie.

Scougall was dumbfounded by the news; his mind raced through the previous night, in particular his memories of Thirlsmuir. He recalled the fine cut of his jacket, the exemplary wig, the quiet but determined voice. There was also the note delivered by the deformed boy.

MacKenzie prompted him to use his shorthand to record Stirling's words. He put down the pamphlet, sought his notebook and took another chair, trying to contain the flood of emotions.

'I was at work last night, adding the finishing touches to a chapter, pondering the thorny question of rebellion, when I received a message from Rosehaugh.'

MacKenzie smiled ruefully. Stirling had been writing a history for years, one which was always close to completion, but never sent to the press.

'The position of Montrose in the late 1630s troubled me,' he continued. Scougall failed to see what this had to do with the death of Thirlsmuir, although he knew Stirling was fond of the nobleman.

'I was thinking of parallels with today,' he continued. 'The Whigs are grown in confidence since the Indulgences. Edinburgh is full of schemers, fanatics plotting armed insurrection. They tried in 1685 and they will try again given the King's difficulties.'

Scougall nodded, but said nothing. Despite his cynical attitude, Stirling was an important man in the government. Scougall was not as vociferous in his condemnation of Episcopacy in his company. The King was facing something more serious than a few difficulties. His people were turning against him; they were rebelling.

'If you could get to the point,' MacKenzie said affably.

'As I made my way down the Bow, I reflected that the King's policies were folly,' Stirling continued. 'Fools like Perth and Melfort care nothing for the wellbeing of the kingdom.'

'Archibald, get to the point!'

'I'm sorry, John. The last thing anyone needs just now, especially after the killing of Kingsfield, is a murder. Rosehaugh's note told me a body was found in a storeroom at the bottom of Niven's Wynd.'

Stirling described what he had seen in the chamber. 'The first thing I noticed in the room was a sweet meaty aroma, so powerful it almost made me retch. I'm sorry to say it was a familiar one – burnt human flesh.'

Scougall stopped his note taking in shock. MacKenzie said a few words in Gaelic under his breath.

'The body was discovered at about nine o'clock by a Mr Guillemot who rents the chamber from a merchant called Hunter.'

Scougall emitted a groan. The mention of another figure from the association caused his heart to miss more than one beat.

'I know it's a shock, Davie. Please keep up with your notes.' MacKenzie noticed his consternation, but attributed it to the disturbing details.

'I stood a yard away,' continued Stirling, 'observing the body. It was mostly burned black, although the head and feet were unscathed, owing to the victim's height. He wore a fine pair of leather shoes and a lace cravat. As I looked at the face, I realised it was Francis Leslie of Thirlsmuir.'

'I've had legal dealings with him,' said MacKenzie, looking pensive, although he felt calmer than he had since the news of Ruairidh's conversion. Scougall wondered what he meant, but continued to take notes.

'I knew him also, John. I found him a distant figure who said little, although loquacious in parliament. Whatever his character, the manner of his death is obscene. It's bad enough to kill, but to desecrate a body in such a way. There are of course significant political implications. His father Pittendean is suspected of siding with the Presbyterians. The murder of his son is a very worrying development.'

Scougall knew Thirlsmuir supported the Prince of Orange. There was no doubt about his father's position. He must also be plotting against the King.

'Could you describe the room?' asked MacKenzie intently.

'It was rectangular with a high vaulted ceiling, possibly twenty yards by ten, full of shelves crammed with boxes of wigs.'

'Were the wigs made locally?'

'The box I opened were full of Tippendale wigs from London.'

Scougall recalled Kingsfield's headpiece lying on the High Street. Here was a fact, a piece of evidence, whatever you wanted to call it, which linked the two killings.

'It might be a coincidence, sir. Kingsfield was wearing the same kind of wig when he was shot. I picked it up from the street and returned it to his servant.'

'There's a further unsettling detail,' continued Stirling. 'The right hand of the victim was missing, removed by a sharp implement applied through the bones of the wrist.'

'What was the cause of death?' asked MacKenzie.

'A blow to the back of the head by a blunt instrument in Lawtie's view. The hand was then cut off, the corpse strung up and burned.' Stirling sighed. 'The details cannot be made public.'

'What about the Town Guards?' asked Scougall.

'Money will have to be distributed. Anyway, Rosehaugh was still at his desk, despite the late hour. He believes the political situation is precarious. He wants the perpetrator, or perpetrators, caught as quickly as possible. An arrest will diffuse the atmosphere in Edinburgh considerably. I'm to put all other business aside and have my men attend to it. He told me to discuss the case with you, saying your counsel might prove useful. And here I am, seeking your wise advice again, John.'

MacKenzie filled three glasses with claret and handed one to Stirling, before walking to the window. He looked down on the High Street deep in thought.

'The King's position is increasingly desperate,' Stirling said despairingly. 'Edinburgh's full of zealots who want to bring down the government.'

'I agree that the King is in a tricky spot. His policies are madness in a land which abhors the Papist. He's learned nothing from the demise of his father whose troubles began in Scotland. But let's not lose heart. He still controls the army and the nobles are loyal. William of Orange is a Dutchman, not a Scot or Englishman. The situation may be improved with a little wise policy.'

'There's more, John.' Stirling's face darkened as he reached into his jacket pocket. 'I found this letter addressed to Rosehaugh near the body. Rosehaugh received another in the same hand a few days ago. I can make nothing of them.'

MacKenzie read them both carefully, before handing them to Scougall.

'I don't understand sir... what are they?'

'You must make copies now, Davie.'

'The wine is good, John,' Stirling began to relax after unburdening himself. 'How many happy times have I enjoyed your hospitality in this oasis? You're right. We must ponder things deeply.'

'Let's first consider the victim,' MacKenzie returned to his seat. 'What can you tell us about him?'

'Francis Leslie of Thirsmuir is... was... Pittendean's third son. He was forty years old; married to Jean Scott, a daughter of Scott of Hardenfauld. He held the estate of Thirlsmuir in Fife from his father and represented the shire in parliament. A gifted speaker in the chamber, he was often in London on his father's business. Pittendean is travelling to Edinburgh to attend... what is left of his son's body. There are two older brothers: Lord Glenbeath, the heir to the title, and James Leslie, a soldier on the Continent. The family are suspected of supporting the Prince of Orange, although they still claim loyalty to His Majesty in public.'

'What about Thirlsmuir's movements before he was killed?'

Scougall continued to take notes nervously, terrified that Stirling had found something out about the association. He tried to think about how he might explain his attendance.

'He arrived in Edinburgh the day before yesterday, staying in his father's house in the Canongate. Yesterday afternoon, he met Archibald Craig, his man of business, in the Royal Coffee House at about two in the afternoon.'

Scougall tensed again. Here was another character from the secret club. He recalled his fat little hands counting the donations.

'Thereafter his whereabouts are not known,' said Stirling.

Scougall stole a look at MacKenzie. Thankfully, he did not see his discomfort.

'What about the fellow who found the body?' MacKenzie asked.

'Guillemot is a Huguenot refugee, now a merchant in Edinburgh. He made the discovery at about nine o'clock in the evening. The flames were already extinguished. He raised the alarm. I was there by ten.'

Scougall's mind flashed back to the association. Thirlsmuir had said little before the note arrived. He recalled the boy's face through the door. The same urchin had handed out the proclamation at Stuart's execution. Guillemot was a vague figure in his memory. He remembered only his French accent and exotic wig.

'Rosehaugh does me great honour,' said MacKenzie, taking his seat again. 'I'll apply my full attention to the case. Have you spoken to Craig?'

'He's a kinsman of the family of Pittendean, hailing from a village nearby, trained as a writer and employed as man of business. He met Thirlsmuir yesterday to catch up with news and prepare for developments, as he put it.'

'Developments?'

'Political developments, most likely – the progress of the Prince in the south.'

'Who does Guillemot rent the chamber from?'

'A merchant called Andrew Hunter who's well known in town. He's trustworthy and of good credit. The Huguenot took the storeroom a few weeks ago. His family have suffered under the persecution in France. I've not spoken to him yet, but I've heard he's an honourable trader.'

'Is there anything else?'

Stirling took a sip of wine and thought for a moment. 'An old woman called Bessie Troon who lives in Niven's Wynd saw two men outside the storeroom in the late afternoon.'

Scougall reflected that Thirslmuir must have passed straight from the association to his death. How was he to tell all this to MacKenzie? He had sworn an oath of secrecy to the Presbyterians.

'What about relations between Thirlsmuir and his family?' asked MacKenzie.

'He was close to his father. I know not how he got on with his brothers.'

'Perhaps we can meet tomorrow in The Periwig. I need to read Lawtie's report and visit the scene of the crime.' Despite the horrendous nature of the crime, MacKenzie felt better. He could still see the black bird circling in the distance, but it was not coming nearer for now.

17

Investigations in Niven's Wynd

SCOUGALL WANTED TO tell MacKenzie everything, but an opportunity did not present itself and it was in his character to put things off. He decided to wait for a time when the shock would not be so great, when his friend's humour was conducive.

After breakfast in The Periwig they walked down the Bow to the Cowgate, a long narrow road running parallel to the High Street on the south of the city. Buildings rose precipitously above the dark artery through which livestock entered the Grass Market. Copious piles of excrement lent richness to the air outside St Magdalene's Chapel, an ancient religious edifice, now the centre of Presbyterian worship in the city.

'Was he attending a meeting in there? It's now a nest of vipers, Davie?' asked MacKenzie provocatively.

Scougall knew he was teasing him and did not fall into the trap. 'Many Presbyterians worship there now, sir.'

'The council has provided a sanctuary for those plotting against the King! Let's turn our attention to Bessie Troon first. According to Stirling's report, she saw two figures standing here, a tall man and a short one.'

Niven's Wynd was only a stone's throw away. About twenty yards up the slope they found a door on the right with the initials AH carved into the lintel – the storeroom of Andrew Hunter where the body was discovered. MacKenzie tried the door but it was locked. A bairn was watching them across the way.

'I'm looking for Bessie Troon, my boy.' MacKenzie opened his hand to reveal a penny. The boy's face lit up.

'I'll tak you, sir.'

They followed him into a stinking stairwell. The cries of children and the screams of a drunken argument echoed downwards as they ascended six flights of delapidated stairs. Having delivered them to a door on the top storey, the child sped off with his earnings.

A young woman dressed in filthy rags and carrying a baby answered.

'I'm looking for Bessie Troon,' said MacKenzie.

The woman eyed them suspiciously. 'What dae you want wi her?'

'We want to talk to her about the killing in the storeroom across the way.'

She disappeared into the grim interior and a few moments later, a tiny woman appeared with a thin weathered face. 'I'm Bessie, gentlemen. Come awa in.'

They followed her down a short hallway into a large room with a low ceiling. There was a damp stale odour about the place. The walls were stained green and the floorboards were filthy. There was a hearth, although the fire was not lit. A few cooking utensils lay on a small table. Scougall counted five box-beds against the walls.

'The wee one's ill, sir. He's going tae dee like the ithers,' she said without emotion.

A bairn was asleep in a bed, emaciated and pale, perhaps only a couple of years old, lying in grey sheets.

'I believe you've already spoken with Mr Stirling?' asked MacKenzie.

'No, sir. Not Stirling. Anither man.'

'Meikle?'

'That was him. An ugly brute.'

'I'm helping with the case. I like to hear everything myself. Sometimes the smallest detail is important, Mrs Troon. You told him,' continued MacKenzie, 'that you saw two men at the bottom of the vennel at about four o'clock yesterday afternoon. Tell me everything you can remember about them. Meikle only noted that one was tall and the other short.'

'I was on ma way tae the cludgie. As soon as I was ootside I saw them staundin there thick thegither, ye ken, talking about some great matter. They paid no attention tae the likes o me. I couldnae hear what they said, but the tall ane looked fashed and the wee ane was trying to explain something, moving his hands aboot. Then all of a sudden the vennel was full of folk. There was a young wumin going up the way and a man coming doon. The man looked at the pair as if he was aboot tae say something. He didnae stop but entered the storeroom. The woman kept on her way. I mind thinkin, it's busy in the wynd the day.'

'Thank you, Bessie. You've a keen eye. Could you describe them to us?'

'The small ane was dressed much like you, sir.' She nodded to Scougall. 'He wore a black jacket and breeches wi a short wig. He looked like a clerk, but with a great belly on him, a fat face and small een. The tall ane was a gentleman. There was nae doubting that. He wore a suit with gold trim, a long wig and blue necktie. I mind thinking he was a guid looking man. I didnae want tae stand there gawping all day, so I left to dae ma business. When I came back they were awa.'

'What did the man coming down the wynd look like?' Scougall asked.

'He was smairt tae, a merchant with a muckle wig, the like of which I've never seen, like a bush on his heid. I'm telt it's the fashion. He opened the door of Hunter's store, closing it behind.'

'And the woman?' asked MacKenzie.

'She was just a maid. I did nae ken her.'

'Has anything else happened out of the ordinary round here?'

'It's so busy these days, sir. All kinds o folk are in town. The chapel doon there is like the Links on Race Day. I've never seen the Cowgate sae busy. Some say a prince has come tae save us frae the Papists! I pray they're right.'

Not far from the top of Niven's Wynd, a crudely painted sign depicting a wig hung above a doorway. In the window, periwigs in a host of colours and sizes were displayed on wooden heads. Scougall touched his own headpiece, reflecting how unfashionable it was compared to those on display. He could not quite get used to the idea of wearing one. His mother viewed the wig as an affectation of the Godless. Why would you cover up the hair on your head with that of some other poor creature? There was logic in what she said, but she knew nothing of the world of fashion. Her reply that fashion from France was the mark of a Papist stung him. It could not be denied that wigs were a foreign import. MacKenzie had told him how the nobles started wearing them after the Restoration, aping the French. It was ridiculous when you thought about it. They were often made from the hair of the poor. But men of business wore them and he wanted to be a man of business. He had told his mother, but she was not satisfied. 'Your father never wore a wig.' 'How am I to find a wife without one,' he had replied. 'You don't need a periwig to find a bedfellow in Musselburgh.' This was no doubt true, but if he sought a wife in Edinburgh he would need one, or he would be the laughing-stock of the town. Every notary wore one. Morrison had a very fine piece, no doubt purchased in Amsterdam. Perhaps it was time to buy a new one, just a run-of-the-mill periwig, a simple bob, not too expensive and not too cheap, but an improvement on the one he wore.

'Let's see if we can have a few words with Mr Guillemot,' said MacKenzie.

Scougall was struck with fear at the prospect of meeting the merchant in case he referred to the association. But he could think of no excuse and sheepishly followed MacKenzie into the shop.

The interior was crammed with hairpieces of all kinds: dress wigs, campaigns wigs, travelling wigs; in a variety of colours, sizes and styles. A large mirror rested against one wall. A middle-aged man emerged from a doorway at the back wearing a resplendent wig. Scougall dropped his head, praying that he would not remember him.

'Welcome, gentlemen,' Guillemot said in a thick French accent. 'You arrive just at the right moment. A delivery of fine merchandise from London arrived only a few hours ago. I'll bring some through from the back. Please be seated.'

'We're not customers, sir. I'm John MacKenzie, Advocate, and this is David Scougall, Notary Public.'

Guillemot bowed in an exaggerated manner. Scougall recalled the vow of secrecy and prayed the merchant would keep it.

'It's a pleasure, gentlemen, a pleasure to make the acquaintance of such fine men of Law.'

Guillemot was more confident in his shop than he had appeared in the club. Fortunately he acted as if he had never seen Scougall before in his life. It was so convincing Scougall was not sure if he simply did not remember him. As a newcomer to the city he had doubtless met scores of folk.

'Your wig is a fine specimen, sir. Is it a Jasper of London?' Guillemot asked MacKenzie.

'That's correct, Mr Guillemot.'

Scougall recalled that he had purchased his from Shield's stall in the Luckenbooths in a deal which included six featheries. The periwig was thrown in as a sweetener.

'But, sir,' addressing Scougall as he stood petrified, although

Guillemot continued to give no indication they had met before, *'C'est ne pas bon.* A young gentleman who seeks the ladies' attention should not wear such an accoutrement.'

Scougall blushed, reflecting that he received little attention from any ladies. Perhaps this was due to his second-rate wig! A new one might impress Agnes.

'All in good time.' MacKenzie's change of tone stopped the merchant in his tracks. 'We're not buyers of your wears today. We investigate the death of Thirlsmuir.'

Guillemot straightened his back, adopting a serious demeanour. 'I'm forgetting myself. I take every opportunity to sell! You must have many questions. I found the body myself. *C'est une affaire terrible, n'est pas?*'

'Who do you rent the chamber from, Mr Guillemot?' asked MacKenzie.

'Monsieur Andrew Hunter is an upstanding merchant of the burgh. I recently arrived in your good toon, as you say. I learn the Scots tongue quickly, *n'est pas?* I was forced to flee the persecution in my own land. I've lost my beloved wife and child to the Papist oppressor. I seek a new life in Scotland. The council gave me permission to open a shop. With the little capital I took out of France, I set myself up in the trade I know best, importing wigs from France, Amsterdam and London. I aim to improve the fashion of this place. In time, I'll start making them here, stopping the drain of money from the kingdom. Then I'll pay the women of Scotland for their hair and export when the Privy Council permits.'

'These are sizeable premises, why did you rent the storeroom?' asked MacKenzie.

'So I could hold more stock! Business is booming, gentlemen. The chamber was perfectly situated, only five minutes' walk away. As you get closer to the Cowgate, rents fall considerably.'

'Where do you live, sir?' MacKenzie probed.

'I have chambers on the third floor of this building, also rented from Hunter, a fine and generous man.'

'What happened to your wife and daughter?'

Guillemot looked down at the floor. 'Both lost in the chaos that's swept through France since the revocation of the Edict. My land swims in Protestant blood! My beloved wife slain and my daughter lost. I hope she is alive somewhere, but I've no word of her for two years.'

'What age is she, sir?'

'She'll now be eighteen. A beautiful creature.'

'I have a daughter also, Monsieur Guillemot. She's twenty. It must be very painful for you.' MacKenzie waited a moment before continuing: 'Which part of France are you from?'

'Mazamet in Languedoc. *C'est tres belle.* I believe I'll never return home.'

'Why did you come to Scotland? I thought most of your people settled in London?'

'It's true, Monsieur. Hundreds are gone there, maybe thousands from across France. But one of your countrymen, a merchant called Alexander Douglas who settled in France, told me about the city of Edinburgh. When I arrived in London I saw there were many of my countrymen there, so I decided to go north to the land of Douglas where there would be less competition in the wig business.'

'Tell us what happened on the day of the murder?'

As MacKenzie asked the questions, Scougall busied himself taking notes.

'I was in the shop for most of the day. I visited the storeroom at about four o'clock in the afternoon to get some stock. I don't have a servant yet, so I must carry the boxes back myself. I returned in the evening. That was when I found him.'

'Did you notice anything out of the ordinary on your first visit?'

Guillemot hesitated for a moment before answering. 'I did see two gentlemen in conversation at the bottom of the wynd. I remember observing one of their wigs was of the highest quality while the other wore a cheap piece. I was about to take the opportunity to tell them my shop was only two hundred yards away, when I heard one curse violently. I thought it not an opportune time, so I entered the chamber.'

'Could you describe them to us?'

'One was a fine looking *gentilhomme*, as we say in French, dressed in a silk suit with a gold-fringed jacket. The other was shorter, not a gentleman, perhaps a clerk. I think you would describe him as fat.'

'Which of them was cursing?'

'The taller one, sir. I was struck by the vehemence of his swearing and the anger of his expression. When I came out ten minutes later he was gone, but the other was standing across the Cowgate beside the chapel reading a pamphlet. I bid him good day and made my way back to the shop.'

'Could you describe your second visit?'

'I closed at six o'clock and ate my evening meal. At nine I decided to fetch a couple of boxes from the storeroom to save me the trouble in the morning.'

'Do you usually go there so late?'

'No, the Cowgate can be boisterous at that hour, but I could not sleep. There was so much noise on the High Street caused by the rabble. When I got there, I was surprised to find the door ajar. I was sure I'd locked it in the afternoon. Fearing a thief was inside, I enetered slowly. I was struck by a strange smell which reminded me of roast boar. I was horrified to find a body on the spit rather than a pig. The fire was out but it was still smouldering. I found blood on the floor beside the fireplace. I was unsure if the fellow was dead or alive but a quick look at him told me he'd breathed his last. I sought the town guards at once.'

'How many keys do you have?'

'Two were provided by Hunter. I keep one on my belt and the other under the counter.'

Guillemot ducked down and began to rummage behind the wooden counter at the back of the shop. 'It's gone!'

'Did anyone else know you kept it there?'

'I don't think so.'

'One last question, Monsieur Guillemot. Did you know Thirlsmuir?'

Guillemot caught Scougall's eye for an instant.

'I didn't know him, although I've heard he was a man of importance, the son of an earl. *C'est terrible*. I believe the Catholics are behind it.'

By the time they made their way back down the wynd with Guillemot it was late in the afternoon. The walls that rose steeply for ten storeys on each side cast the narrow lane into darkness. Piles of excrement, human and animal, lay at the sides, the stink becoming worse as they neared the Cowgate.

'I hope the streets of Mazamet were kinder on the nose!' exclaimed MacKenzie.

'Like all great cities, your streets have, how do you say, a particular reek. But I've heard your city is soon to have lighting?'

'Lighting!' Scougall repeated, incredulously.

'It's true, Monsieur Scougall. The council is placing lanterns in the High Street and Cowgate to illuminate the town. It may usher in a new age of enlightenment, *atteindre l'illumination, n'est pas?*'

Guillemot opened the door of the storeroom and lit the candles on the walls, revealing the cavernous interior. The fireplace and spit were at the far end; the room was packed with shelves containing an assortment of boxes.

MacKenzie made straight for the fireplace which he examined closely. He opened a few of boxes and looked under the shelves. Scougall followed his example, looking for anything out of the ordinary.

After about ten minutes MacKenzie ushered them both to the door. 'This is where Thirlsmuir was struck on the head. The bloodstain on the wall must be from the strike. Then he was dragged to the spit. Observe the two lines on the floor made by the heels of his boots.'

Scougall and Guillemot followed him to the fireplace where he showed them a larger bloodstain. 'The hand was cut off here. The killer must've had significant strength to hoist him onto the spit. Thirlsmuir was not a small man. But why was the hand taken?'

'Could it be a warning,' suggested Scougall.

'It caused great effusion of blood, possibly covering the killer's clothes. This was not a spontaneous murder following an argument or fight. If that was the case, we would've found him with a smashed skull in a corner of a vennel or dumped in the Nor Loch. The killer wanted him to be found, wished to display the manner of his death, desired to cause maximum offence. He wanted us to notice the hand and find the letter. He wanted us to ponder the meaning of the killing.'

'It's surely the act of a madman!' cried Guillemot.

'We would regard the person as mad. This isn't like the shooting of Kingsfield. We're dealing with something quite different.'

'Do you believe the Papists are behind it, Monsieur MacKenzie?'

'I don't know, yet.'

'The Papists will do anything, torture and kill in any manner!'

'That may be so, but the evidence doesn't tell us if the killer's a Papist or not,' continued MacKenzie. 'We may be dealing with a person compelled to kill. On the other hand, the display of the body was designed to have a political impact. The victim was not an unknown urchin, but the son of one of the great nobles in the land. It could be a conspiracy to destabilise the government.'

Scougall was convinced the Papists were responsible. They wanted to provoke the Presbyterians by killing Kingsfield and slaying Thirlsmuir. MacKenzie did not know all the facts on this occasion.

18

Pittendean House

THEY PASSED THROUGH the Nether Bow Port into the Canongate, stopping at the gates of an imposing mansion about halfway down on the north side. It was set back from the road by about thirty yards, a large three-storey house harled in ochre with crow-stepped gables.

'It's one of the finest dwellings in Edinburgh. Pittendean has spent a fortune on it,' said MacKenzie as they approached the front door.

An impeccably dressed servant who spoke with an English accent showed them into a large hallway into which light flooded from a huge cupola above. MacKenzie reflected that servants from the southern kingdom were becoming more common. It was a way for the nobles to show off their position, aping the English aristocrats when local servants cost a fraction of the price. They ascended a broad staircase onto the first floor.

The chamber they were shown into at the back of the house was less grand, although it did provide a view of the gardens and fields to the north of the city. The earl's private sitting room had a homely feel; there was a welcoming fire, a few chairs, table, bookcases and desk. It was all quite informal.

An old man rose from an armchair beside the fire. He was not above five feet in height and swamped by a huge periwig which encased a lined face. MacKenzie bowed and Scougall followed suit.

'Welcome, gentlemen.'

'Thank you for seeing us, my lord, especially at such a terrible time for your family,' began MacKenzie.

'I'm robbed of a fine son; a fine son in his prime. Scotland has lost a devoted servant.' Pittendean sighed as he beckoned them to sit in two richly upholstered chairs by the window.

'This is your assistant, MacKenzie?'

'Davie Scougall, Notary Public – an exemplary penman and golfer,' said MacKenzie.

'A fine game which I was much taken with in my youth, Mr Scougall. Now I cannot walk far enough to complete a round. I sit at cards or read a history for my entertainment, when I've time. There's always so much business to attend to. Politics is an all-consuming profession. I can understand why my son James became a soldier. He's plenty of leisure when he's not fighting – too much. His debts are huge – gambling bills in Paris, tailors' bills in London, furniture bills in Amsterdam.'

Scougall nodded, but said nothing. He was beginning to feel hot. A roaring fire burned in the hearth. He had always sweated profusely, an affliction which he was often teased about.

'It's strange how children from the same family,' continued the Earl, 'have such different characters. Take my eldest, Glenbeath. A gentler man you couldn't find, happiest on his horse hunting with his hounds. He cares nothing for politics, or, some say, for his wife and family. Thirlsmuir, on the other hand, had a hunger for public life. He loved the horse-trading, argument and debate in parliament, and a little intrigue when it was called for. My daughters are as different as crab apples and quince. Sarah a sensible girl who has caused me not a moment's grief in her whole life. She was married at fourteen to the man chosen for her, though twenty years her senior. Whereas Sophia has a mind of her own, refusing all the matches I suggest. But she's my favourite. I've spoilt her, so I'm to blame.' He took a deep breath and sighed before continuing: 'How's your daughter, MacKenzie? I've heard she's betrothed to a Highland man? A match, how will I put this, which may take as much as it provides.'

'I must take account of my clan as a Highland man, my lord. But the match is a sound one from a personal point of view. My daughter's much taken with him.'

Scougall felt a twinge in his chest at the thought of the pair. He did not know if the Earl's smile indicated that he knew about the difficulties in which Ruairidh found himself.

'What think you of the family, Mr Scougall?'

Scougall hated the way nobles only noticed you when it suited them. Perhaps a change of regime would bring them down a peg or two.

'I believe the family's a fine thing, sir.' It was an inane thing to say but he could think of nothing else. Pittendean seemed to ignore him anyway. He was sure he had asked just to keep him on his toes, to remind him, despite his diminutive height, of his authority.

'What do you make of the progress of the Prince, gentlemen?' asked Pittendean.

'He'll be in London soon,' Scougall blurted out, which he immediately regretted as it was clear from the way he said it that he looked upon the prospect favourably. MacKenzie had told him a score of times not to give anything away when questioning a suspect. Pittendean, although a grieving father, was apparently viewed by him as one, although he could not believe he would kill his own son and burn his body, or have someone else do so.

'Is your intelligence good, sir?' The Earl seemed interested, although Scougall caught a disgruntled look on MacKenzie's face.

'It's only what I've heard in the coffee houses, my lord. I know no more than any other whether it's true or false.' This was a lie, but he could not tell him he had intelligence from a group of conspirators, which had included his own son. The thought increased his anxiety and he felt sweat dripping from his oxters. He was glad Agnes did not see him in such a liquid state.

MacKenzie intervened, saving him further embarrassment. 'How does your lordship stand at this delicate time?'

Pittendean pulled himself up in his chair, lent forward and spoke in a whisper. 'I must watch what I say to you, gentlemen. Whichever way the wind blows, I'm still Earl of Pittendean.'

Sitting back, he laughed, then pulled a cord beside his chair. The presence of his son at the association suggested his support for the Presbyterians, thought Scougall. But what if he was playing a double game, letting them think he supported William, while remaining loyal to the King?

'Rosehaugh has asked me to speak to you.' Pittendean's tone changed, his smile disappeared. He looked old and vulnerable. 'He says you're to be trusted. As you can imagine, rumours about the manner of my son's death are causing disquiet. The official view is that he was stabbed. The truth is a gross insult to my family. I want the perpetrator, or perpetrators, caught and punished. The Presbyterians howl for Popish blood and the Papists blame Protestant fanatics. The death of Kingsfield has unhinged things. Everything is on a knife edge. Edinburgh could explode at any moment, so we need to get to the bottom of this quickly. I'll answer your questions as long as you keep off politics. My lips are sealed on that subject.'

'I realise this will be painful, but could you tell us what happened yesterday?' asked MacKenzie.

'It was a day like any other. Thirlsmuir arrived from London in the morning. In the afternoon he met Craig in the Royal Coffee House. After that he appears to have gone missing. I can find out nothing about his movements thereafter. I arrived in town this morning from Fife.'

'How long has Craig been in your family's employment?'

'His father was a servant of my house. Craig was trained in the law to serve us as secretary. I believe he's devoted to our interest.'

'Was there any disagreement between him and your son?'

Pittendean thought for a moment before answering. 'Their relations could be strained at times. My son was demanding and could be impatient. But Craig could stand up for himself.'

'Was there anything in particular they argued about in the days before his death?'

'Are you suggesting he was responsible for killing my son? How would his interest be served by such an act? He would lose everything.'

'Your son and Craig were seen arguing in the Cowgate near St Magdalene's Chapel in the late afternoon, close to the storeroom where his body was later found. It may be nothing, but I must cover everything for Stirling.'

'It's likely they were arguing about... strategy.'

'Strategy?'

'Craig was less cautious than my son. He's a great hater of the Papist, a view inherited from his father.'

'There was nothing he spoke of that might indicate the nature of their meeting?'

'All I'll say is that it was to discuss developments in England which change by the day, if not the hour. It's no secret that St Magdalene's is a centre of... political activity. As a family we must keep abreast of what's happening. My people look to me for leadership at this... dangerous time.'

'Can you think of anyone who might have wanted him dead?'

'Assassination is not uncommon in this land. Look at the fool who shot Kingsfield. Feuds flare up and burn out. In the Highlands they still occur regularly, though not as vehemently as they once were. But to desecrate a nobleman's body in this way – thank God my dear wife is dead. This is not a feud but the act of a madman.'

Pittendean looked beyond them out of the window. 'We lost our eldest child, years ago, when he was a boy. My wife never recovered.'

'I didn't know, my lord. I'm sorry for it. I know the pain you must have suffered,' said MacKenzie.

After a few moments, Pittendean turned to them again: 'Please continue, gentlemen. I was lost in thoughts of the past.'

'Who are your political enemies?' asked MacKenzie.

'I would have placed Kingsfield himself amongst them.'

'Are you at law with anyone?'

'There's a tiresome case against Soutra which has dragged on for years. He may be a Papist, but I can't believe he would kill my son and desecrate his body to recover a few thousand pounds. I'm at law with a handful of others, but why would they kill him? It'll hardly improve their chances in court!'

'Would it be possible to get a list of your creditors and debtors?'

'Craig will be able to help you.'

'I'm sorry to ask this question, but how were relations in your family?'

'My eldest son is soft in spirit. My youngest is a soldier on the Continent. They had little to do with Thirlsmuir. The idea they were involved is preposterous.'

'There was nothing in your son's history that might have left him... vulnerable.'

'I can't think of anything. He was dedicated to one thing in life – politics. He was a fine speaker in parliament. Under a union between Scotland and England, a greater stage would have opened up for him. Who is to represent the House of Pittendean now? Glenbeath cannot, so I must encourage James, who is weak. I'm too old for the game of politics.'

There was a knock at the door and a large well-dressed man entered. From his features he was clearly related to Pittendean.

'Here's my eldest son, Lord Glenbeath.'

'My brother's death's a great shock, a great shock to us all,' said Glenbeath.

'I'd like to talk to you, my lord,' said MacKenzie.

'That will not be possible, sir. I leave tomorrow to take my brother's body home for burial.'

'My son will give you a few moments of his time,' Pittendean said firmly.

'It's not convenient, Father. I've much to do, too much to do.'

'You'll make time for your brother's sake.'

'If you insist,' he said in an aggrieved manner.

Pittendean rose and bid them farewell. MacKenzie waited until he had left the room.

'I'm sorry to ask this, my lord Glenbeath, but where were you on the night your brother was killed?'

'You think I killed him! What right have you to question me in this manner?'

'I've been asked by the Crown Officer to aid his enquiries.'

Glenbeath looked suspiciously at MacKenzie, then at Scougall. 'I accompanied my father to town this morning.'

'Can you think of anyone who might have wished your brother ill?'

'Wished him ill!' Glenbeath repeated in a scoffing manner. 'Many wished him ill. I wished him ill. He was an arrogant dolt. He thought I was a despicable creature.'

Scougall was shocked to hear him speak so heartlessly of his deceased brother.

'I wasn't devoted to business like him. I prefer... the pleasurable things in life. I've no interest in causing a stir in parliament. He didn't understand... my appetites. But he was not as perfect as my father believes. All men have a vice.'

'What vice are you referring to?'

'The vice of gambling from which he could not free himself. I enjoy the table like any man, but he would spend hours there. He often won handsomely, but also lost badly. I believe his debts were kept hidden from father.'

'Who's the money owed to?'

'There are many – usurers, moneylenders, those in the shadows.'

'Why did he borrow from them?'

'He had tried the patience of legitimate lenders – lawyers like you, Mr MacKenzie.'

'Do you have any names?'

'I'm not part of that world. I don't share the obsession some have with games of chance. They'll risk everything on the turn of a card or the savagery of a cock in the pit. I wouldn't be surprised if an unpaid debt is behind this. I know how such lenders operate if they're not repaid. First there are warnings, followed by threats of violence. Finally, they kill without compunction.'

'Would they burn a man's body for an unpaid debt?'

'They have no legal way of recovering money other than the threat of violence or the use of it. They don't lend by bond written by notary. Everything is sealed by word of mouth and shake of hand. It's possible he was being made an example of. Seek out the moneylenders of the city. You may find his killer among them.'

'But you don't know any of them?'

'I'm sure it will be easy to find out who they are. Usury was always in fashion.'

'You said relations with your brother weren't good?'

Glenbeath turned to look out the window and hesitated before answering. 'I half expected him to kill me one day so he would inherit the title.'

'Were you jealous of him?'

'You misunderstand me, Mr MacKenzie. It wasn't jealousy. It was hatred. He despised me. I despised him. But I did not kill him. I was at home in Fife.'

19

Lodgings of a Papist

DRESSED IN BLACK mourning, Jean Stuart stood at the window with her back to them. As she turned, the devastation of sorrow was visible on her drawn face. 'Thank you for coming, gentlemen,' she said in a soft emotionless voice.

MacKenzie and Scougall sat by the fireplace in the sparse chamber.

'Alexander spent little on the encumbrances of life,' she continued. 'He'd no need of luxuries, so devoted was he to the cause in which he believed. He worried about soul, not body. He forgot everything else, even his mother who loved him like no other.'

'We acted as witnesses as you requested, madam,' MacKenzie said solemnly. 'Your son met his end with dignity. We'll deal with all the outstanding legal issues with your permission.'

Scougall recalled the terrible image of Stuart's twitching body on the gibbet; his screams for the woman who stood before them; his hand lying in the dirt. It would be too painful to tell her that in the last moments of his life he did not cry out for God but sobbed for her. He recalled Thirlsmuir's hand, removed after he was killed. Were they connected in some way?

She remained at the window, looking vacantly down on the High Street as she spoke. 'I can't think upon it. I can't let my mind dwell upon it. No mother should know such pain! How can God allow such butchery? How can God let a mother suffer as I have?'

'He didn't suffer long. I have Rosehaugh's assurance.'

She continued in a trance-like voice. 'I'm left with nothing.' She turned to look out of the window again. 'I hate this stinking city. I miss the view of the hills from my own chamber.'

MacKenzie nodded. The mountains of his native Ross-shire had a special place in his memory.

'Mordington is abroad, fighting in wars I don't understand,' she continued. 'I try to avoid thinking about the present. I can't do it for long. My son's portrait haunts me.'

MacKenzie observed a small picture of Alexander Stuart opposite the window.

She suddenly dropped to her knees and howled. 'How could he do this to me? Why would he wound me so?'

MacKenzie went to her, helping her back to a chair where she sat staring down at her hands. At last she spoke. 'I can understand that he might've done it to spite his father, but why would he destroy the life of his loving mother?'

'The young are transported by the strength of their beliefs, madam. We can't change their minds. When did he convert?'

There were tears on her cheeks as she spoke softly. 'I heard three years ago. The news was like a knife thrust through my heart. I knew others were doing likewise; even some of the great men in the land were turning to the old faith to seek favour with the King. But the thought that my only son served Antichrist was too much to bear.'

Scougall shared her terror of a conversion in the family. He could not imagine that his twin sisters would turn to Rome, but Satan could tempt the Godly. He resolved to warn them when he saw them next.

'For a long time I heard nothing apart from an odd letter,' she continued. 'I wondered if he had left Scotland for good as a few were sent from France. I feared I would never see him again. Then after a long silence of over a year, another arrived. It declared his love for me, but proclaimed that God had told him he must do a great deed to further the cause of the true religion. I wasn't to worry. All would be well.'

She turned her face towards them. MacKenzie saw that she was still a fine-looking woman. She must have been a rare beauty in her youth. She would make a comfortable bedfellow for a widower.

'Although I was relieved to hear from him, I felt a great weight of foreboding. I sensed he was lost to me for good. I sobbed in my chamber and contemplated ending my life. But I was still a mother. I had to travel to Edinburgh where the letter was posted. I'd try one last time to persuade him. I'd keep trying to turn him back to me. But when I got here, I heard Kingsfield was slain and Alexander taken to the Tolbooth. This is how he repays me!'

'I hear one of the priests is beaten by the mob,' she continued.

'It's only what he deserves. I hope the other suffers under Rosehaugh as my son did. And the rest of the Papists in town – I've heard Seaforth's brother is fled to the Highlands!'

Scougall wondered what she would have said if she had known MacKenzie's daughter was betrothed to him. 'Your son isn't the only convert to Rome, madam. It's a tragedy afflicting many families,' he found himself saying as he thought of Elizabeth.

'The divisions caused by religion are absurd – and they call themselves Christian,' said MacKenzie. 'Alexander swore under torture no one told him to kill Kingsfield.'

'Someone planted the idea in his head!' she said bitterly. 'He was a gentle man. He was not a killer. Somebody drove him to do it.'

'Do you have any idea who might have done so?'

'I know nothing of the company he kept since he was lost to me. Everything was a secret. He lived in the shadows. As I said, a couple of letters came from France, another few from London.'

'Can you remember where in France?'

'I'll check when I return home and let you know, if you think it's important.'

'There are other Papists in Edinburgh, madam,' Scougall proposed timidly. 'There's a college of Jesuits in the Abbey.'

'He told me nothing about his associates.'

'Is there anything in his letters that might provide a clue?' asked MacKenzie.

'They are all vague, full of his new-found happiness, love of God and delight in serving the true Church. There's much about transubstantiation and his love of the Mass. Perhaps you might find something in his papers on the table there. He left little else except that foolish confession.'

'I tried to dissuade him from publishing it, but his mind was made up.'

'Your notary might examine them. A few debts are outstanding. You have my authority to settle everything. I'd like the business completed before I return south. I must plead before the council to have his body taken down from the West Port, so I may have him back for proper burial. I want a place where I can talk to him, overlooking the hills where he played happily as a boy.'

'May I recommend caution, madam,' interjected MacKenzie. 'The fever against Papists burns more ferociously each day. The wheel turns towards Presbytery. Make a formal request to the council, but don't pursue it vigorously. Once events have come to a head, I'll take up the case. Quiet determination will prevail above protestation. The council will not make any decisions at the moment – everything is paralysed because of the political situation. The Court of Session doesn't sit and business has ground to a halt because of the invasion. I'll do all I can to have his body returned to you.'

'He's not a traitor! The thought of his body impaled on the city gates is appalling! Why in God's name do they place him there? He was persuaded to do it by others!' She broke down in tears again.

MacKenzie rested his hand on her shoulder. He saw her son swinging from the gibbet and felt an overwhelming sympathy for her. But Stuart had shot a man in cold blood. He had been punished for committing murder, even if encouraged by another.

'You'll get him back. He'll be buried in the kirkyard at Mordington. Be assured, we'll do all we can, madam. I suggest you travel south as soon as possible. The rabble grows stronger each night. They'll soon turn their anger on those related to Papists.'

Scougall thought of Ruairidh laughing with Elizabeth during dinner at The Hawthorns. He was an arrogant soldier who had converted to further his career. He wondered if his love of his new religion would drive him to kill for it.

20

Conversation in Parliament Square

MACKENZIE STOOD BENEATH the huge equestrian statue of Charles II outside the Session. The King's elder brother was represented as a Roman Emperor on horseback, laurel wreaths around his temples, a baton in his right hand. But Charles II was no emperor. MacKenzie had kissed his hand at court in London in 1663. Charles was affable and amusing although duplicitous. In those days Lauderdale ruled the roost in Scottish affairs. The King hated the country because he was forced to sign the Covenant at his coronation. He had never returned to his northern kingdom. Who would have thought that his brother James would become King and make such a botch of it?

As the Session was not sitting, Parliament Square was quieter than usual. He nodded at a few lawyers of his acquaintance. At last the corpulent figure of Archibald Craig waddled towards him. He knew Thirlsmuir's man of business by sight.

'May I have a word, Mr Craig?'

'It's nae every day the Clerk of the Session wants tae speak with me.'

MacKenzie noticed Craig's skin was greasy. His small round nose was sweating like cheese.

'Might I have a few words in private?' MacKenzie addressed him as if he wanted to talk about a point of law.

'I've a meeting tae attend, sir. I'm late already.'

'It's about the death of your master.'

'I've already made a statement tae Mr Stirling. I've naething mair tae say on the matter. On whose authority do you act? I thought you were a servant of the Session, nae an arm of the Crown Officer.'

'I've been asked by Stirling to delve deeper into the killing as the Session is risen. The case has caused much consternation in government circles.'

'Rosehaugh should be shaking in his boots,' Craig scoffed.

'It must be a grave shock for Pittendean?'

'It sets back the affairs of oor family. The Earl is auld and his eldest son has nae appetite for public life. James is a soldier in distant lands. It has damaged oor plans.'

'Your plans,' MacKenzie repeated.

'Thirlsmuir was destined for great things. Did you hear him speak in the chamber?'

'I heard him once or twice.'

'He was glorious there – men were wont tae listen tae him. His lordship wants his speeches published for posterity.'

MacKenzie reflected that they would make a dull volume. It was difficult to convey the power of oratory on the printed page. 'Where do the family stand at this juncture?'

'I've naething tae say tae you about politics, sir. I'm only their man of business. I dealt with the mundane issues.'

'I've heard you were much more than that, Mr Craig.'

'I only serve the family of Pittendean.'

MacKenzie moved forward, forcing Craig back towards the plinth of the statue, towering over the small clerk, who was forced into a corner at the side of Parliament House. 'Tell me about the day of his death.'

Craig was annoyed to be penned in, but MacKenzie would not let him through. At last Craig spoke: 'I met him in the Royal Coffee house at three o'clock. I left about four and returned tae Pittendean House. There's little mair tae add. The Papists are responsible for the murder. Thirlsmuir saw through their treachery.'

'Why would they kill him in such a manner?'

'They serve Antichrist, do they not? Is that nae enough? They slay women and children in cold blood. Have they nae done it often in Ireland and France? They wouldnae hesitate tae kill in the most brutal manner.'

'How were relations between Thirlsmuir and his older brother?'

Craig ruminated for a while before answering: 'the Earl would be the first tae admit his eldest son is a strange fish. You only have tae spend a few seconds in his company to see that. But he's a harmless fool. All he wants tae do is… hunt.'

'Will he not benefit from having his brother out of the way?'

'I see the direction you take me doon, Mr MacKenzie. I'm sure Glenbeath played nae part in his brother's death. He couldnae kill a goose. The sight of blood disturbs him.'

MacKenzie straightened his back and his tone altered, the smile disappearing from his face, his affability melting to coldness. 'Why were you in Niven's Wynd with Thirlsmuir just after four o'clock on the day of his death if you returned to Pittendean House as you said?'

Craig tried to remain calm, but he was clearly shaken and weighing up what to say. 'I was nae there, sir. As I telt Mr Stirling, I returned tae my chamber to attend tae business. In the evening I was in the Targe Tavern with friends. They'll vouch for me.'

'We have a witness who saw two men. One was tall and handsome. the other short and fat.' MacKenzie wanted to get under his skin. Sometimes you had to play the scoundrel to flush one out.

'Your witness is mistaken. I wasnae there. There are many short fat men in the city.'

MacKenzie's demeanour altered again. He smiled urbanely. 'Thank you, Mr Craig. Pittendean said you'd provide a list of his creditors and debtors.'

'I'll attend tae it as soon as I hae time, sir.'

MacKenzie gave him a friendly tap on the shoulder. 'If only the King would call a parliament so the nation could air its grievances,' he added provocatively, waiting to see what the response might be.

'We're agreed on one thing. But I fear he'll nae do so. This will only be solved by force of arms.'

Golf on the Links

SCOUGALL COULD NOT remember a time when he did not have a golf club in his hands. His father and mother did nothing to encourage him. Indeed his mother viewed the game as a sin; not among the first rank, like fornication, theft or murder, but a sin nonetheless. Spending too much time on the course was a waste of time when you could be earning money or worshipping God. His father did not swing a club often, but his grandfather, also called David Scougall, who he was named after, was one of the finest golfers in the east of Scotland. He had no doubt inherited his skill from him. If there was a place where he was at ease, where he was himself, and not some other feeble creature, it was on the Links. He might be a tongue-tied fool in society, but on the course he spoke articulately with his clubs and there were few who could drive as far.

'Thank you for meeting me, John. Can it only be a few weeks since we sat together at The Hawthorns. I presume you've heard the news about Ruairidh?' said Seaforth as he stepped out of his coach. Two heavily armed retainers clad in plaids dropped down from the back and remained in close proximity to him.

'I've only heard what's spoken on the street,' replied MacKenzie sternly as he placed his ball on the first tee. 'He was flushed out of a Papist den by the mob. He's suspected of complicity in the murder of Kingsfield.'

MacKenzie swung in an inelegant fashion, the club stopping for just too long at the apex, but he made good contact. 'It's not the kind of news a prospective father-in-law wants to hear about the man his only daughter is to marry.'

Scougall felt awkward to be in their company. It was surely a private matter between them, although he observed smugly Seaforth's mediocre shot, hit with a violent hook. His game appeared as misguided as his religious position.

'My brother had nothing to do with the killing. Stuart was known to him, but the fool acted alone. Ruairidh will be safer in Brussels or Paris for a time. Tell Elizabeth she can't see him until things settle down.'

Scougall took his lead scraper and drove solidly down the middle. The ball came to rest a good sixty yards ahead of the others.

'The King's position grows weaker by the day,' said MacKenzie as they headed off down the fairway. 'The mob grows more vehement each night. We must put the marriage on hold, my lord. It would be unwise to make hasty decisions at this juncture.'

'Ruairidh's sorry for not being honest with you. He converted in the Low Countries after wrestling with his conscience for months. I believe the match is still a sound one.'

'Has it anything to do with furthering his career as a soldier under a Papist King?' asked MacKenzie, anger bubbling underneath his cool exterior. A Gaelic proverb came to him: *Faodaidh fearg sealltainn a-steach an cridh' an duine ghlic, ach còmhnaichidh i'n cridh' an amadain.* Anger may look in on a wise man's heart, but it bides in the heart of a fool. They were wise words. He tried to conquer his feelings.

'I believe not. He lived a dissolute life before. Now he's a reformed character.'

'A dissolute life?'

'He was prone to… the table… and the bottle.'

'And the whore?' added MacKenzie.

'He's a young man, John. He's sowed his wild oats. Who among us can say he hasn't done so? I'm sure even Mr Scougall has strayed from the path of righteousness occassionally.'

Scougall was appalled by the suggestion. He did not gamble and had never visited a whore. He had perhaps imbibed too much wine on occasion and once drank a large quantity of whisky from which he suffered greatly the next day. That was hardly a dissolute life. 'I believe I've not, sir,' he said in a pathetic manner.

'Now he'll be answerable to a higher power,' added Seaforth.

MacKenzie wanted to shout out what a scoundrel he was. But Seaforth was his chief. Kinship was a trap as well as a source of succour. 'Did you know he had converted, my lord?'

'I'm sure you'll not understand, being an irreligious man. The Catholic religion brings great peace for a convert, like returning home after years of exile. It's worth risking everything for.'

Scougall could not believe the hypocrisy of the vain fool. He almost applauded as Seaforth fluffed his second shot, sending a huge divot into the air. The ball came to rest only ten yards away.

'We've been misled,' said MacKenzie sternly.

'It can't be helped. My King's a Catholic. I owe obedience to him as God's anointed on earth. To oppose him is a mortal sin, not a small one like misleading a cousin.'

MacKenzie had to smother his ire. There might be grim satisfaction if he could engineer an end to the match. Elizabeth would be heartbroken, but saved from ruin. Another husband could easily be found.

Seaforth played his third shot, his ball bouncing along the fairway and coming to rest thirty yards away.

'Where's Ruairidh?' asked MacKenzie as he approached his ball.

'I assure you, he had nothing to do with Kingsfield's death. The Catholic brotherhood came together to pray. Kingsfield's name was never mentioned. The priests were harmless men of God, not plotters. One has paid sorely already. The other is taken into custody to be tortured. The remaining priests in the city plan to leave as soon as they can.'

'What does he make of Alexander Stuart?'

'He thinks him a foolish fanatic.'

'What of the death of Kingsfield?'

'What do you mean?'

'Who'll benefit from it?'

'Not the Papists in Scotland, John. Their position is weakened. Perth and Melfort are furious. Kingsfield was an arrogant oaf with enemies on his own side but we Catholics were better off with him alive.'

'Who might benefit among the Presbyterians?'

'A warrior is removed from the fray before battle is begun. Those vying for leadership will be rejoicing; Queensberry and Pittendean for example, but also those who are not Presbyterians such as Hamilton, who lurks in London, and Atholl.'

'Is Pittendean weakened by his son's death? He's an old man.'

'Yesterday I saw him talking with Lord Basil, Hamilton's brother, at Holyrood House. He's a political animal to the soles of his feet.'

'Could the Presbyterians be involved in the assassination?'

'They must persuade a Papist to kill for them. Do you believe the killings are connected?'

MacKenzie hit another powerful shot. It seemed to hang for a moment against the blue of the sky before falling onto the green.

'One is a premeditated assassination before a score of witnesses. The killer makes confession and is executed. Stuart told us nothing more of his motives. The slaying of Thirlsmuir appears the act of a madman. I'm privy to all the details, which are monstrous. But something doesn't quite fit. Perhaps it's just the times.'

Scougall thought again about the connections he knew about – the boy who delivered the note and Stuart's testament; the make of London wig worn by Kingsfield and kept by Guillemot in the storeroom. Behind it all was the association.

'The government must regret sending the army into England. Scotland's left open to insurrection,' said MacKenzie.

'The militia will protect the kingdom,' replied Seaforth.

'The Presbyterians are well armed. The cellars of Edinburgh are stacked full of weapons. The door of the kingdom is left open.'

'The Scots army must help the King,' continued Seaforth. 'The Prince of Orange must be crushed in England first. If he takes the south, Scotland will fall and Ireland too.'

'If the King called a parliament and negotiated he might regain the people's trust. They don't want to rise up against him. They don't want another civil war. Remember the devastation of the last one.'

'I fear it'll be decided in the field as all such struggles are. We can't negotiate with rebels. They must be crushed.'

'But the rebels have widespread support among the people. The King has none.'

'It's only a minority in Scotland who support them, a rabble from troublesome parts of the kingdom. Claverhouse showed what can be done... with a little force.'

Scougall hit his second shot straight as a die, high into the sky. They followed it with their eyes to an almost unimaginable height before it fell to land just in front of the green, bounced a couple of times and came to rest within ten feet of the hole.

On the green, Seaforth putted home after four attempts. 'One hole will suffice today, gentlemen. I've other business to attend to.'

'I must see Ruairidh,' said MacKenzie solemnly.

'I'll ask him before he leaves.'

'He's still in Edinburgh?'

'I've said too much. There are spies everywhere and possibly assassins.'

Scougall observed the two shifty Highlanders at the edge of the green. As Seaforth picked up his ball he spoke directly to him for the first time: 'You must be pleased with developments, sir?'

'I'm a golfer, my lord. I've no interest in politics.' This of course was true, for in the game of golf there was no shady halfway house, no subterfuge and mistrust, just a simple desire to get a ball in a hole in the lowest number of shots. It was a game of purity, whereas politics was corrupt.

'I could be the next target of an assassin,' Seaforth continued. 'The gates of the city are watched. Each ship leaving Leith is searched. The Presbyterians have spies on every road. It's too dangerous to move him at the moment. When the time's right, I'll get him out.'

'He might tell us something useful about Thirlsmuir's death. Stirling has asked me to help with the case.'

'It might be possible. There's just one other matter.'

MacKenzie knew he had fallen into a trap. There would be a meeting with Ruairidh, but there was a price. There was always a price when dealing with the nobles.

'My funds have dried up. The merchants change all their money into gold and silver. Some take cash out of Edinburgh and bury it on their estates. No one wishes to hold bonds or notes. No one will lend me anything unless at exorbitant rates. I must rely on the generosity of my clansmen.'

It was no wonder that the moneylenders would not lend the spendthrift a penny, thought MacKenzie. They would never see any of it again. It would be spent in London shops or the bawdy-houses of Paris. 'I'll see what I can do, after I've spoken to him.'

'You drive a hard bargain, John. Two hundred pounds sterling would see me through the next few months.'

Scougall was shocked by the size of the request, a reflection, no doubt, of Seaforth's desperate finances. The bonds of kinship were like the filaments of a spider's web. It was impossible to be free of them.

'There's another matter. I need to know the names of the principal usurers in the city,' said MacKenzie.

'Credit's scarce at the moment,' Seaforth continued, 'but a couple still lend. One is a merchant called Adam Moffat; the other a fellow just returned from exile called the Lamb.'

'The Lamb?' repeated MacKenzie.

'Baillie of Lammington, a laird from the Borders.'

Scougall realised he could not put off telling MacKenzie much longer.

22

A Body in a Bawdy-House

SCOUGALL GRABBED HIS cloak and followed MacKenzie and Stirling. They passed down the High Street and made their way through a warren of closes to an inconspicuous door in Weir's Land.

'I've nae touched onything,' the woman in a low-cut scarlet gown who answered the door said defensively. She was in late middle-age, her face covered thickly with powder and rouge. She smiled at Stirling with an expression full of recognition. Scougall realised he was a customer of the house. Why did he need a whore when he had a wife? It was the road to damnation. He recalled the verse from Proverbs 7:27: *Her house is the way to hell, going down to the chambers of death.*

'Where is he, Maggie?' Stirling asked solemnly.

'I've nae seen you for a long time, sir. Come this way, gentlemen.'

They followed her up a spiral staircase and down a passageway to a door. Maggie shook her head. 'I cannae go in. I've nae had a deid ane in ten years. Deid anes are bad for trade.'

The small chamber was simply furnished with a bed, table, chair and cupboard. An awning hung on the wall opposite the door. As their eyes adjusted to the gloom, a shape on the bed became visible. MacKenzie took Stirling's candle and lit another on the table. He slowly pulled back the white sheet which covered it.

A naked body was lying face-down on a mattress drenched in blood. Scougall turned away in disgust. 'Who is he?' he gasped, repulsed by the large hairy buttocks.

MacKenzie held the candle above the head to reveal cropped red hair. A pile of clothes and a periwig lay beside an expensive pair of boots on the floor.

'How was he killed, John?' Stirling asked from a safe distance behind.

MacKenzie examined the body closely. 'It looks like he was garrotted. Observe the indentations on the mattress on either side. The killer sat on the victim's back when strangling him. There are bruises around the neck and marks left by a cord. The blood is from an injury to his front. We need to turn him.'

The dead man was as heavy as a sack of coal. At last, the three of them managed to tip him over. A dreadful wound in the groin was revealed.

'He's been castrated!' cried Stirling.

'Not just castration, Archibald. All his organs are removed.'

'A second murder, or a third! Rosehaugh will be appalled.'

MacKenzie turned to Maggie who was still in the passageway. 'Who is he?'

'Dr Black, sir. Dr Isaac Black, a medical man, a travelling fellow. It was his first visit tae ma hoose. He said he was just back frae foreign lands.'

The name struck Scougall like a punch in the guts. Two members of the club slain hideously. It could not be a coincidence. A terrible thought swept through him. His own life might be in danger. Were all those who attended being punished for plotting against the King, for questioning the natural order established by God? He cursed himself for agreeing to accompany Morrison.

'Who was he with?' asked MacKenzie.

'A new lass frae France. She didnae look strang enough tae kill a man like that.'

'Where is she?' asked Stirling.

'There's nae sign of her since the body was found.'

'Where does she live, Maggie?'

'Baxter's Land, I believe.'

'What's her name?'

'Christine, she called herself.'

'Christine what?'

'Just Christine.'

The three of them searched the chamber meticulously. There were bloodstains on the floor and wall beside the bed. MacKenzie got down on his knees and moved the candle along the floorboards to look underneath. A couple of old dresses hung in the press. Stirling pulled back the awning to reveal a small window about two feet square. He opened the shutters and looked out. The neighbouring tenement was about ten feet away across the wynd.

There was a sheer drop of above twenty feet.

'Could a woman have the strength to strangle a man as large as Black?' asked Scougall trying to compose himself.

'It's possible she was aided by a man. He might've been waiting in the room, or she may have let him in.'

'Where could he hide?' asked Stirling.

'Maybe in the shadows behind the door. The cupboard doesn't look big enough.'

'Did the killer escape through the window?' asked Scougall.

'But it's tiny,' Stirling said.

'A small woman might've squeezed through.'

'Perhaps they just left through the door.'

'We're three storeys up. A descent would be treacherous, requiring someone undaunted by heights, perhaps an acrobat of some kind.'

'They have high mountains in France,' Scougall said without thinking.

'It all looks too tidy,' MacKenzie replied. He turned to Maggie. 'Was there a letter left in the room?'

'Nothing, sir.'

Stirling left the house to summon Lawtie and inform Rosehaugh, while MacKenzie and Scougall retreated to Maggie's howff, a small cave of a room on the ground floor which was her office. They sat on a threadbare settee.

'Will you share a glass with me tae calm yer nerves, gentlemen?'

'Thank you, Maggie,' said MacKenzie.

'Your tall friend has gone?' she asked.

'Mr Stirling attends to business.'

Maggie gave a knowing smile. 'He's a fine gentleman, Mr Stirling. A gentle giant of a man.'

Scougall could not believe that he was sitting in a bawdy-house, sharing a glass of wine with a whore.

'How did you find yourself in this business, Maggie? I'm sure there are easier professions to follow,' MacKenzie asked affably. As she filled their glasses with foul-tasting wine, she told them her story. Scougall sat with his notebook on his knees, taking down her words, appalled by the narrative of depravity, but moved by her sad history. She counted her cash as she spoke, recording the amounts on a piece of paper, the strokes of her quill slow and deliberate. She said she could barely read or write but had a sharp eye for money.

'Tell us what happened tonight, Maggie,' said MacKenzie when she had completed her story.

'The doctor arrived at about six o'clock. I went through in my mind who I had tae offer. Jenny was nae weel, Jessie six months with child. Perhaps the new lass frae France would do. She was a bit strange looking with an uncanny face, but they all like fresh meat.'

'The doctor staggered into the howff. He was drunk. He smiled at me. "Ah Maggie," he said, slurring. "What do you have for a poor man on this summer's night? I'm inflamed with passion. My soul's burning for it."

'I said "Come awa in, sir. Have a seat in the howff. I'll pour you a glass. Let me hae a wee word with the new lass frae France. You ken the French are expert in the airt o love.'

"She's travelled far to be with me tonight. I'm honoured, Maggie."

"'She's fled persecution in that country, sir. You'll be the first to hae her in the kingdom of Scotland."

'I left him for a moment, made my way quickly tae her room, the chamber where his body lies. She was combing her hair at the glass. I told her she had a customer and she asked his name. "He's a doctor," I says, "a Dr Black." She smiled at this as if she recognised the name. "Then he will be my first customer in Scotland." "He'll be up presently," I said tae her. I returned tae the howff and telt him the room, reminding him of the price. He finished his glass, put doon half and aff he went. It was a quiet night, just a couple of ither customers ouer the next few hours. I dozed for a while. When I woke I realised he'd been with her almost three hours. I usually check tae mak sure the lassies are content for things tae continue, so I knocked on the door at about nine-thirty. Nae answer. I knocked again. Nae answer. And again. I thought they'd maybe fallen asleep so I tried tae open it. It was locked. I was annoyed. I had told the lass tae keep it unlocked. I had tae fetch my ither key. As soon as the door was opened, I saw blood everywhere. I couldnae look at the body, so I got a girl tae put a sheet ouer him. I told her nae tae touch onything and sent for the guards.'

'Tell me about Christine,' said MacKenzie intently.

'She came to see me last week, looking for work, a poor refugee frae France, she said. She had come tae the city with her bairn. She knew the trade from her younger days. She was a bonnie looking thing, thin-like. She begged me to gie her a chance. She feared working the streets in a town she didnae ken.'

'Was there anything else about her? What did she wear?'

'She was dressed in an auld red frock. She didnae hae much of a chest, thin-like, as I said, but some men like that. I would nae usually tak a girl withoot recommendation. But she looked desperate and business is doon over the last few months. Folk are fired up wi politics, nae fornication. I've lost a couple of girls. So I telt her I would tak her on trial. She turned up on time, an hour before the doctor appeared.'

'Did she bring anything with her?'

'I think she carried a bag, but I dinnae ken what was inside it.'

'What size was it, Maggie?'

She indicated with her hands a couple of feet long.

'Was it made of this?' MacKenzie removed a piece of linen about an inch square from his pocket. 'I found a snag attached to a nail on the floor beside the bed.'

Scougall had not noticed him coming upon it.

'That looks like it, sir.'

'And you said she lived in Baxter's Land.'

'That's what she telt me. I've nae idea if it's true.'

'What was her surname?'

'She told me. A French name but I cannae mind it.'

'How regular a customer was Black?'

'It was his first time in ma hoose.'

'Had you ever seen him before?'

She hesitated. 'No, sir. I would've remembered a gentleman like him.'

MacKenzie sat forward and smiled. 'I need you to do something for me, Maggie. It may not be to your liking. I want you to write a list of all your customers over the last month, as many as you can remember. I realise it'll be difficult. Your clients desire anonymity. But if you want business to revive, we must catch the killer quickly. I will, of course, keep the names secret and destroy the list when the case is solved.'

'I'm slow at writing, sir.' She did not look keen. 'I'll dae my best. Do you think the killer is ane of them, working with Christine? Ma ither lassies are aw terrified.'

'That's what I aim to find out, Maggie. But I'll need your help.'

She said that she would do what he asked. He then told her that he wanted to speak with the other girls.

'There are only two, Janet Stratton and Isobel Young. I'll get them for you.'

MacKenzie questioned both but found out little. They had no recollection of anything particular during the evening. Janet recounted how she was summoned by Maggie and in terror placed a sheet over the corpse. Isobel could not face entering the room. Neither of them knew anything about the French girl.

23

Scougall Makes a Confession

SCOUGALL SAT NERVOUSLY beside the fireplace in MacKenzie's study, looking up at the paintings on the only wall not lined with books. One was a portrait of Grissell Hay whose death they had investigated the year before; the other was MacKenzie's wife. There was a remarkable resemblance to his daughter Elizabeth, the same dark hair and striking blue eyes.

'I'm sorry for keeping you, Davie,' said MacKenzie as he entered. 'I've had a long meeting with Stirling. Some more wine? The news from England is not good... although you may disagree. The King's supporters are melting away. His daughter Ann has left London for the north.'

MacKenzie withdrew a bundle of documents from a leather case and spread them on the table. 'We need to take stock; stand aside from the fervour on the streets, take to the balcony and observe the dancers from above; apply the faculty of reason to the evidence, although there's not much.'

He took a seat at the table before continuing. 'A young Papist commits murder on the High Street of Edinburgh, confesses his crime and is executed. Why did he kill, Davie?'

Scougall wanted to tell him about the association immediately, but felt compelled to answer. 'He was possibly driven by hatred of a father whose abuse encouraged him to seek revenge.'

'But who was pulling the strings? And there's the connection with Ruairidh MacKenzie.'

'Is he still to marry Elizabeth?'

'I've been misled by my chief. I'm also angry with myself for not being more cautious. I know you were unhappy about the negotiations.'

Scougall could not understand MacKenzie's loyalty to his clan. He did not know if there was a chief of the Scougalls, although there were many folk of the name throughout the kingdom. None were landed men, nobles or lairds; all belonged to the middling sort, although a distant relative was an artist of renown who had painted the famous Marquis of Argyll. He did not know what to say, so he took a sip of wine, looking for the courage to begin. 'I was worried you were giving away too much money, sir.'

'It's entirely possible that the killing of Black is unrelated. There was no letter. Let's turn to Thirlsmuir.'

'It may be a blood feud, sir.'

'But most killings of that kind are by pistol or sword. Roasting a body on a spit is not common in family fights. We're dealing with a killer who wallows in destruction, one who exalts in murder, not a person who kills on the spur of the moment. On the other hand, it could be a political conspiracy.'

'Surely only a man possessed by the Devil, a servant of Satan, could kill in such a manner!'

'It's not Satan we seek but a man or woman, Davie!'

'A woman could not emasculate a doctor and hoist a laird onto a spit!'

'A strong woman is capable of doing these things or a woman helped by a man. Now let's examine the letters again. There must be something in them.'

Scougall looked down at his hands. They were shaking. He could put it off no longer.

'I must tell you something, sir.' He tried to look worried, so MacKenzie would understand that he had something serious to say.

'What is it, Davie?'

'I fear you'll not be pleased with me.'

'What have you done?' MacKenzie smiled, raising his head to meet Scougall's eyes. 'Something very foolish?'

'I've attended an association, sir.'

MacKenzie's smile disappeared. 'I didn't realise you were a political man. I didn't think you plotted with Whigs!'

'I don't plot, sir. I'm not cut out for politics. I don't like the business. But I don't support the King. I cannot do so. His policies go against all we have fought for since the Reformation.'

'There's a difference between not supporting his policies and siding with those who seek to get rid of him by force, even by killing him. I don't support them, but I could not countenance armed rebellion.'

'I've only been there once, sir. I didn't like those who attended.

They use the mob to do their bidding. They turn its anger on and off like water from a pump. I didn't support the assault on Innes.'

'You were there?' MacKenzie wore an expression of incomprehension. 'I can't believe you were part of a rabble which took the law into its own hands. I've heard the priest was badly beaten. It may yet be an act of murder if he doesn't recover.'

'I wasn't involved, sir. I stood at the back. I attended... reluctantly. I didn't know what was going to happen.'

'But you did nothing to help him.'

'He was a Papist priest!' Scougall felt tears welling up. 'What was I to do? The crowd would have turned on me if I'd come to his aid.' He was ashamed to admit that he had had no intention of doing so. The priest was a servant of Antichrist. He could never bring himself to help such a person.

'He was an unarmed man set upon by a mob.' MacKenzie looked disgusted.

'George Morrison persuaded me to go. He's an old acquaintance from Musselburgh, recently returned to Scotland. He said it would be good for business.'

'What business?'

Scougall had not intended to tell him everything about his dealings with Morrison.

'He wants to establish a company of merchants to trade with the Indies. He says the opportunities are great. He's asked me to be his man of business.'

'His man of business! What of your work for me as writer? Is that not good enough for you, Davie Scougall?'

'It is, sir. I have much to thank you for, much indeed. But am I not to rise? The company might prosper. The opportunity might not come along again.' He felt wretched.

'So you seek to raise money from the club. The fanatics are to be your investors!'

'No. That isn't the reason. I accompanied him because he asked me to. We seek money from anyone who'll provide it. You may invest if you wish.'

'I wouldn't give a penny to such a nest of vipers!' MacKenzie cursed violently in Gaelic. 'I can't believe that after all I've done for you, after all we've been through together, I'm repaid in this way. You plot with Whigs behind my back!'

Scougall bowed his head. He knew there was worse to come.

'There's more, sir.'

'More? Tell me!' MacKenzie snapped. 'You're to be made Sheriff of Haddington after the rebellion?'

'I should have told you. I've wrestled with myself for days. I couldn't sleep. Golf has brought me no comfort. I'm ashamed of my conduct, but I couldn't find the right moment. It's been an unbearable burden. There were always interruptions. I didn't know where to begin...' He was mumbling feebly and his face assumed the rich hue of port. Tears were on his cheeks. He felt humiliation like a dagger in his guts.

'What are you talking about, Davie?'

'I've kept important intelligence from you.'

MacKenzie fell silent for a few moments, before asking: 'What do you know?'

'Thirlsmuir and Black were members of the club.'

'Two of the men you plotted with are murdered and you forgot to tell me!' There followed a stream of expletives in Gaelic.

'I'm sorry, sir.'

'Get out!' MacKenzie shouted. 'Get out of my sight, boy!'

Scougall had never seen him so enraged. As he rose, he stammered another pathetic apology and began to take his leave.

'Sit!' bellowed MacKenzie.

Scougall retraced a few spaces and dropped down obediently.

'This case is more important than your ridiculous antics. You've been a fool, Davie Scougall! You've let me down... But here's something, at last. Tell me everything you know and don't hold anything back.'

Behind his mask of anger, MacKenzie's mind was spinning. The killing of two men from the club was of great significance. Excitement burned through him and he felt his confidence returning. He could see in his mind's eye the black bird receding further into the distance.

Scougall shared everything he could remember of the night at the association, in particular the identity of all those who attended. He apologised again and again until MacKenzie told him to shut up. When he had asked his questions, they shared a bottle of wine. Scougall was relieved to take refuge in claret. Quite unlike himself, he drank deeply, seeking the oblivion of inebriation. Only when they had finished the second bottle and begun a third, did he forget his stupidity.

'You've made your confession like a Papist!' MacKenzie slurred. Scougall laughed. He was drunk. But he felt much better having unburdened himself.

24

A Walk in the Country

SCOUGALL MADE AN effort to say little that might be deemed controversial as they walked down Leith Wynd to the north of the city. He was eager to make amends for his deception. They passed the Correction House where the poor were put to work and the College Kirk, before leaving the city through Beggar's Walk between the Nor Loch and the North Craigs. They found themselves among open rigs, the path meandering northwards through some pleasant countryside. At a junction they turned west along a well-worn path which afforded views of the city to the south and of Fife across the Firth to the north.

'The fresh air will blow away our hangovers. Tell me again about the note, Davie.' MacKenzie was in good spirits having slept soundly.

Scougall was feeling unwell but focused all his attention on remembering every detail from the association. 'The door opened without a knock towards the end of the meeting. One of the guards entered. He handed Thirlsmuir a note. He read it quickly, whispered something to Craig, took his hat and left.'

'There was no sign of the hat in the storeroom. Was there anything else, Davie? Think.'

He tried to recall the scene. He had looked up as the guard left. 'Yes – outside was a boy in the shadows.' He had forgotten to tell MacKenzie the previous evening.

'Would you recognise him?'

'The same child handed out Stuart's paper on the day of his execution. He has a harelip.'

'You told me no one knew of the location except those who attended. However, the person who gave the boy the note knew where they were meeting. You know what this could mean, Davie?'

'I'm not sure, sir.'

'The killer could be one of those at the meeting.'

'But why would a Protestant slay other Protestants? Why would he send Thirlsmuir a note if he was at the meeting?'

'He wanted Thirlsmuir to leave, but did not want to draw attention to himself. He may have appointed the boy or got someone else to do so. We must, of course, assume that those who attended didn't tell anyone else. We can't be sure of that, but given the sensitive nature of the discussions it's possible. We need to find the boy as a matter of urgency. He may lead us to the killer.'

'Is it possible a Papist has infiltrated the association?

'The person may be Papist, Protestant, or neither. At least we've a theory to be working with. One of those sitting round the table could be responsible. Let me recall their names – Black, Lammington, Grimston, Craig, Johnston, Guillemot, Quinn, Thirlsmuir and Morrison. Of the nine, two are dead.'

'It's not Morrison, sir. I can vouch for him.'

'But you've only just met him again after many years. You know little about him.'

'I know his sister. He's a merchant, not a murderer!'

'I hope we can rule him out, Davie, but they're all suspects at the moment, with the exception of you. I base this supposition on knowledge of your character.' Scougall was pleased to see him smile.

'What about the guards?'

'Morrison told me one was Lammington's man and the other Grimston's.'

'You said yourself the same pair carried off the priest. Thirlsmuir was dead by then. I don't see how they could've killed him.'

'Morrison and Johnston were also with the mob, so was Craig.'

'Then we might be able to exclude them, unless they arranged for someone else to carry out the killing.'

'What about Ruairidh MacKenzie?' Scougall asked tentatively, hoping not to sound as if he was gloating.

'Seaforth's adamant he had nothing to do with Kingsfield's shooting.'

'But he's a Papist, sir.'

'Seaforth will arrange a meeting so we can question him. Is there anything else you can remember?'

'There's one other thing. The note was left on the table. Craig knocked it onto the floor.'

'We must visit the room as soon as we're back in town.'

They reached the top of a small knoll and stood in silence, taking in the panorama to the south, the great castle on the right, the spires of kirks and high tenements, the Nor Loch before them like a black rag, the long sentence of Edinburgh taking the eye from the castle rock to Arthur's Seat which guarded the city like a crouching lion.

'All appears quiet from here,' said MacKenzie. 'But what plots are being hatched, what murders formulated over there?'

He turned to look north across the Firth. 'I long for the Highlands. Let's return when these troubles are over.'

Scougall's prejudices against the Highlands had been accentuated by a violent assault at the hands of caterans on a journey to Glenshieldaig, the retreat of a MacLean chief, a couple of years before. The thought of another visit was not appealing. He knew what he would find – high mountains, bog, rain, wind and whisky, which he had no taste for; the people were little influenced by the church, often keeping barbarous customs, which included the worship of deities other than the one true God. He longed to experience the wide world, rather than freezing in a Highland keep. But he must work his way back up in MacKenzie's estimation. He forced himself to smile. 'It would give me great pleasure to see your ancestral home, sir.'

'Splendid. I've business outstanding in Ross-shire. We'll make a journey to Ardcoul as soon as this case is over. You'll meet my brothers. We'll enjoy some leisure – golf and perhaps hunt in the hills.'

Scougall had never hunted in his life. But his feigned enthusiasm seemed to improve MacKenzie's mood. He patted him affectionately on the shoulder.

'Let's turn over a new leaf, Davie. I accept your apology for your stupidity. I'm sorry I was so angry with you... We must agree to differ on politics.' He nodded towards Edinburgh. 'Revolution's in the air. A revolution which you support and I do not. I'll not change your view about bishops and you'll not alter mine about Presbytery. The issue will be resolved by men who have stronger convictions than us. They'll risk their lives for Presbytery and fight with every fibre for their King. They're the men who make history. We're only observers of it. We must hold on to what we share as men, especially the rule of law. History teaches that revolution will not be the end of change. Some hope for greater transformation –

fundamental reform of the constitution, including a closer union with England.'

Scougall was about to say that such a union was a sound idea. It would lock two Protestant realms together and provide markets for Scottish goods in England and its plantations. But he remained silent. He knew that MacKenzie believed it would be a disaster. Scotland would be a conquered land run entirely in the interests of England.

'I fear that everything is pre-ordained, sir. There's nothing we can do to change the course of events. The killer's actions are predetermined. We're all being slaughtered one by one.'

MacKenzie smiled mischievously. 'A Presbyterian ponders pre-destination. Forget such preposterous metaphysics. We have free will. I assure you, Davie. Nothing's set in stone. Th effects of last night's wine have dampened your spirits.'

But Scougall had heard it often enough in church. Only a few were saved and assured a place in heaven as the Elect. Most were condemned to Hell. He had not considered the details before, but now that he feared for his life, he saw there was logic in it. 'I've sinned against the Lord. There's nothing I can do about it.'

'Forget the pronouncements of the clergy, Davie. How do they know anything more than the next man? It's a ridiculous theory,' MacKenzie scoffed.

But Scougall was trapped in a laberynth of theology.

'A murderer of a most brutal kind is in the city. We must find him or her, before they kill again.'

Scougall nodded solemnly. 'I must apologise…'

'No more apologies. Let's turn our minds entirely to the case. You still have much to tell me. I want to know everything you can remember about the association. Last night you spoke through the fog of wine.'

MacKenzie led the way down the track as Scougall went over everything again.

'Both Thirlsmuir and Black were leading figures in the movement,' said MacKenzie as they approached St Cuthbert's Kirk in the shadow of the castle. 'Their deaths open the field for others. Could a power struggle be behind this? We've already met Guillemot. What motive could he have?'

'I can't think why a newcomer to the city would commit murder in a place which has welcomed him.'

'I want you to speak with young Johnston. Learn as much as you can. Leave Grimston and Lammington to me. Then we'll seek out Quinn and Guthrie. First, tell me something of Morrison and his sister.'

'George and Agnes are Musselburgh folk. He's an enthusiastic merchant and Agnes...' He was looking for the right words, but what ones could describe her – fine, comely, buxom, bonnie, blithe, beautiful, wholesome. None of them were quite right. None would quite suffice to describe her or Elizabeth. And another question troubled him – was Agnes one of God's chosen?

'Agnes... Agnes will be my wife... I hope... but I haven't asked her yet.'

'May I give you a piece of advice, Davie. Ask her before someone else does,' laughed MacKenzie.

Scougall had not considered she would have other suitors. The thought of a rival or rivals was dreadful. He would have to act soon or risk losing her.

'I'll ask George tonight. Her father's dead. You're right, sir – what on earth am I waiting for?'

'By the way, I collected this from Maggie Lister this morning.'

MacKenzie handed him a grubby piece of paper. On it was a list of names scrolled in a child-like hand. There were also a series of strange doodles down one side which looked like an elephant's head and trunk. Scougall recognised two names on the list – Stirling's was not unexpected, but the other was. Lammington had visited the house on the day Black was killed.

Back in town, Scougall retraced the route he had taken to the association. Eventually he found the old apartments. The door was open. They climbed the spiral staircase to the third storey and walked down the passageway to where the guards had stood. The door of the chamber was ajar. No one was inside; the bottles and glasses still lay on the table untouched since the meeting.

'I was sitting here, Morrison was beside me, Thirlsmuir next to him,' said Scougall. He got down on his knees to search on the floor and spotted a ball of paper beside the wall. Fishing it out, he handed it to MacKenzie.

'Three letters cut from a pamphlet: the capitals S, T and M.'

'Why is it presented like that?' asked Scougall.

'The killer leaves little behind. We can't observe the handwriting.'

'What does it mean?'

MacKenzie reflected for a few moments. 'STM. St Magdalene's Chapel, perhaps. It may have simply been a request for him to go to there.'

Quinn's shop was opposite Guillemot's at the head of Niven's Wynd. Scougall was reluctant to face the Irish shopkeeper. If they had not been told already by Guillemot, the association would surely find out he was aiding MacKenzie. He entered timidly behind him.

The shop was an oasis from the stinking city, suffused with an overpoweringly sweet smell, completely at odds with the reek of the streets outside. It was like stepping inside a rainbow as the light from three large windows was reflected through a myriad of bottles and phials. Scougall was relieved to see a woman serving behind the counter, a thin creature wearing spectacles.

'May I help you, gentlemen?' She spoke in an Irish accent similar to Quinn's.

'You're a citizen of Dublin, madam?' asked MacKenzie. 'I'd recognise that voice anywhere.'

'I'm a Dubliner born and bred, as is my brother.'

'What brought you to Edinburgh?'

'My brother wanted to leave Ireland. Why do you ask, sir?'

'We work for Crown Officer Stirling.'

She hesitated for a moment, eyeing them suspiciously before continuing, 'Andrew's worried about the future of Ireland. The Papists and Protestants are at each other's throats. It's different in Scotland where only a handful of zealots follow the Whore. In Ireland we are outnumbered. The Papists take every opportunity to abuse us. He thought we would be safer in the country of our ancestors. There's no future for Presbyterians like us in Ireland.'

'Now you bring your sweet-smelling liquids to Edinburgh. You'll find our city in much need of perfume!' replied MacKenzie.

Scougall remained silent, praying that Quinn would not appear.

'The city's been very kind to us. We bring you golden vials full of odours.' She beckoned them to look round.

'May we speak with your brother?' asked MacKenzie.

'A fever has taken him. It should burn out in a few days, hopefully. He rests above us.'

She pointed to the ceiling.

'Then, may we speak to you, madam...'

'Helen Quinn.'

'I'm John MacKenzie and this is Davie Scougall. We're helping the Crown Officer investigate the death of Lelsie of Thirlsmuir. Niven's Wynd is full of newcomers to the city. Your neighbour Guillemot is a refugee from France.'

'Yes, Mr Guillemot is a Huguenot.'

MacKenzie's demeanour lost its playfulness. 'Thirlsmuir's body was found in his storeroom at the bottom of the wynd.'

The woman nodded gravely. 'A terrible business.'

'What's your opinion of Mr Guillemot?'

'I've only shared a few words with him, but he keeps a pretty shop. I've heard he's suffered much; lost his wife and daughter in the persecution. My brother tells me he's a good neighbour. Surely you don't think he's responsible?'

'We must leave no stone unturned. Have you noticed anything out of the ordinary in the wynd of late? Has anyone unusual visited your shop or Guillemot's over the last few weeks?'

She was silent for a moment, before raising her hand to her mouth. Scougall noticed red lipstick was thickly applied. What was this profession of perfumer? Was the natural odour of women not good enough, must it be covered up? It was another thing his mother disapproved of. Folk should smell like folk, not flowers. But Quinn and his sister were good Protestants. He wondered if Agnes used perfumes. Elizabeth applied them often, always smelling sweet. But the odour could be overpowering in a confined space. He began to crave fresh air, still feeling fragile after the overindulgence of the night before. And her brother who had sat near him at the club was ill with fever. He wanted out of the place. It could be plague, after all.

'I can't think of anyone in particular,' she continued. 'Customers come and go. I can't spend my time gawping at the window. There's so much work to be done preparing our perfumes. I'll ask Andrew if he's seen anything suspicious. Where may I contact you, Mr MacKenzie?'

'Libberton's Wynd, Madam Quinn. Even the smallest thing might be important.'

Scougall was pleased to see him head for the door.

'Just one more thing, madam. Where was your brother on the evening Thirlsmuir was killed?'

'We spent the night together here. He was suffering from the first signs of fever.'

Scougall knew she was lying, but why would she not. None of those who attended the association would admit to being there.

'There's something I've just remembered, sir. I've seen an old whore in a scarlet dress lingering outside Guillemot's shop a few times. She was maybe just looking at the wigs. But I do remember thinking, there she is again, I wonder what her business is.'

The next morning, Scougall worked methodically through Stuart's papers in his office. They were mostly dull accounts, bonds and invoices, only a few of which were not settled. He carefully examined each, observing the florid hand which had written them and thinking about the young man's terrible fate. At eleven o'clock he stopped for a break, leaving his office briefly to buy a couple of venison pasties in the Luckenbooths. He was feeling ill-at-ease and returned quickly to the task at hand.

As he picked up the next document, a sheet of paper dropped onto his desk. He was surprised to see a letter; the only one he had found in Stuart's papers. It was written in Latin. He translated it to himself slowly.

A few seconds later he was running down the High Street. After looking in Ninian Parker's and Mrs Kendall's, he found them in the Serpent Coffee House.

MacKenzie was pleased to see him. 'Archibald was keeping me abreast of developments, Davie. Glenbeath was at home in Fife as he claimed. There are a score of witnesses. However, the latest news from the south is disturbing.'

'I've found something, sir.'

'Take your time, Davie. Catch your breath first.'

'I must apologise to you both. I found this letter in Stuart's papers.'

'What is it?' Stirling's eyes glanced across the epistle. 'It's in Latin.'

Scougall whispered. 'It's from Thyrus Gonzalez de Santalla to Alexander Stuart.'

'Who?' Stirling looked perplexed.

'I'll give him his full title, Mr Stirling. The Superior General of the Society of Jesus – Praepositus Generalis, the leader of the Jesuits! He's the most powerful Papist in the world after the Pope himself!'

'A letter from the Superior of the Jesuits to Alexander Stuart,' Stirling repeated.

'The letter orders him to kill Kingsfield!' Scougall looked round furtively lest anyone overhear them. 'Stuart had orders from the highest authority of the Catholic Church after the Pope to slay the Duke in broad daylight so that many might witness the demise of an enemy of the true religion.'

MacKenzie's eyes darted through the text, nodding as he translated the Latin. 'What do you think, Archibald?'

Stirling examined the letter carefully again. 'It might be authentic.'

'But why would the Jesuits want Kingsfield killed rather than Crawford or Melville who are more important figures on the Presbyterian side? And why would the leader of the Jesuits concern himself with such a matter?'

'I don't know, John. At least I have something for Rosehaugh – we've little else so far. Here's evidence that foreign Papists were behind the killing, interfering in Scottish affairs.' He dropped his voice. 'The release of this information would be incendiary. I must show the letter to the Advocate immediately. We must keep it secret, gentlemen.'

Stirling took his hat and bid them good day. Scougall watched him depart through the smoky interior before handing another sheet to MacKenzie.

'I quickly made a copy, sir.'

'Well done for thinking ahead, Davie,' he smiled.

Scougall was pleased by the praise. He was more convinced than ever that a Papist plot was behind the murders of Black and Thirlsmuir.

25

A Late Sermon

SCOUGALL RETURNED TO his lodgings and sat with Mrs Baird chatting over a bowl of vegetable broth. He made an attempt to read after retiring to his chamber but made little progress with a recent purchase, *The Chains of Episcopacy Exposed*. His mind kept returning to the killings.

At eight o'clock he was relieved to receive a visit from Morrison. 'There's an opportunity to meet some investors tonight, Davie,' he said excitedly.

In a dingy court off the Lawn Market, a battered door opened onto a dilapidated hallway. The sound of clapping and cheering got louder as they approached another door. Scougall recognised one of the guards from the association who nodded at them knowingly as he allowed them into a packed hall. A man was addressing the audience in a refined voice from the stage at the front. Each sentence was met with rapturous applause. Scougall felt his uneasiness grow. He was worried that the association would already know he was working with MacKenzie on the case.

'It's the Earl of Glencairn, one of the leaders of the Presbyterians,' whispered Morrison.

'Our deliverance comes. God will shine upon us. The Deliverer will be in London soon. Bishops will be banished from Scotland!' There was a great cheer as he left the platform.

Next on stage was James Guthrie. He began his sermon by addressing the corruption of the government, moved on to the evils of the Papist religion and finished with a prayer that Scotland would be delivered from the Whore of Babylon, ushering in a new age when the Covenant would be proclaimed throughout the realm again. Scougall was used to long sermons, but he soon lost interest in what the minister was saying and let his eyes wander round the hall. Gradually, he spotted all the association: Lammington at the far side beside Quinn who was miraculously recovered; young Johnston close to where they stood among a group of students; Craig at the other side with Guillemot, who was easily identified by his lavish wig. The gaunt figure of Grimston was at the front of the throng, nodding seriously at every word.

After about half an hour, Guthrie brought his sermon to a climax. There was resounding applause, shouts of support and cries of condemnation of King James. The audience coalesced into small groups or drifted off to taverns throughout the city. Lammington nodded to him in a friendly manner. Johnston was speaking to Grimston. Guthrie was gathering his papers together. He decided to take his chance. Excusing himself from Morrison, who was talking to an acquaintance, he approached the old minister. He forced himself to do so, wanting to recover MacKenzie's approbation.

'I must compliment you on a fine sermon, Mr Guthrie.'

For a second Guthrie did not recognise him. 'I ken you, sir. But I can't recall your name. Where hae we met?'

'Davie Scougall.'

'Yes, of course. Scougall of Musselburgh. I meet so many folk these days; so many return tae Scotland awaiting deliverance. The revolution will come, sir. I hae God's assurance.'

'It was the night Thirsmuir was killed,' Scougall added.

Guthrie hesitated, his expression becoming grave. 'Thirlsmuir was a great loss tae the cause, Mr Scougall. He was a man of great... presence.'

'Are we all in danger, sir?'

'How mean you?'

'Dr Black is also slain.'

'God smites those who disobey him. Seek forgiveness for thy sins. Prayer will protect you, as it has saved me over many years of strife. I fought at Drumclog with sword in hand, smiting for the true church. I've faced Claverhouse's dragoons in the field. Now the Papist assassin lurks in the shadows, but God will conquer Satan. Trust in God, sir.'

Scougall forced himself to continue with his questioning. 'Are you convinced a Papist is behind the killings?'

'Why would Presbyterians kill each other?'

'It could be someone in the association.'

'Are you suggesting there's a spy in our midst?'

'Or the killer's not a Papist.'

'Come, Mr Scougall. Why would a Presbyterian kill his ain kind? The Papists are responsible. They are everywhere in the city. Although we flush mair oot each night, they take sanctuary in Sodom and Gomorrah at Holyrood. We'll take it soon with God's help.'

'How would they know where we met?'

'They have spies also. They seek to destroy those who fight Antichrist. Lammington and Grimston attack malignancy with ardour. Thirlsmuir was mair a man of politics, blown sometimes by the wind. He was nae as devout in heart. His faither doesnae proclaim his support yet. He sits on the fence, waiting tae see what becomes of the Prince of Orange. Black was weak, a sinner…'

'Black was a…?'

'Black is nae loss tae the cause of righteousness. He moved between the factions, kenning everyone in the movement. But he was a man of dubious… moral character. It was nae surprise he was found with a knife in his back in a bawdy-house. He was a great fornicator and abuser of women. We must be as a shining light. We must cleanse the nation of sin. The association is stronger without him. Trust in God.'

Scougall felt Guthrie's burning self-righteousness. Although he sensed the minister wanted rid of him, he tried to move the conversation towards the other characters. He was no doubt an annoying clerk asking piddling questions when great issues were at stake. But he would persevere by flattery.

'I found your sermon instructive and uplifting. I'll return to my lodgings and pray with ardour all the longer tonight.'

There was a flash in Guthrie's eyes. 'I thank you kindly, sir. The Mass will nae be heard much langer in Edinburgh. We'll cleanse the streets… with Papist blood.'

'I've heard Lammington was owed money by Thirlsmuir,' Scougall asked casually, deciding to take MacKenzie's direct approach.

'Deep are the bonds that bind the gentry. You must excuse me, sir. I'm tired after my sermon. I must rest.'

'I've heard Lammington will lend to anyone… even Papists.'

'You're wrang, sir. It's impertinent tae mak such an accusation. I see you're trying tae turn me agin him. Are you Grimston's creature?'

'It's only what I've heard in the coffee houses. I've been told he'll lend to anyone at high rates.' Scougall was aware of a slight change in the way Guthrie spoke to him. There was a hint of respect. He realised Grimston was a man to be feared.

26

Purchase of a Periwig

SCOUGALL OBSERVED HIMSELF carefully in the glass after his ablutions the next morning. He was taking more interest in his appearance since meeting Agnes. He was not pleased with what he saw. His jacket was threadbare, his shoes worn through and his coat had served him since he was an apprentice notary. He decided it was time to visit a tailor.

In William Kellie's shop he spent thirty pounds Scots on a new suit. He had never spent so much on one before, but was very pleased with it and agreed to call later in the week to collect it. He visited a cobbler in Warrender's Close where he purchased a pair of leather shoes with silver buckles. He would soon be a man of business if the company was launched successfully. He must dress like one.

As he stood outside the shop looking at the wigs in the window, he was surprised to see Morrison inside arguing with Guillemot. He knew they were acquainted from the association, but was surprised by the heated nature of their debate. Morrison was shouting, while Guillemot gesticulated wildly. He would have crept away had his friend not spotted him through the glass; his angry expression melting into a smile.

Scougall entered the shop and greeted them apologetically.

'I wish to purchase a wig, Mr Guillemot.'

'Watch yourself, Davie. Monsieur Guillemot drives a hard bargain,' laughed Morrison, his anger seemingly dissipated. 'I'll leave you to make your purchase,' he said giving Guillemot a sharp look. 'Drop in tonight to see us, Davie.'

Guillemot waited until the door was shut. 'He wants me to sell at no profit. He doesn't understand the quality of my goods.'

Ushering Scougall towards a chair in front of the glass, he took up position behind, looking down at his headpiece with disgust.

'It's time this was replaced, Monsieur Scougall. It's not fit for a gentleman.'

Disappearing through the back for a couple of minutes, he returned with a box, from which he removed an impressive wig.

'I can't afford such a piece,' said Scougall.

'But you've not tried it on yet.'

He removed Scougall's wig carefully and replaced it with the one from the box, adjusting it gently into place with spindly fingers. Scougall caught the unpleasant odour of his breath, a common affliction of the French, he thought. Once it was secured in place, Guillemot's hands remained on his shoulders. Scougall did not care for such intimacy. It struck him that if the merchant was the killer, he could easily take the opportunity to attack him.

'Come, Monsieur Scougall. Look at yourself. Behold the wonderful craftsmanship of Tippendale! *C'est bon, n'est pas?*'

The extravagant wig put his humbler bob to shame. In the glass he saw himself transformed from humble clerk to a gentleman. He imagined what he would look like in his new suit and shoes. The folk of Musselburgh would not recognise him. He would no longer be Davie Scougall clerk, but David Scougall, secretary of the Indian Company of Scotland. But did he have the confidence to wear such a wig in public? He saw himself walking down the High Street laughed at as a buffoon, an inflated pudding, puffed up with his own importance, the street boys shouting: 'Davie Scougall, Davie Scougall, wig as lang as an apple strudel!'

'I can't afford a Tippendale, sir.'

Guillemot's hands caressed his shoulders. This was perhaps an affectation of a wig merchant, he told himself. A fear flashed through his mind that the Frenchman was a sodomite. The sin was common in the land of King Louis where the King's brother was said to be afflicted by the perversion.

'For you, I'll make a special price... as you share my... political views. We're brothers fighting the good cause.' This was the first time he had referred to the association. 'How does one pound sterling sound to you?'

'I'd expected to pay closer to twenty pounds.'

'I choose to make no profit on the transaction for a special friend.'

Scougall surmised he would be making a substantial loss. But he would need a new wig if he was to be a man of business, if he was to become a gentleman. He could wait until the requisite moment before wearing it; perhaps keep it for a special occasion – his engagement party for instance!

'I'll take it, Mr Guillemot. It's very kind of you.'

Guillemot removed his hands and allowed Scougall one last look in the mirror.

'You've chosen wisely, sir. Let me put it in a box, so you can take it home.'

Scougall's previous purchases were restricted to books, golf clubs and featheries. In a single day he had bought a suit, shoes and wig. In his mind he saw himself parading through the shops of Covent Garden. One day he might have his own coach and horses.

'Don't forget my generosity... when the time comes,' Guillemot said casually as he presented him with the box.

'How do you mean, sir?'

'If I need help in the association... but I see you understand me... say no more. I can rely on you.'

Scougall was not sure what he meant.

'I'll see you again soon.' Guillemot gave him a knowing nod which reminded Scougall that he had intended to question him about the killings. It seemed a bit ungrateful to turn to the subject of murder after the bargain had been made.

'The demise of Dr Black is terrible,' he said as he rose to his feet.

Guillemot nodded gravely. 'It's a tragedy, *n'est pas*? The Papists show no end to their cruelty. They'll kill, slaughter and maim the Protestant. But the news from London is good.'

'Are you a friend of Morrison?'

'I know the young gentleman. We've made a number of business transactions.'

'What's the nature of your business?'

'We haggle on price, as all merchants do. I want to pay low, he asks high.'

Scougall did not know Morrison traded in wigs. He didn't know much about his interests. 'Grimston's a strange fellow,' he added.

'Lammington and Grimston are neighbours in the border lands. Both seek to rise. This will be their chance – a new king on the throne distributing offices and pensions. Those supporting the old King will fall, leaving the field open. I'm with Lammington. As you are also,' he said knowingly.

'I don't side with either...' Scougall finally realised the meaning of his remark.

'I only ask that you vote with him when the time comes.'

'Vote?'

'If there's a vote in the association. It's important we support Monsieur Lammington. Grimston has no interest in trade. Religion is everything to him. It'll be better for us, as men of trade, if Lammington's our leader.'

Scougall had already paid his pound. He felt like he'd been bought.

'I've heard Lammington's a usurer?' He adopted MacKenzie's method of provocation. It was pure supposition based on Seaforth's belief that he was active in the money market.

'He's just a merchant who helps those without cash. He lent me a small sum, so I could establish my business. I came to Edinburgh with nothing.'

'I've heard he threatens those who don't make repayment on time.'

'I've never been in that position, Mr Scougall. But a moneylender must be forceful or some will never repay. Monsieur Lammington's an honourable man. Grimston, on the other hand, is a relic of the past.'

'What of Quinn?'

'Quinn is a foreign man like me. He's suffered, as has his sister. I'm told the Papists seek revenge in Ireland and many Protestants flee Dublin. Those in the north, who are of Scottish descent, seek help from their brethren here. William is petitioned to come to their aid.' He paused for a moment before adding: 'Quinn is also with Lammington.'

'Then it seems Lammington has most support. Where did Black and Thirlsmuir stand?'

'Thirlsmuir stood for himself, a rival of Lamminington and Grimston. I know not who Black favoured.'

'I hope it'll be over soon. I support the aims of the association, but I want peace.'

'I could not agree more, sir. Violence is not good for the trading interest. Who thinks of wigs when everything's uncertain? But a great change awaits the Kingdom – a glorious transformation. Monsieur Lammington assures me of that.'

'I hope you're right. Do you know Craig and young Johnston well?'

'You're inquisitive, Mr Scougall.'

'It's just my legal training, Mr Guillemot.'

'Johnston's a firebrand with all the hot-headedness of a fool. Craig works tirelessly for the House of Pittendean, putting family interest before any other. The great men use them to direct the mob as they are well-connected with the youth of the town. I'm with you and Quinn and Morrison. We're men of business who want to build a better future for this land. It makes sense for us to be on the right side when revolution comes.'

27

An Awkward Request

'I CAN SEE FROM your expression you're not pleased to see me, Davie.'

'It's not that, Elizabeth. It's not safe for you in Edinburgh at this time.'

'Not safe! I'm to remain in the country while my friends suffer here,' she said defiantly.

'I'm only repeating what your father's told me. I've advised my own family to stay at home until calm returns.'

'I've no time for calm. I need your help. I hope you're still my friend.' She said this adamantly, staring intently at him with her piercing blue eyes.

They had communicated secretly before by letter when she had used him as a way of finding out about her father's affairs. However, on this occasion Scougall was already in such trouble he wanted no other reason to sour his relationship with MacKenzie. Before he could say anything else she was sitting beside him at his desk.

'Do you know my mother died on the day I was born?'

Scougall did not know what to say.

'She was newly married,' she continued. 'She was looking forward to life. She was anticipating the joy of motherhood.'

'I'm very sorry, Elizabeth,' was all he could think of saying, although he knew it sounded trite.

'Yesterday I saw a premonition of my own death.'

He did not like the way the conversation was heading.

'I saw myself dying in childbirth just like her, leaving my son alone in the world.'

'That will not happen to you. You'll be fine,' Scougall said, although the thought of her having a child with Ruairidh MacKenzie was abhorrent.

'I love him, Davie. My father's accepted the match, although

I know he had doubts because of Seaforth's finances. Everything was almost settled. I would lie with him in Brahan Castle on our wedding night.'

The thought of them lying together in a cold keep was disgusting.

'Then yesterday I received a letter. At first I wondered what romantic subterfuge had encouraged him to have someone else, perhaps his man, write the address. But my joy was short-lived.'

She opened her purse. He did not want to read it, but he had no choice.

My dear Elizabeth,

You must forgive me my dearest love. These are trying days for all of us and we must all make difficult decisions. I've not been entirely open with you. When I was last in France, I was converted to the Catholic faith of my brother. It's the old faith of Scotland, the one followed by all Scots until the reformers turned us from our natural course.

I wanted to tell you at The Hawthorns but my brother bade me say nothing as negotiations were at a sensitive stage. Now, alas, I fear we will never marry.

You may have heard of the terrible events in Edinburgh. Kingsfield was killed by a young convert to my religion. I was known to the assassin from secret meetings. These were harmless prayer sessions but we were discovered by the mob. Father Innes was brutally assaulted and Father Pryde taken into custody to be tortured.

I'm now a hunted man. If I'm caught, I'll be tortured too, despite my brother being a privy councillor. They believe I had something to do with the Duke's death and suspect me of involvement in the killing of Thirlsmuir.

I can assure you my love that I'd nothing to do with these murders. But the mob calls for Papist blood. If I'm apprehended I'll be torn to pieces.

I can assure you that my conversion has made me a better man. I've confessed all my sins and am at peace with God. A great weight is lifted from my shoulders. I hope in time you'll come to realise the Church of Rome isn't to be feared, but is a vessel of God's love through Jesus Christ.

I pray you can forgive me for keeping this from you. I dearly hope we may still marry. I assure you of my love for

*you and respect for your father. I ask you to apologise to
him and I hope one day to call him father-in-law.*

*I cannot say where I'm bound. Once I'm in safety I will
write.*

Your loving cousin,
Ruairidh MacKenzie

When Scougall looked up, he saw she was crying. He was sorry for
her pain, but felt nothing but hatred for him. 'I'm sorry, Elizabeth.
I fear he may have fled abroad already.' He dared not say he knew
he was still in Edinburgh.

'I want your help to find him, Davie.'

'But, Elizabeth… your father wouldn't want me to… I've no
idea where he's bound…'

'You're to be my eyes and ears in Edinburgh. I know you're
working closely with father. I need to know where Ruairidh's
going.'

'You can't… you mustn't go after him… it would be folly… if
you married him… it would be…'

'I will follow him. I must follow him. I'll be his wife even if we
have to live in exile. I love him, Davie. Do you not understand? I've
no choice.'

'But you'll be marrying a Papist against your father's wishes!'

'I care not if he's a Papist!'

'He's betrayed you. He's treated you with disrespect. He's a
foolish…!'

He realised he had overstepped the mark. He had spoken with
venom, but he could not help it. He knew in his heart that Ruairidh
MacKenzie was a rogue.

'I didn't know you had such strong feelings for him,' she replied
coldly.

He wanted to tell her it was because he cared for her. He wanted
to say that she was the most beautiful creature in the world. He had
always loved her, ever since he first set eyes on her that day at The
Hawthorns. But he could not.

'I'm sorry, Elizabeth. I can't help you find him.'

'Then I have misjudged you, Mr Scougall,' she said bitterly. 'I see
we're not friends, after all. You're prejudiced against him because
of his religion. You're no better than the members of the mob who
roam the streets. I bid you good day.'

He pleaded with her to remain so they could talk further, but she stormed out, slamming the door behind her. He knew in his heart that he had done the right thing. He would never help her find a Papist husband.

28

Questions Over Coffee

AFTER A LONG search MacKenzie found Lammington sitting on his own at a table in a corner of the Serpent Coffee House in Brotherstane's Wynd.

'Will you take a cup of coffee with me, sir? I need to speak to you on a legal matter.'

Lammington raised his head. He looked surprised but nodded affably, moving along the bench to let MacKenzie sit beside him.

'What do you want with me, Mr MacKenzie?'

MacKenzie smiled. 'How have you found Edinburgh since your return... from exile?'

Lammington looked at him carefully. 'I like it very much. I now worship as I wish. It's been a long hard struggle. I have... our King to thank for that.'

'Are you a supporter of King James?'

'I support his policy of toleration. Now, I'm very busy today, sir. What do you want of me?'

'I'm working for a client. I'm investigating the killings of Black and Thirlsmuir. I believe they might be connected to the assassination of Kingsfield.'

Lammington eyed him suspiciously. He took a long draw on his pipe and exhaled slowly. 'I've heard both were fine men taken in their prime. Why would you want to ask me about them?'

MacKenzie moved closer to him on the bench and dropped his voice to a whisper. 'I hear they're members of your little gathering.'

'What on earth do you mean?'

'They both attended your association; a club of like-minded gentlemen, a group of Presbyterians who plot against the King. I want to find out if it's a coincidence both were slain?'

'They were well known as loyal servants of Presbytery. Black was recently imprisoned in the castle by the government. Thirlsmuir was a leading man of the realm. But I didn't ken them weel.'

'Have you ever met them?'

'I may have passed a pleasantry with them but I've never had dealings with either. Your intelligence is mistaken, MacKenzie.'

'Do you know Cockburn of Grimston?'

'I ken him, but I've little to do with him. His family hold land just to the north of my own. We are both returning exiles. My estates were forfeited and sold to another. I hope to have the transaction rescinded by parliament, but it's a slow process. Perhaps you don't understand me. Trade is my passion. I've returned frae exile to improve my lands by applying the methods of the Dutch in agriculture and to grow my trading interests. I've no stomach for politics.'

'Are you acquainted with James Guthrie, minister?'

'I've heard a couple of his sermons. He's not amongst the first rank of preachers.'

'What about Peter Guillemot and Andrew Quinn?'

'I've never heard of them.'

'Archibald Craig?'

'He was Thirslmuir's man of business. He's known to me but not intimately.'

'What of young Robert Johnston, student at the college?'

MacKenzie could tell that Lammington was trying to contain his anger as he puffed quickly on his pipe.

'I've nae time for such meetings. If you ask me, the Papists are responsible for the killings. They're still protected in the Abbey. All I want is to settle my affairs so I can return hame and live at peace on my lands.'

MacKenzie could tell that Lammington was itching to leave, but he had him trapped behind the table. 'I've heard you'll benefit from the killings.'

'I'm unaffected by their deaths. Who is the client you represent?'

'The mother of Alexander Stuart.'

'You shouldnae waste your time representing Papists.'

'His mother is no Papist.'

Lammington took his hat, indicating that he wanted to be gone. But MacKenzie did not rise to let him pass. 'I'm told you have extensive moneylending interests.'

'That's public knowledge. I provide credit on security. I put idle funds tae work for the benefit of all. Many lawyers are engaged in the same business.'

'They are, sir. Indeed I've sums lent out myself. It's just I've heard you are willing to lend to those with poor credit.'

Lammington looked unsettled. 'I lend a little to such men and charge a higher annual rent for the risk – that's the principal of sound business.'

'Do you lend to Papists?'

Lammington was silent for a few moments. 'I've provided money to a few over the years.'

MacKenzie nodded knowingly, wanting to leave this in the air. It would not look good for a worthy Presbyterian to be known as a lender of last resort to the servants of Antichrist.

'Did you lend to Thirlsmuir or Black?'

'I've already telt you, Mr MacKenzie. I was not well known tae them. I've other business to attend to. I thank you for the coffee.'

'There's just one more thing, sir. Did you visit Maggie Lister's house on 26 November... the day on which Black was killed?'

MacKenzie detected a flash of panic in his eyes.

'Ah, Maggie Lister's where Black was found.' Lammington took up his pipe again. 'I'm a man like any other, Mr MacKenzie.'

'Could you confirm you were there on the day he was killed.'

'I was there in the early evening. Indeed, I recommended the establishment tae Black. I arrived about four o'clock and left an hour later. I was with a whore named Janet Stratton, a fine wench. I swear I saw nothing of Black.'

MacKenzie rose from the bench allowing him out. He sat for a while deep in thought as he finished his coffee. He now had to track down his neighbour Grimston. It proved easy to find his favourite drinking den in a close off the Cowgate where he took a bottle of wine at the same time every afternoon.

MacKenzie took up position in a corner and waited. At three o'clock Grimston arrived with his servant. MacKenzie was in luck as the laird took the table beside him. He was relying on the fact that Grimston did not know him. MacKenzie glanced over at the large knuckles of Grimston's right hand as he sat clutching his glass like a claw. He sipped his wine and pretended to attend to the papers in front of him while focusing all his attention on what Grimston said to his man.

Grimston took a pamphlet from his pocket. 'Look at this, Syme.'

'I cannae read, sir.'

'I ken you cannae. I'll read it for you… listen. The King's fled London like a poulet… the time approacheth. The time's at hand. We'll have our glorious revolution, will we not? I've waited lang. I've worked haird. I'll nae let the likes of Lammington tak the prize. What's he done tae deserve such accolades? I fought on the battle field for Christ Jesus, while he sat in a change house lending money tae ony who sought mammon.' He took a long swig of claret. 'I must hae something on him… to persuade the ithers of his sinfulness… to show his true character.'

A youth approached Grimston's table.

'What do you have for me, Johnston?'

MacKenzie took up his quill. He did not pen a brief, but noted the exact words spoken by Grimston. It was a useful trick which made it look like he was distracted by work. Here was a bit of luck at last, he thought, the opportunity to listen to a conversation between two members of the association. All he had to do was sip his claret.

'I've followed him, sir. I've a list of aw his movements over the last week. You're correct about his appetite… for women… he's visited the houses of Maggie Lister and Jessie McDade.'

'He's a fornicator, Mr Johnston!' thundered Grimston. 'Those who dedicate their lives to lust must be punished, as it says in the Bible… This man cannot lead us. When we've enough evidence, we'll confront him before the others. The association must know his true nature. Keep watching him for a few mair days. I've something to show you.' He bent down and took a bundle from a sack on the floor. 'I used it at Bothwell Brig. I shot a dragoon through the heart. It aims true.'

Johnston took the gun in his hands lovingly, weighing it carefully. He pictured himself firing at a Papist, the dull thud as the bullet entered the body. He saw himself killing the dominie, revenging himself for the years of abuse.

'It'll be yours when the time comes. You'll vote with me, Mr Johnston?'

'Of course, sir. I stand with the righteous.'

'You're a good fellow. Now be aff with you. Speak with the whores. Learn everything you can of the fornicator. Here's something tae loosen their tongues.' He handed him a few coins. 'Then we'll be rid of him.'

29

A Liberal Education

AS HE APPROACHED the decrepit two-storey building, Scougall wondered what he might have achieved if he had attended the College of Edinburgh. He did not have the privilege of a university education; rather, at the age of fourteen, he left Musselburgh grammar school to be apprenticed as a notary public. The profession of advocate might have been open to him and perhaps marriage to Elizabeth.

Passing through an arched passageway, he entered a large untidy courtyard, where an old servitor told him classes finished in five minutes. When the bell rang, students spilled out of doors on every side, screaming like the rabble he had been part of on the High Street, speeding out to hunt down victuals in tavern or booth. He noticed the lean figure of Robert Johnston approaching. In the light of day, he saw he was a youth of perhaps thirteen or fourteen with a face still covered in plooks.

'To what do I owe this pleasure?' Johnston asked.

Scougall was not well versed in the art of subterfuge, but remembered MacKenzie's parting words. 'Adopt the role of fanatic, Davie. You're a believer in the cause of Presbytery. Play it well and we'll learn much.'

'Can we talk, Mr Johnston?' He adopted a serious but friendly air.

'We're nae supposed to speak outside the club to avoid suspicion falling on us. There could be spies watching. Antichrist has eyes everywhere.'

'I heard something is planned for tonight.'

'You want some sport do you?' Johnston's face lit up. He looked around furtively and dropped his voice. 'We'll pay a visit tae a tenement in Gray's Wynd where Patrick Brown bides, a suspected Papist. We're tae smash his windows and piss on his door; nothing too much, not yet.'

'A suspected Papist?' Scougall did not like the idea of urinating in public.

'He's been seen in their company.'

'Count me in, Mr Johnston. When are you meeting?'

'Eight o'clock. You'll hear the drum on the High Street.'

'We must hound the Beast out of Scotland!' said Scougall raising his fist as he repeated a few stock phrases on the lips of the rabble. 'The odour of Antichrist must be expunged!' He had no difficulty in expressing the views of a devout Presbyterian. He was only articulating his own deepest fears. As MacKenzie would have said, the emotions were unqualified, unrefracted through the lens of reason, a pure response to the fear of Satan. However, the act of playing a role distanced them from him. He saw them for what they were – fear, hatred, anger, resentment, blood-lust – all part of his makeup too.

'We'll gie the fucking Whore something tae think aboot,' added Johnston. Scougall wanted to upbraid him for swearing, for using the words of the gutter, but he contained his disgust.

'Are you the master of the mob, Mr Johnston?' He knew the question would appeal to his vanity.

'I pull the strings on the street. I ken aw the students and apprentices in the city. They'll be rewarded when the time comes.'

'When the time comes?'

'When bishops are banished frae the realm and the church restored tae the glorious constitution of 1638. That's reward enough for me. But the boys want drink money. I disperse funds provided by Craig.'

'Where does he get it from?' Johnston spoke more readily than he had expected. He was perhaps just a young fool, the plaything of others, like Alexander Stuart.

'Where do you think it comes frae? The Earl himself!'

'But he's not declared.'

'He hasnae made his position known in public, but he's a supporter of the cause.' Scougall saw that the world of politics was one of duplicity.

'Was Thirlsmuir slain by them?'

'The Papists feared such a devoted servant of the Covenant. His death was a warning to stop the struggle on the street and allow the Whore free reign. But this is the Land of Knox and Melville, valiant men of God who fought for the true kirk!'

'Did they kill Black as well?'

'I'm sure they did. They'll keep killing. They'll keep killing Protestants who stand against them. They'll bring Irish troops intae Scotland as they did under Montrose. But we'll vanquish them. The nation stands united against them as they did in the days of the Covenant. If we stand thegither there's naething we cannae achieve.'

'We'll fight them together, Robert,' Scougall added, but Johnston did not like being interrupted. He was a teller of tales not a listener.

'Have you heard the Prince will soon be in London? If James Stewart flees, the government in Edinburgh will fall. Papists like Melfort will be put tae the sword.' He pulled back his jacket to reveal a dirk hanging from his belt. 'We'll extirpate every last one.'

Scougall wondered why the boy felt such hatred, enjoying as he did, the benefits of a college education. He recalled MacKenzie's words that men of violence rise during times of strife; those who kill without compunction, caring nothing for God's laws, caring little for Presbytery or Bishop. Men who crave only power over others. Johnston was perhaps capable of killing Thirlsmuir or Black, after all. But he could not think of a reason why he would do so, unless told by another.

'Be careful, Mr Scougall. Papist spies are everywhere. Some will tak money frae baith sides... I'm promised a pistol by Grimston. You'll need a weapon when the revolution comes.'

Scougall was a poor swordsman and did not own a dirk or gun. He could swing an iron but not a rapier, although he did have a good eye with a pistol. Perhaps he would need one for protection.

'What else can I do, Mr Johnston?'

'Proclaim your opposition to Antichrist! And provide money. But don't look sae worried. Our time comes. A glorious conflagration will consume this city. Out of the night we'll rise. The Papist will be vanquished frae the realm!'

The boy's eyes sparkled with fervour.

'We'll be victorious, Robert. Our time comes. It will be glorious, indeed. We'll free our country from the oppressor,' added Scougall.

He bid Johnston farewell and made his way to the Cowgate intending to drop in at St Magdalene's Chapel. Inside, he found himself in a hive of activity rather than a place of peaceful meditation. For a few moments he stood admiring the vaulted ceiling, stained-glass windows and timber panelling. When he lowered his gaze he saw Quinn's lithe figure coming towards him.

'It's Mr Scougall, is it not?'

'Yes, sir. How are you feeling?'

'I'm recovered, thank you. A brief malady, thank God. I'm restored to health. The news from London is good. My sister told me you visited the shop with the tall lawyer MacKenzie.'

'He's helping Stirling investigate the killings.'

'A terrible business. I see Mr Craig wishes to talk to you. Drop into our shop sometime. I'll provide you with a little perfume for your lady.'

'It's good to see you again,' said Craig interrupting in a friendly manner.

'Is there any news?' asked Scougall nervously.

'William will be in London soon. The King loses support across the country.'

'You agreed to provide a list of Pittendean's debts.'

'Of course, my lord mentioned it, but I'd forgotten. There are so many other matters to attend. I'll see that it's done, although I'm very busy at the moment. It might be a day or so.'

'I've something else to ask you... It's a delicate matter.'

Craig beckoned Scougall into a quiet corner.

Scougall forced himself to say something. 'It's a difficult time to borrow. I'm told a man might obtain funds from Lammington without security.'

'It's a dangerous time to extend credit, Mr Scougall. But there are always ways, if you're willing to pay a high enough price. Are you in need of funds? I could have a word with him.'

'I've heard he uses brutal means to secure repayment.'

'He'll use any means to get his money back if it's not redeemed. I don't believe violence is one of them. He's a merchant like any other. He likes to lend to those who are likely to repay.'

'Did Thirlsmuir pay his debts on time?' Scougall was surprised by his own forwardness.

Craig looked taken aback by the question. 'Are you suggesting he was killed for not paying a debt to Lammington? That's ridiculous, sir.'

Scougall could not believe his luck. He had found out that Lammington was Thirlsmuir's debtor.

'It's just what I've heard, idol gossip I'm sure. I'm looking for a small sum to tide me over the winter. I'm owed money by a few clients who are late in settling their accounts. I only need about a hundred pounds Scots.'

'I'll mention it to him. It should not be a problem for a... loyal servant of the cause.' Craig's face broke into a knowing smile.

Scougall nodded appreciatively and was on the point of excusing himself when Craig moved closer. 'You must make sure you're on the right side, Mr Scougall. If you were thought to be on the wrong one, you'd be punished.'

The colour drained from Scougall's face.

'I'm sure you would not be disloyal to the association. We know about your connections to Stirling and MacKenzie. Sometimes it's necessary to prove your loyalty.'

Scougall nodded vacantly.

'You're known to Rosehaugh?'

He nodded again.

'Rosehaugh is a defiler of the Godly who has tortured dozens of Presbyterians. It would be nae loss tae the nation if he was dispatched, if he was... struck down, perhaps in his office in the Tolbooth – a blow to the back of the head. It would be easy. His demise would be looked on favourably by the association, by the whole movement, by everyone who holds the cause of Presbytery dear. It would prove beyond doubt your loyalty. Think upon it, Mr Scougall.'

Scougall had no time to say that it was against the Lord's Commandment to kill, as Craig moved on, whispering as he passed: 'Think about, it. That's all. The time will come, Mr Scougall. You must choose the right path.'

30

Sanctuary at Holyrood

AS THEY WANDERED up the High Street in the gloaming, Scougall told MacKenzie what he had learned from Johnston and the request made by Craig.

'We're making progress at last, Davie. We know that Johnston is Grimston's creature and that Craig and Pittendean are knaves of the first rank. I doubt if we'll receive a list of the debts.'

MacKenzie stopped in his tracks and thought for a few moments. 'We must take the initiative ourselves. After breakfast tomorrow, search through the Books of Council and Session, beginning with the most recent volume and working backwards. Find all the transactions involving Pittendean and keep an eye out for anything connected with the association.'

Scougall agreed to undertake the task, although it would be a laborious slog through hundreds of pages. He would have to make an early start. Morrison had decided to hold a meeting to raise money from investors in the afternoon. 'The capital raising is tomorrow afternoon in the Royal Coffee House. You would be very welcome, as would any of your acquaintances.'

'I look forward to hearing the business case.'

Scougall was pleased to hear he would come. 'Is there any word of the boy, sir?'

'He seems to have melted into thin air. Stirling tells me his mother is Bessie Troon. She's not seen him for a week. I fear he may be at the bottom of the Nor Loch. I've asked to have all the association watched, but the guards are needed to maintain public order. More trouble's expected on the street. I'd like the lodgings of all the suspects searched, but Stirling says it's not possible for political reasons. We'll have to wait and see what happens.'

A crowd was gathered in the Lawn Market beside the Weighing House at the top of the High Street. Scougall was relieved to see it was not Johnston's rabble. Laughter and applause rose from the throng rather than abuse. A small wooden stage had been constructed on the street.

'Is it not time Edinburgh had a theatre, if only a temporary one,' smiled MacKenzie. 'One of the great pleasures in life is to be distracted by a play. Sarre's players have been given a licence by the Privy Council to perform for the people.'

Scougall viewed the theatre as frivolous and ungodly entertainment. 'Such a festival of dolts will stain the good name of this town!'

'We can't hark back to the days of Cromwell when all theatres were closed. It would broaden your mind to observe a play, Davie.'

Scougall was annoyed by the suggestion that his mind was narrow and might benefit from watching a gaggle of fools impersonating others. If you wanted drama, you could do a lot worse than listening to a sermon; the best preachers knew how to hold a crowd's attention. 'There's enough drama in the Bible,' he replied.

MacKenzie was already walking towards the stage. Scougall could make nothing of it. There were a host of characters: a king and queen, soldier, fool, harlequin, but what it was all about, he could not work out. Mighty speeches were made, songs sung, jokes told. The bows of the actors and the crowd's applause seemed endless. When it was over, they passed to The Periwig where they sat at their usual table.

MacKenzie said nothing until he had finished his wine. 'We've one more meeting tonight, Davie. I've arranged to see Ruairidh in the Palace. I want you to accompany me.'

Scougall was looking forward to bed and had no desire to see him again. 'It's surely not my place, sir.'

'I want you there, as a witness.' MacKenzie hoped Scougall would be a restraining influence on him. He was not sure that he could control himself.

The High Street was still busy despite the late hour; groups of artisans and students were loitering at every corner, while homeless beggars roamed aimlessly searching for a morsel to eat. They walked the mile from the Castle to Holyrood House in silence; MacKenzie deep in thought.

Holyrood Palace was at the foot of the High Street. Two tall towers dominated its façade on each side, with classical columns enclosing a large door. MacKenzie reflected that it was one of the principal residences of Scottish kings, although diminished since James the Sixth inherited the English Crown in 1603 and took up permanent residence in the south. Many lamented that Scotland no longer had a court. The nobles had fled south, adopted English manners and left Edinburgh to the lairds and lawyers.

Scougall viewed Holyrood as an enclave of Popery where the followers of Antichrist took refuge. The Abbey Church, an ancient structure at the side of the Palace, was converted into a Chapel Royal. It was where the Order of the Thistle convened, a Jesuit school was established and the Mass celebrated. The whole place was a den of iniquity, a cancer in the heart of the kingdom where the Devil feasted on the soul of Scotland.

The guards at the gates had been warned to expect them. Inside the Chapel, Scougall observed the ornate furnishings and elaborate carvings with disgust.

'Fine craftsmanship, indeed,' said MacKenzie. 'Grinling Gibbons is an artist of the first rank.'

Scougall said nothing, his puritanical nature revolting against the exuberant scupltures.

At the far end a priest was conducting a service. Scougall could hardly believe that he was witnessing the Mass. It was still a capital offence according to the statute book of Scotland! The Papists called it transubstantiation, the blasphemous belief that the bread and wine were literally transformed into the body and blood of Christ.

When the ceremony was over, the priest disappeared into the shadows and another figure rose from the pews beside him. He turned and walked towards MacKenzie and Scougall. It was Ruairidh MacKenzie. When he reached them, MacKenzie did not remove his hat, a grave insult to a member of the aristocracy.

'I'm sorry. I should have told you everything. I must assure you...' Ruairidh mumbled.

Scougall was not prepared for the violence of MacKenzie's outburst: 'You've treated my daughter disgracefully. I ought to run you through with my sword. There'll be no marriage now!'

'I've suffered much... for my religion,' Ruairidh continued. 'I love her... as I believe she loves me. When this is over, we can, maybe...'

'You've lied to me. You've lied to Elizabeth. We'll never trust you again.'

'I beg your forgiveness. I had to follow my... conscience. My heart told me I did right. The old faith pleases me in a way the Protestant one never did. I'll do anything to keep Elizabeth's hand.'

'You would disclaim your religion?'

'I could not.'

'Then the marriage will not take place!'

'I beg your forgiveness.'

MacKenzie knew he would have to play a long game. Elizabeth was devoted to the rogue. If the marriage was delayed, the life of a soldier was unpredictable. He might be slain on a foreign battlefield.

'My brother tells me you've some questions. I'll answer them all... truthfully.'

MacKenzie gathered his thoughts, containing his anger, directing his mind towards the case. His tone softened. Scougall removed his notebook and stood silently at his side. 'Tell me all those who attended the meetings.'

'There were different people each time. We didn't discuss politics. There were no plans to kill anyone. We talked only about our souls.'

'How often did Stuart attend?'

'He was there a few times. He was an intense fellow. He asked difficult questions of the priests, touching on points of theology which I didn't understand. He never mentioned Kingsfield.'

'What about the priests?'

'I don't know them well. My brother told me to attend. He said it would help him. A title is promised him. I might become the brother of a duke, perhaps gain my own reward. Elizabeth would benefit too. I'll serve the King loyally whatever happens.'

'What will you do now?'

'There are enough soldiers to defend the Palace for now. But the situation is becoming precarious. I'll have to get out soon... I still want to marry Elizabeth when this is over.'

'Is there anything you can tell us about Kingsfield's death... anything about Stuart... or about Thirlsmuir and Black?'

'I recall one thing. Father Innes said something that I thought little of at the time, but now seems unusual. He said a number of times that Stuart was destined to do great deeds in the service of God.'

MacKenzie finally took off his hat. 'Tell your brother that Davie will prepare a bond for two hundred pounds *Scots*,' he said, emphasising the last word. The loan was not to be made in sterling.

It was only a twelfth of the amount Seaforth sought. He turned on his heels without saying anything else.

Scougall hoped it would be the last time that he ever saw Ruairidh. As he walked out, he prayed that Elizabeth would not follow him into exile, but after their conversation, he feared that she would.

31

A Capital Fund

DESPITE THE UNCERTAINTY in the city, Morrison believed they should go ahead with the launch of the company. Scougall thought they should wait, but his friend was adamant. Money was at hand due to the disruption of trade, especially among the wealthier merchants and lawyers. They advertised by word of mouth a meeting on the afternoon of 2 December at the Royal Coffee House.

Scougall only mentioned it to a few acquaintances with little enthusiasm, believing that there was a good chance it would be unsuccessful. He was therefore surprised to find a large crowd in the smoky interior of the coffee house. There were not enough stools for everyone to sit on, so many were forced to stand at the back.

He took a seat beside Morrison at a large table reserved for them. He had been asked by him to say a few words and was feeling nervous. He did not like speaking in public and not slept a wink the night before.

'I'd like to thank you for attending, gentlemen,' Morrison began confidently as he took to his feet. 'What I have to share with you this afternoon is an opportunity of the first rank, one which comes along rarely in a lifetime.'

Scougall looked round the arc of dour faces. These were not folk come to watch a play but serious men of trade.

'Firstly, I'll explain the case for the company,' continued Morrison, 'then I'll address the timing of our fund raising. Mr Scougall will say a few words before distributing the articles of association. Finally, we'll open the subscription book.'

Scougall was impressed by the relaxed manner in which he spoke. But his nerves were getting the better of him. There was no way out. He had chosen this path, seeking wealth and status. He must keep thinking of the long-term goals. He might eventually be able to buy an estate. Agnes would be his wife. They would entertain MacKenzie, and perhaps Stirling, in the country air. Never again would he be the source of mirth or mockery.

'Is it not an ill-advised time for such a half-baked venture?' asked an old merchant who was well known as a cautious trader.

'Not at all, sir. If you'll allow me, I'll answer your question in good time.'

The man nodded, but looked disgruntled.

'As many of you know, I've recently returned from Holland where my family were exiled. During those dark days I studied the Dutch trade. They are more successful than any other nation in this field of human endeavour. It's surely time to apply the lessons in Scotland. Wealth is built on trade, especially the foreign trade, and it's to trade we must look if we're to prosper too. Much has been said about why Scotland is poor. Many lament the lack of money in the kingdom. The trade with Africa and the East Indies is a vast one. There's room for us to take a share. Scotland can prosper, gentlemen. Scotland will prosper.'

There were murmurs of agreement. A couple of younger merchants clapped their hands enthusiastically.

'Once we've raised a fund, we'll hire a ship in London and sail it north to Leith. We'll fit it out with the finest manufactures the nation can provide. We'll recruit a captain with experience of the Indies trade and employ a crew. There are plenty looking for positions in Scotland, men who have sailed under the flags of other nations and brought the fruits of wealth to them. Now they'll do the same for their native land. We'll sail our ship to the Indies, aiming to make land at Batavia to sell the cargo and buy spices, before returning to London. I believe the returns will be as much as six or seven times, perhaps even ten times. Think, gentlemen. For a hundred pounds sterling promised to the company today, you'll earn six or seven, or even a thousand pounds in a year's time.'

There were a few sighs of amazement and some cheers. Scougall did not know where Morrison came up with the figures, but he was impressed by the response they elicited. He relaxed slightly and let his eyes wander, recognising a number of faces. He spotted his old friend Robbie Dundas and also his nemesis on the golf course Hector Stoddart. Grimston was sitting at a table staring intently at Morrison. Lammington was standing at the back, smoking his pipe. There was also Quinn and Guillemot sitting together. Guthrie was at a table with another minister. He was heartened to see MacKenzie in the far corner.

'We'll sell our spices in Amsterdam or London,' continued Morrison. 'Shareholders will receive a cut and may reinvest as much as they want in the next venture. The following year we'll send two ships to the East and lobby parliament for an act giving the company a monopoly on trade to the Indies, just like the Dutch and English companies have. More investors will come in and we'll raise enough for more ships. Think gentleman, our company will have a fleet of mighty ships! You'll own a share in a fleet! We'll build them in Scotland, creating work for craftsmen, rather than Dutch or German shipwrights. In time, we'll become a global trading company sending Scottish goods around the world, returning with spices for the markets in London, Europe and Edinburgh!'

There were more nods of agreement and a few more claps.

'We've calculated that one thousand five hundred pounds sterling will be sufficient for the voyage. Mr Scougall has prepared articles describing the constitution of the company, outlining the rights of subscribers and the process by which directors will be elected.'

Scougall wished his family were there to see him. Davie Scougall, whom many in the parish of Musselburgh expected little of, who was known as dour Davie, afflicted by shyness, although proficient with a golf club, was raised to such heights. If only the bullies in the school yard could have been there. They would not be laughing at him now, or poking him with a stick or throwing stones at him. He tried to contain a smile. Although he recalled that Morrison was one of the worst of them.

'We seek investments of ten, fifty or a hundred pounds sterling,' he continued. 'I want to end by quoting a few words of a fellow countryman who's well versed in the world of trade, a dear friend who regrets he cannot be with us today. Some of you may have heard of William Paterson. Here's what he has to say – It will be manifest that trade is capable of increasing trade, and money of begetting money to the end of the world.'

There were a few more claps and cheers.

'Before I ask you to subscribe, I'll put my own name to the venture. I intend to invest two hundred pounds sterling. The sum is the entire wealth of my family. My good friend Davie Scougall will provide one hundred pounds, his life's saving.'

There were cheers from all corners of the coffee house. Many who were there only for a drink or pipe at the bar turned to listen. It was almost all the money Scougall had in the world. He had told Morrison it was as much as he could afford, although he failed to mention another twenty-three pounds ten shillings in cash and a few loans which brought his remaining assets to about twenty-eight pounds. He had saved the sum over many years and judged it represented the writing of about four thousand instruments of sasine. He would of course receive a salary for his work for the new company. A sum of fifty pounds sterling per annum was mentioned, more than sufficient to allow him to reduce his work as notary. He stole a look at MacKenzie whose expression told him that committing so much money was risky. He should invest a smaller amount, not put all his eggs in one basket. No doubt some pithy Gaelic aphorism would be quoted to support such a view. But he did not care. He would have to take risks if he wanted to rise. No capital could be created without risk. He felt like a man at last, rather than a stupid boy. He believed his mother was wrong. He could be a good-looking man. If he was not, why was Agnes interested in him? He had never been more certain about anything in his life. He was no longer the lugubrious clerk who did everything he was told. He was a man of business in his own right.

'Please pass round the articles, Davie.'

He had drafted them carefully and Morrison had arranged for them to be printed. It was the first time he saw his words in print and it gave him much pleasure. He spoke his words deliberately. 'I've considered carefully this investment opportunity. I believe it offers all thinking men of trade a first class opportunity to make a good return on their capital,' and it was over. With relief he turned to Morrison's beaming face.

'I'll now open the floor to questions, gentlemen.'

'Will the ship be insured?' asked a lawyer at the back.

'We'll buy insurance in London,' replied Morrison. 'I believe it'll cost about seven per cent but will cover us in case of difficulties.'

'What goods will you take to the Indies?' asked a merchant.

'Whatever Scotland can provide of quality at a reasonable price – the best linen and woollens... We'll buy as much as the ship can hold.'

'I've goods for sale,' replied the merchant. 'You can buy from me, sir.' There were laughs around the coffee house.

'I've fine linen,' said another.

'And I, too!'

Scougall knew they hoped to benefit by selling their own goods to the company. But would they invest their money in it?

'We'll buy from all who can provide quality products,' added Morrison.

'What will you do if the Dutch don't allow you to trade at Batavia?' asked Lammington.

'We will be allowed. The demand for spices in Europe is vast, the supply plentiful. If we can't gain access to the port, we'll find traders who will buy for us. However, I've been assured by Dutch friends we'll not sail home with empty holds.'

'What if the ship sinks?' asked Grimston, taking to his feet to ask the question.

'We'll send a second ship. But it won't sink, sir. We should not focus on the risks, rather the opportunities. If we stressed the risks we would remain at our firesides, jealously berating the success of others. Look at the Dutch who are careful and sober men. There can be no reward without risk.'

'God bless the Prince of Orange!' someone shouted from the back. There were other cries of support and a few curses against the Papists.

'Who'll captain the voyage?' asked another merchant.

'We'll have a Scottish captain. There are many to be had.'

'My brother-in-law's an experienced sea-faring man,' replied the merchant.

'All candidates will be considered, Mr Hunter.'

'Will the political situation delay the venture?' asked another.

'I'm not a political man, sir. But change is in the air. Others plan similar ventures. I've heard that great men seek to launch a fund. If we are first to raise capital, we'll have a considerable advantage.'

'Who else seeks such a venture?' probed Lammington.

'Pittendean is known to have an interest, as does Tweeddale and his family.'

There were no more questions. Scougall realised it was the moment of truth. They would fail if no one was willing to promise money. He opened the subscription book and passed a quill to Morrison. When he finished writing, he looked up brightly: 'I've signed for two hundred pounds sterling.'

There were claps and cheers.

Scougall took the quill without hesitation. He signed his name and the amount.

'Mr Scougall is in for one hundred pounds. Now, who else is with us? Who's with us, gentlemen?' Morrison asked enthusiastically.

'I'm with you, sir,' said Hunter. 'I'll provide one hundred pounds sterling.'

'I thank you, sir. You'll not regret it.'

Cheers went up for Hunter was known as a canny man of business.

'I'm in for one hundred pounds, also.'

'And me, sir.'

'And me, for fifty.'

'And me, for a hundred!'

'I'll invest ten pounds, sir.' Grimston's gruff voice came from the back.

'Put me down for a hundred pounds,' added Lammington.

A host of others came in including merchants, lawyers, clerks, soldiers, doctors and even a few ministers. Craig, Guillemot and Quinn were among those who invested. Scougall realised that courting the association had paid dividends. All of them subscribed except Johnston. Even Guthrie made a pooled investment of ten pounds with another clergyman.

'Do we have any others?'

'I'll put in a hundred pounds. Our nation needs confident men of trade. I wish you all the best in your venture.' Scougall was delighted by MacKenzie's vote of confidence. He looked down at the list on a scrap of paper, quickly adding up the subscriptions.

'We have two thousand pounds sterling, gentlemen!' It was five hundred pounds more than they had hoped. Scougall was amazed how such a vast sum was raised in the blink of an eye. God was surely shining on them. He had supported the Dutch, now it was the time of the Scots. They were a blessed nation, just as the ministers said. Their success was surely pre-ordained. He could not help blurting out: 'We have a fund, gentlemen. We've raised a capital fund! We have our capital!'

'I thank you all,' continued Morrison. 'The first call will be for half the amount subscribed. Please make your payments at Mr Scougall's office before the fifteenth of December.'

MacKenzie had copies of the killer's letters on the table in front of him. He had been reading them for the hundredth time.

Scougall's repetition of the word 'capital' drew his attention to the letters at the start of two paragraphs in the first letter: T and U. He had a sudden revelation. His eyes darted through the rest of the letter as he noted down the capitals at the beginning of each paragraph. They spelled THIRLSMUIR. It was so obvious now. He grabbed the second letter and noted down the capitals. He was relieved to see they spelled JOHNSTON and not SCOUGALL.

When the crowd of investors had dispersed, MacKenzie approached them. 'May I congratulate you, gentlemen. You'll have money to launch your company, but I'll lose a loyal clerk.'

'I'll still have time to write the odd instrument for you, sir.'

'It's a wonderful opportunity for Davie, Mr MacKenzie,' added Morrison.

'It is indeed. Will you have coffee with me?' MacKenzie indicated to a servant that they would each have a cup. 'I've one or two questions... of my own.'

'I would encourage you to stand in the election of directors, sir,' said Morrison.

'I've no desire to be a director.' Scougall saw MacKenzie's good humour was gone. He waited until a servant brought three cups. 'My questions don't concern trade, Mr Morrison.'

Scougall had forgotten about the killings in the excitement.

'Don't worry, Davie,' said Morrison, as relaxed as ever. 'I'd expected to be questioned by Mr MacKenzie at some point.'

'What did you do after you left the mob on the night Thirlsmuir was killed?'

'I went back to my lodgings. I was in bed shortly after nine o'clock. My sister will vouch for that.'

'Why do you think Thirlsmuir and Black were slain?'

'I've no idea. I'm not a... political man. Trade is everything to me. I attended the association to make contacts from a trading point of view. Many of them have become investors.' He took a sip of coffee before adding 'Papists are surely behind the killings.'

'What was your sister doing that night?'

'Agnes would never!' Scougall blurted out, stunned that MacKenzie could consider her a suspect.

'Calm yourself, Davie. Mr MacKenzie must ask his questions. My sister was at home all evening.'

'Is there anyone who can vouch for her?'

'I don't think so, but I'll ask her.'

'Have you ever been a customer of Maggie Lister, Mr Morrison?'
Scougall bowed his head in embarrassment.

'I've not, sir. I've no appetite for whoring.'

'She's made good money from your association of Presbyterians.'

'I'm a man of trade. Nothing more, nothing less.'

MacKenzie watched him closely. There was something he did
not like about him. 'I've only one more question. Have you ever
borrowed from Lammington?'

'I have not.'

'Then you are one of the few men in this city who hasn't,' smiled
MacKenzie, his demeanour lightening. 'How do you fund your
trade, sir?'

'I use my own capital. I've no need for moneylenders.'

When Morrison left, MacKenzie placed the letters before
Scougall on the table. 'I've something to show you, Davie.'

Scougall was amazed by the discovery.

'We must warn Johnston immediately,' said MacKenzie.

'He believes his life is in danger as a leader of the rabble. I'd
almost forgotten.' Scougall took out his notebook. He had a list
of bonds from the Books of Council and Session showing that
Pittendean was a substantial debtor of Kingsfield. The loans
stretched back over a number of years.

MacKenzie examined his notes. 'The original debt was for
20,000 merks,' he said. 'Each year it was rolled over for a larger
amount at a higher rate of interest. The unpaid interest was added
to the principal. It would be impossible to escape this spiral of debt.
In 1680 Pittendean owed Kingsfield 20,000 merks. The sum is
swollen to more than 100,000.'

'But the debt has not been erased by the Duke's death. The same
sum is due to Kingsfield's heir,' said Scougall.

'Kingsfield's grandson is a boy of four. If Pittendean can secure
the perquisites of office, he might alleviate his financial position
significantly. It will also give him leverage in the Court of Session
when his debts are considered.'

'There's more, sir. A man called Sir Thomas Mann is a witness
to each bond.'

'I've not heard the name before, Davie.'

'Neither have I. Nor have any of my fellow notaries. He's
described as a merchant in the documents.'

MacKenzie smiled. 'STM – Sir Thomas Mann.'

32

A Night on the Town

'IT'S BEEN A success beyond my wildest dreams, Davie. Two thousand pounds will be in our hands in a few days!' Morrison was in exultant mood. Scougall was invited to a celebratory dinner in their lodgings, a small apartment of rooms on the second floor of Sleich's Close.

'I did very little, George.'

'A few serious words were enough to persuade the waverers. I provided the vision; you kept their feet on the ground. And you brought in Dundas and Stoddart and of course MacKenzie. It's just as the great Paterson foretold – you must strike when the iron is hot when raising a fund. It's not about rational argument. It's all about pure emotion. Come, drink up.'

Morrison filled his glass as Agnes entered the dining room carrying a tray. 'George has told me everything, Davie. The great and the good gathered round the table – your words of sense.'

Scougall recalled the couple of sentences he had practised again and again before his glass. He had never thought he could speak in public. But the subscription book sat in his office full of promises of money from a list of more than fifty subscribers. He could not believe how fortune had shined on him since meeting her. He took a slice of the pie. It tasted delicious. All his hard work was paying off at last. He was to rise and he had found an admirable bedfellow.

'What will you do next, George?' she asked, making herself comfortable at the table.

'We must arrange a meeting to elect directors. We also need an iron box for the cash. You might obtain one, Davie. Once we have the money, we'll transfer some to London to pay for a ship. I know a man who will do this cheaply, a London merchant of sound credit called James Smith. We'll travel to the city ourselves soon.'

Scougall had never been outside Scotland before. The thought of visiting London was exhilarating. He had risked his life on a journey to the Highlands, but this would be a trip towards the heart of civilisation, rather than the bosom of barbarity.

'If the King's regime falls, as I hope it will, the great men will flock south like geese. We'll follow in their wake. A glorious future awaits us.' Morrison took a tartlet from the tray, bit into it and complimented his sister on her cooking. 'I must be off,' he said, still munching. 'I need to negotiate bills of exchange. Agnes will entertain you until I return.'

Scougall had not expected to be left alone with her. He watched her clear the table, admiring her pretty face and comely figure, imaging what it would be like to be married, what it would be like to sleep with her. In the midst of his joy, however, doubts bubbled to the surface, feelings which often came over him during happy reflections, like a slice or hook after ten straight drives on the golf course. He wondered if she could find anything attractive in him. In the coffee house he had felt like a man of business, now he was a plain clerk again, hardly the company director yet. He found himself short of words, as usual. She disappeared into the kitchen. He could at least look MacKenzie in the eye, having confessed his foolishness. He would have nothing more to do with the association. As Morrison had said, it was not politics that interested them but money. He was stirred by his speech in the coffee house. He had said that he cared not whether a man was Presbyterian, Episcopalian or Papist. If he had money to invest he stood with them. This was surely a new brotherhood laying aside religious differences in the pursuit of wealth. They would not take the Papist's Mass, but they would have his cash!

Agnes returned carrying a delicious-smelling dish of roast mutton in blood. How appealing her cooking would be after Mrs Baird's familiar fare. He wanted to ask her there and then if she would consider him as a husband, but something held him back. It would be better if he broached the subject with Morrison first. As her father was dead, it was only right. He would do it in a casual way, a few words enquiring if she had any suitors, establishing his interest. Watching her across the table, he felt blissfully happy.

'George tells me you're helping Mr MacKenzie with the murders.'

Scougall was struck by how little he was affected by the killings. 'I've worked with him on other cases.' He did not want to boast, but it was the truth.

'What do you do?'

'I take notes in shorthand. I jog his memory. I propose ideas. Sometimes they are stupid ones, but he says having someone to talk to is helpful. We must consider all possibilities like a game of chess. Even the slightest detail can be important. Stirling often relies on him. I'm pleased to say he puts his faith in me, to some degree.'

'You're changed much from your boyhood in Musselburgh.'

'I was a shy child, Agnes.'

He recalled an image of himself at school, a lonely ridiculed bairn. The cruelty of children knew no bounds.

'You appear less shy each time we meet.' She smiled, but her expression changed as she heard the beat of a drum outside. Another night of protest was in store, a night of violence as Johnston had promised. One that he was supposed to be a part of.

'I hope it'll be over soon,' she said. 'It frightens me. Some of those attacked are not Papists, but good Protestants. The innocent are being targeted too. Everyone is terrified.'

'Things will come to a head soon,' he assured her. 'The Prince of Orange is almost in London. There will be elections in Edinburgh for a Convention of Estates to decide the government here.'

'I've already lost my parents. I couldn't bear losing George... or you, Davie.'

'I'm sure the Papists are behind the killings,' he stated bluntly, shocked by his own confidence, unsure if it was the wine talking, as he had drunk three glasses of sack. 'I know you're unsure about MacKenzie. It's not his fault he was born in the Highlands where he was exposed to unfortunate influences. What he seeks above all is the truth. He'll not rest until the killer's found.'

'I believe him to be an honourable man, if you say he is, whatever the name MacKenzie signifies to Presbyterians. If only life might return to normal, people could go about their business and turn their attention to... other matters.'

He wanted to say something about marriage, but could not think of the right words. 'The kingdom's going through a transformation,' he said finally. 'I'm passing through one too. I used to be tongue-tied, but you and George have woken something in me. A new sun is rising in my life. Despite all the killing, I'm hopeful for the future.'

'I am too, Davie.'

She returned to her seat from the window. As she went to pick up his plate her hand touched his for an instant before she withdrew it. He looked into her dark eyes and felt an effusion of joy course through him.

Morrison was back half an hour later. 'Let's have a nightcap. I know just the place.'

'I've an early start tomorrow, George.'

'Let's celebrate our success over a glass or two of claret. I've something to tell you.'

'And I have something to ask you,' Scougall added, but he did not think Morrison heard him.

An hour later he watched Morrison down his umpteenth glass. 'I'll show you the sites of London, Davie. You'll be amazed... we'll visit Amsterdam and Hamburg... and maybe the Indies... and Africa... Agnes will look after the business here.' His eyes were glazed. He was more than a little drunk. Scougall was not sober. Four glasses were a great deal for him.

'Let's drink to the new company!'

Scougall wondered if it was a good time to raise the subject of marriage, but decided he should wait until his mind was clear, although he had an overwhelming urge to let the world know of his love. He was on the cusp of saying something, when Morrison stood up, taking his hat.

'Let's risk a few pounds. I feel lucky tonight!'

Scougall was not sure what he meant, but followed obediently as he staggered out of the tavern, knocking into everyone, avoiding fights with apologies, laughter and slaps on backs. They crossed the High Street and made their way down to the Canongate through hoards of inebriated revellers screaming their hatred of the King. Johnston's drink money was spent already. The mob had done its business. They turned into a vennel leading to the south-west of the burgh, and found themselves in a teeming warren of closely packed tenements. Morrison was meandering like the River Forth. At last he found the door he was looking for.

At first Scougall could not tell the nature of the place. They stood in a large room full of men sitting at tables in subdued conversation. A couple of fiddlers played in a corner in a restrained manner. It was all very different from the frenzy of the streets outside. Servants wandered round pouring wine and serving food. His shock at the realisation of where they were was only partly diminished by the wine he had drunk. Gambling dens were the haunt of sinners where the Godless risked everything on the roll of a dice or the turn of a card. The tables were full of all sorts of folk – nobles, lairds, lawyers, merchants, soldiers. He looked round their faces. Some exhibited the agony of loss, while others expressed the joy of success. A few were as impenetrable as stone. As his eyes adjusted to the candlelight, he began to recognise some of the countenances. He had written instruments for many of them over the years. He had an overwhelming desire to be quit of the place, but Morrison grabbed his arm and led him to a table.

'Come, Davie. There are seats here.' Once they were settled, he whispered in his ear. 'Do you have any money? I've spent mine. Will you lend me a pound or two?'

Scougall pulled a few coins from his pocket. 'That's all I have, George.'

'You must have more. I feel lucky tonight...' He leaned close and whispered: 'We could borrow some more, only a few pounds mind... on the security... on the security of the subscriptions.'

Scougall's face wore a look of horror at the suggestion and Morrison rolled his head back in laughter. 'I only jest. I only jest.' He grabbed the coins and turned to the banker. 'Count me in, Mr Law.'

But Scougall knew it was no joke. A young man with a pock-marked face dealt from a deck of cards. 'And you, sir?' he asked politely.

'I don't gamble.' There was muffled laughter around the table. 'He doesnae gamble!' repeated a man in a long wig. 'Then why on earth are you here, sir?' There was more laughter.

'I don't know.' Scougall was beginning to feel unwell.

'Gentlemen.' The laughter drained away as the banker shuffled the cards and dealt them deliberately.

'There you go, Davie!' Morrison moved two coins across the table. 'My debt's repaid already. I knew my luck was in.'

'I want to retire,' Scougall said taking his hat.

But Morrison was not listening. An expression of the utmost seriousness had spread across his face despite his inebriation as he pondered his next hand.

'Goodnight,' Scougall said, wanting to be out of the place as quickly as possible.

'I'm sorry, Davie. I want to stay a little longer. I'll see you tomorrow.'

Scougall was relieved to take his leave. As he made his way out, staggering slightly, he heard a familiar voice behind some curtains. He stopped in his tracks and stole a quick glance through a gap. Lord Glenbeath was deep in conversation with another man at a private table. As he turned his head Scougall realised it was the abuser of the Presbyterians – Graham of Claverhouse. It was a strange combination. Glenbeath's father was a suspected Presbyterian; Claverhouse was the loyal servant of the King.

33

A Witness Comes Forward

STIRLING ASKED TO meet them in Greyfriar's Kirkyard at noon. He chose the secluded spot because he feared spies were everywhere. He no longer trusted his own guards who were in cahoots with the Presbyterians. Edinburgh was splitting at the seams, every tavern packed to the gunnels, every coffee house stowed out. It was difficult to find a place away from the crowds where you could talk without catching another man watching you, weighing you up.

MacKenzie and Scougall were waiting on a small mound among the graves and lavish tombs of rich merchants and lawyers. The spot afforded a good view of the city; the small steeple of St Magdalene's Chapel just below them to the right, the castle looming above and the turrets of Heriot's Hospital visible now and again through the trees. It always pleased Scougall to stand on the hallowed ground where the National Covenant was signed in 1638. He recalled the bravery of a previous generation who had fought against another despot, the present King's father. Charles 1 had tried to force the English prayer book on Scotland. The present King had learned nothing from his father's disastrous rule.

Stirling approached stooping slightly, his tall fleshy body leaning into the wind, as his black cloak billowed round him like bat's wings. 'I've important news, gentlemen.' He waited a moment to catch his breath. 'It's about Innes, the priest who was taken from the Papist meeting. A witness has come forward, a flesher called Bruce. He says he was cleaning his stall in the flesher's market when he heard the mob on the High Street on the night Thirlsmuir was killed. He was about to leave for home when three men came into the courtyard. He ducked behind his booth, fearing it was the rabble. From there he saw two large men carrying the priest. To his surprise they let him down gently and spoke kindly to him. The priest removed outer garments which were placed over other clothes and departed laughing. As the two fellows retraced their steps to the High Street, Bruce heard one of them refer to him as 'Cathcart'.

'That was the name I heard at the association,' said Scougall.

'He must be in the pay of the Presbyterians, pretending to be a priest, but working for those who oppose the King. There's double-dealing going on here,' said MacKenzie.

'Is it connected to the other killings, John?' Stirling asked, perturbed.

'I'm not sure, Archibald. Use your contacts to find out what you can about Cathcart.'

'Is he the killer?' asked Scougall.

'I don't think so. But he's a part of what's happening.'

Stirling looked around, observing the scene, enjoying the peace and quiet for a few moments. 'I still find it difficult to believe Montrose signed the Covenant here.'

'People change their mind,' said MacKenzie.

'He opposed his King, but became his staunchest supporter.'

'We can never tell how we'll act during a crisis. It takes time to think things out.'

Scougall knew MacKenzie referred to his recent deception. 'I'll not displease you again, sir,' he uttered.

'There are difficult choices for us all, Davie.'

Stirling rested his hand on Scougall's shoulder. 'Friendship counts above everything. Remain loyal to your friends... whatever happens. I'll keep you informed, gentlemen.'

'Have you warned Johnston?' asked MacKenzie.

'One of my men spoke to him this morning but he laughed it off.'

They watched Stirling's long back retreat to the gates.

'You must speak to him again, Davie. He has a loose tongue. Find out anything you can about Cathcart but don't mention you know anything about the letters.'

Scougall found Johnston holding court in the College library. He was describing the brutal events of the previous night to a small group of students. Scougall waited in a quiet corner beneath the portraits of Protestant saints Calvin, Luther and Melanchthon.

'I didnae see you last night, Mr Scougall.'

'I was feeling unwell. I heard it was a great success.'

'Too successful, I fear,' he laughed. 'I've a message frae the Crown Officer that my life's threatened like Black and Thirlsmuir,' he added casually. 'It's nae the first time I've received such warnings. It will nae be the last.'

'Let me buy you a pint. I would like to hear more about last night.'

Johnston's face lit up at the prospect of a free drink. 'The scholar always has thirst for beer and wenches,' he smiled.

Johnston suggested they retire to the Ganton Tavern, a drinking den with a reputation as a haunt of rogues. The scene of debauchery and drunkenness which welcomed them repulsed Scougall. Johnston downed pint after pint, while he stuck to wine, sipping slowly, swallowing only a tiny amount. He pretended to be a little drunk as Johnston repeated how the time was ripe for bloody revolution. He joined in toasts to the Prince of Orange, praying that no one would see him in such a place.

The conversation roamed over a variety of subjects but Scougall steered it back to the night the Papists were flushed out by the mob. 'Cathcart must be a fine actor,' he said casually.

Johnston laughed: 'He was brought up as a Papist. His real name is nae Cathcart. It's Robert Pringle. He's a kinsman of a friend of ours.'

'Who is that?'

'He's a cousin of Archibald Craig.'

Scougall was pleased with himself. Here was evidence linking Kingsfield to Pittendean, via a fool, a spy and a fat clerk. Was Pittendean responsible for killing the Duke? But he could not understand how the assassination might be related to the death of his son and the savage attack on Black.

When Johnston went outside to vomit, he paid the bill. In the tiny lane at the back of the tavern, he slapped him on the back and sent him off in the direction of his lodgings, hoping that the killer was not following him. As he watched Johnston disappear into the darkness, fear crept through him. He sloped back home, turning nervously every few paces.

34

A Summons to the Castle Hill

SCOUGALL WAS DISTURBED to see Grimston's servant waiting at his office door the next morning. In the light of day he saw he was an ugly stinking brute.

'He wants tae see you,' he said gruffly.

Scougall could not think of an excuse and was forced to follow him up the High Street to the Castle Hill where Grimston was standing beside a low wall, gazing towards the Pentland Hills. There was little welcoming about him. No pretence of civility reduced the severity of his expression.

'Is it not a fine view?' he said without turning his head.

Scougall observed Greyfriar's Kirk and Heriots Hospital below them; the Pentland Hills topped with clouds in the distance.

'I was there in '66.'

'Where, sir?' Scougall was not sure if Grimston referred to the school beneath them, an institution for orphaned bairns, built at the bequest of a rich merchant George Heriot, or the hills in the distance.

'I was at Rullion Green in November 1666, twenty-two years ago... I left pairt of my arm in those hills!'

Scougall had no idea what he meant until Grimston raised his right arm and brought it down on the wall, making a dull thud.

'I hadn't noticed, sir,' he said apologetically.

'I was trampled by my horse. The surgeon couldnae save it, but I escaped with my life. Many others were hung or sent tae the plantations. I've served the cause lang, Mr Scougall. I've suffered much, fought many battles. I've killed those who sinned against the Lord. I'm willing tae lay doon my life for Presbytery.'

'I think we're very close, sir. I've heard this morning that William...'

'So much suffering caused by Charles Stewart and his Papist

brother,' Grimston interrupted. 'I hae heard he converted tae the Whore on his death bed – both the spawn of Papist bitches! We should nae marry oor princes tae foreign whores.'

'Why did you want to speak with me, sir?'

'Are you a freend of Johnston?'

Scougall was lost for words. Was the boy slain already?

'Are you a freend of young Johnston?'

'I met him for the first time at the association,' he said feebly.

'He kens we battle with Antichrist. This is nae just a struggle for Scotland. It's a fight for aw oor souls.' At this point, Grimston turned directly to him. 'Scotland must be rid of bishops! They're the spew of tyrants. There's naething I wouldn't do tae free this realm frae Antichrist.' He turned to the hills again and spoke calmly. 'I would cut aff ma brither's airm. I would slit ma mither's throat. I would kill ony man that stood in my way.'

Scougall felt he was in the presence of a fanatic.

'I would kill you if I had tae, Mr Scougall,' he said in a matter-of-fact way, as if telling him the price of a loaf of bread.

A blade of fear shot through Scougall as Grimston edged nearer. He could smell his stale breath and the damp reek of his old clothes. He saw his wig was stained yellow with age and noticed a louse nestling there, and another, and another.

'You must understand,' he whispered, 'if you stood in the way of Presbytery, if you thwarted the battle, I would cast you on tae the rocks – watch your skull smashed tae a thousand pieces, the corbies feasting on your brains.' He suddenly held his arm aloft, revealing a metal spike at the end below the cuff of his shirt, and grabbed Scougall's jacket with his good hand. Scougall feared that he was going to be hurled over the rock face but the grip loosened. Grimston took a step back. There was an ugly smile on his face.

'Dinnae worry, Mr Scougall. I ken you're loyal tae the cause, despite your friendship with MacKenzie. I want men who I can trust when the time comes.'

'When the time comes?' Scougall asked hoarsely.

'When the struggle reaches a peak, I need to ken who's with me and who's agin me. You're either with me or agin me. There's nae halfway hoose in the fight between Christ Jesus and Satan. Are you with me, sir?'

Scougall nodded fearfully.

'Side with me when a vote's called in the association. Whatever way I vote, follow. That's aw I want… for now. It's nae much tae ask, is it?'

Scougall found himself replying: 'I'm with you, sir.'

'That's good. That's what I wanted tae hear.'

Grimston looked towards the hills again and spoke quietly with a sigh: 'Lammington's a sinner. He's a drunkard, a gambler and a vile usurer. He doesnae prostrate himself before his Maker. He seeks power over others in this kingdom. How can such a man pretend tae lead the Godly? He's surely nae one of God's chosen like me. I've been promised everlasting life from the start of time. Lammington talks of obedience to God while he seeks the whore to assuage his lust. Oh vile hypocrite! He lusts after power as he desires the body of the scarlet woman.'

Scougall did not know what to say.

'Dr Black was cut frae the same stane. Degenerates, aw of them!'

He was desperate to be away from him.

'The things I could tell you aboot the holy Baillie of Lammington, the tales of debauchery. I've heard it said that…' Grimston did not finish the sentence, but a smile spread across his face. 'When the time comes you'll side with me. You would not side with the hypocrite. I would have tae seek you oot. I'm the Sword of the Lord! It would be naething for me tae tak you. I've ripped oot the black hearts of those who served Satan.'

'I'm with you, sir,' Scougall knew he should be using the opportunity to question Grimston about the killings but he could not summon up the courage.

'Be gone with you, sir,' were his final words as he turned his gaze to the hills again.

Scougall was relieved to be out of his presence. He made his way quickly down the Lawn Market and found himself in the Luckenbooths. He looked at some new featheries in Shield's stall and tested the shaft of a scraper. But he was not in the mood to make a purchase. With an hour to spare before meeting MacKenzie, and little work to be getting on with, he turned into Flesher's Court where Bruce had seen the priest disrobe.

In the courtyard, surrounded by high tenements on each side, the fleshers were hard at work on their carcasses. He watched them hoist slabs of meat onto their shoulders and dump them on the tables. He stood observing the butchery, reflecting that it was a flesher of a kind they sought.

He was on the point of leaving when he saw Quinn enter the court from Merlion's Wynd. He was about to greet him when Lord Glenbeath appeared a few paces behind. There was so much clamour in the courtyard they did not notice him. He watched them proceed down Dickson's Close to the west, Quinn about ten paces ahead of Glenbeath, who was clearly following him.

He did not like to spy on a man, but he could see MacKenzie's angry expression if he let the opportunity slip, so he waited until they disappeared round a corner, before following about twenty yards behind. The thoroughfare was busy, so it was easy to mingle with the crowd and not be seen.

The pair passed down Cuthbertson's Wynd and entered Mitchell's Entry, a close which led south to the city wall. Scougall peeked down the quiet vennel. There was no one else around, so he let them go ahead, watching them stop in the shadows beside the old wall. He moved into the close and ducked behind a couple of barrels. Quinn removed a bundle of papers from his cloak and handed them to Glenbeath. He looked through them hastily before taking something from his pocket. Scougall presumed it was money. Without saying anything else, Quinn headed off along the wall through a narrow passageway to the west. Glenbeath turned on his heels and began to retrace his steps towards him. Scougall's heart jumped in panic as he pushed himself against the wall, praying he would not be seen in the shadows. He closed his eyes and listened to Glenbeath's stick on the cobbles. His footsteps were getting closer and closer. He thanked God when he walked straight past without seeing him.

He waited for about twenty seconds before emerging from his hiding place. Just as he did so, two urchins appeared at the entrance of the close. It was unclear if they meant mischief, but one crashed into Glenbeath, sending the papers into the air. He cursed violently and took a swipe at one with his cane. The boys took flight, speeding past Scougall as he sank back against the wall. There was a hint of panic in the way Glenbeath sought to retrieve the papers.

One sheet blew down to where he was hiding, coming to rest beside a barrel. He would be discovered if Glenbeath came back to fetch it. His mind raced through a series of excuses: he was taking a constitutional beside the city wall; or looking for Quinn; or looking for his lordship. All of them seemed feeble.

Luckily Glenbeath had not noticed. He gathered the rest under his cloak and headed towards the Cowgate.

Scougall waited until he was out of sight. The business of spying did not come easily to him. He looked up and down the vennel a number of times to make sure it was empty, before bending over to pick up the discarded paper. He expected to see a tract or broadsheet of a political nature which were circulating in the city in vast numbers because of the crisis. He was shocked to see a crude etching of two naked men. He felt disgust sweep through him as he realised one was preparing to sodomise the other. He stuffed it in his pocket. A few seconds later he took it out again to have another look. He should surely destroy the vile thing there and then. What if he was found with it in his possession? Sodomy was a capital offence. He was not sure of the punishment for observing the representation of the act. But MacKenzie would be angry if he destroyed a piece of evidence. After all, he had found another link between the family of Pittendean and the association. Glenbeath's interests went beyond the hunt. He was a gambler and patron of illicit prints. Quinn was supposed to be a religious man who had fled Papist tyranny in Ireland. His perfumery business was a façade for something that smelt foul.

35

Weight of a Body

MACKENZIE AND SCOUGALL plodded up the High Street in the pitch black, summoned from their beds in the middle of the night. It was raining heavily and the wind buffeted them as they slipped on the wet cobbles.

The Weighing House was a large building at the bottom of the Lawn Market which housed the city's weights and measures. It was frequented by merchants during the day. Stirling was waiting under the lintel of the door.

They followed him inside without saying a word. In the middle of the main chamber, a body was slumped across a weighing beam.

'Another one,' said Stirling morosely.

As they came closer, they could see that the body was decapitated, a bloody stump of flesh and bone protruding from the neck, an explosion of blood staining the floor around the beam.

'Is it Johnston?' blurted out Scougall.

'Rosehaugh will be ill-pleased,' Stirling whispered.

'As will the family of this poor fellow,' replied MacKenzie, kneeling beside the corpse. 'What do you think, Archibald?'

'The blood loss suggests the head was cut off here.'

'He's a fellow of some means.'

'How so, John?'

'The ring on his left hand must have a value of a hundred pounds. From the look of his gangly frame, he's not above fourteen or fifteen.'

Scougall kneeled beside him. 'It's Robert Johnston just as the letter predicted. He's the youth who controlled the rabble. He's another member of the club.'

'Are you sure, Davie?' asked MacKenzie.

'I recognise his boots. They have a peculiar buckle which I noticed in the Ganton Tavern. I was sitting with him in an alehouse two nights ago!'

MacKenzie rose to his feet. 'He was beheaded by a stroke of axe or sword. The weapon was skilfully wielded – the head was cleaved off cleanly. Is it left here or taken like the other body parts?'

MacKenzie and Stirling made a search of the chamber but there was no sign of it. Scougall stood trembling, unable to move. Johnston was an arrogant fool, but he was only a boy; a zealot for the cause perhaps, but he did not deserve such a fate. Of the ten who attended the association on the first night, three were slain. He had hoped the murders of Black and Thirlsmuir were unconnected. He could not believe it now. They were being killed one by one.

'Lawtie's on his way,' said Stirling. 'I found this on the other side of the beam... I've not opened it yet.'

MacKenzie grabbed the letter. Although it was addressed to Rosehaugh, he did not hesitate to open it.

I wander the streets. I inhale the reek of middens. I listen to the clamour of urchins, the spew of humanity. The time is at hand, oh my children.

Everlasting sinners must repent. The battle approacheth. The Papists tremble in the Palace as they partake of the blasphemous Mass.

Until all is transformed by Him, I prepare the way. I set the wheel in motion. It will spin until the end of time.

Rise when the time comes. I hear the sighs of the restless. I feel the agony of the incarcerated. I hear the screams of the dammed.

The King is servant of Antichrist. The tyrant worships the Whore in Rome. He is a lover of priests. The people will rise against him.

Hasten the end of the rule of Satan through bloody sacrifice. I will kindle their anger. It will be a rebellion of the righteous.

Glorious land, I kill in your name. I kill for Him.

MacKenzie's eyes darted through the text seeking out the capitals at the beginning of each paragraph. 'Guthrie,' he said handing it to Scougall. 'We must warn him, although he may not accept our help.'

'I cannot see Rosehaugh allocating funds to protect a Presbyterian minister,' said Stirling.

'All we can do is warn him and hope we can find the killer. Let's learn what we can before Lawtie disturbs the scene.'

Taking a candle from Stirling, MacKenzie kneeled beside the body again. He removed a pair of tweezers from his pocket and began to prod the wound.

Scougall wandered aimlessly round the room, too shocked to think straight.

'We're dealing with a man who mocks us, who plays games with us, treating murder as sport,' said Stirling in a forlorn voice.

'I can't work out if he's a madman or someone who wants to make himself appear mad,' said MacKenzie.

'The case is going from bad to worse. Johnston was a darling of the mob. His killing will take their anger to new heights. I fear a cataclysm awaits us, perhaps for England and Ireland also.'

'You suffer from lack of sleep, Archibald.' MacKenzie rose to his feet stiffly. 'There's still hope. A settlement may be reached and the King's position retrieved by a few concessions. We can do nothing about that. What troubles me is the lack of evidence. All we have is a piece of linen from the bawdy-house, a boy's face in the shadows, a crumpled note and three letters predicting the identity of those killed except Black. We must look at the letters again… there must be more in them.'

Stirling looked aghast. 'I'm going to make preparations for my wife and daughter to leave the city. They can go to my sister in Fife. I must see to my money. I'll call in loans and raise as much cash as I can in case we have to leave in haste. The horses must be made ready. I would advise you to do the same, gentlemen.'

'Are you not forgetting you're responsible for finding this boy's killer,' stated MacKenzie firmly. 'Think of Montrose. He fought on for what he believed to the end.'

'The killer mocks me. Rosehaugh threatens me. What am I to do?'

'We must go over the evidence again after some sleep. There must be something we've overlooked. I suggest we meet in the Royal at ten o'clock tomorrow.'

Despite the grim discovery, MacKenzie was feeling enlivened. There was no hint of his malady. His mind was clear; the black bird banished for now. Elizabeth's marriage and the political situation would work themselves out.

Only a couple of days before, Scougall was elated by the success of the company and the prospect of marriage to Agnes. There was now a shadow across his happiness. He feared for his life.

36

The Association Reconvenes

SCOUGALL HAD NO appetite for breakfast next morning. Johnston's violent death disrupted his sleep, the severed neck percolating his fitful dreams. In his office, he kept a chair against the door to stop anyone getting in. He only left for twenty minutes to drink a couple of cups of coffee. He was beginning to acquire a taste for the drink which many folk remarked they could not do without as a stimulant to their thoughts. Others thought it a curse upon the nation.

As he sat at his desk contemplating all that had happened, a boy appeared at the door with a note. He recalled the urchin Troon with the harelip. None of his acquaintances on the street had any idea where he was. The curt statement told him the association was to meet again that evening. His heart sank.

He made his way directly to MacKenzie's lodgings.

'You must attend, Davie. We must learn as much as possible.'

'I fear I'll be suspected as the murderer, sir.'

'I will ask Stirling to post guards nearby. More suspicion will be raised if you don't attend. You must continue to play the role of fervent Presbyterian. That will not be difficult,' he said with a wry smile.

Scougall wanted above all to prove himself worthy of his friendship, so he reluctantly agreed. After a meal in his lodgings, he took himself to Milne's Court on the north side of the High Street. As he entered the square, he saw the gaunt figure of Grimston. Summoning up courage, he followed him into a tenement where Lammington's man directed him to a small chamber. Guthrie was sitting, head bowed in prayer, an arc of stools in front of him, half of which were already taken. Scougall sat beside Grimston who nodded gravely without saying a word.

He realised the time was set aside for prayer, so he closed his eyes and begged God to provide him with a sign of the killer's identity. He did not know if Guthrie knew yet about the letter. Rosehaugh was supposed to inform him, but he would surely pay little attention to a warning from him.

As he tried to concentrate on prayer, he heard the door open and close several times. Nothing was said and he kept his eyes shut.

At last Guthrie rose with Bible in hand and began to read with great expression. He was burning with raw passion as he expounded on the justness of their cause, the necessity of rising up against the tyrant and fighting Antichrist to the last.

Scougall's mind drifted. He wondered if MacKenzie was correct in his belief that the killer was among them. If that was so, it could not be Guthrie. He stole a look to his left as the minister began to read from the Book of Job. Grimston was staring stonily ahead. He was a brutal figure, ambitious for a leading role, vehement in his hatred of Lammington. Was he the killer?

Over his shoulder on the left he caught sight of Morrison's large head. He was the man he hoped to call brother-in-law but he was not the pious character he had first imagined, or the poor exile returning to his native land. He was hungry for success in business and fond of gambling. He could not believe, however, that he was a cold-blooded killer. He was dedicated to trade, although there was something suspicious in his relations with Guillemot. There was also the outrageous request he made in the gambling den.

Beyond Morrison was Guillemot. He recalled the bony hands on his neck, lingering in an unsavoury manner. But what was his motive to murder?

To his right sat Craig, the fat clerk who was capable of anything in the service of Pittendean. There was his connection to Cathcart and his request to assassinate Rosehaugh.

Beyond Craig was Quinn, another incomer to the city. He was a hypocrite: pretending to be a devout Presbyterian while supplying vile etchings.

He recalled the image of Glenbeath trying to recover his prints in panic. Was he pulling the strings off stage? Had he killed his brother or was he taking revenge on his father? Why was he on good terms with Dundee, a loyal servant of the King?

On the far right sat Lammington, puffing thoughtfully on his pipe. He was the most charismatic of the group and appeared the most reasonable. Black and Thirlsmuir were rivals, but Johnston was not. There were accustaions of usury and hints of debauchery, as well as his presence at Maggie Lister's on the day Black was killed.

He wondered if the others were thinking similar thoughts. What they would make of him, a hesitant clerk dragged into the association by a boyhood friend who was a colleague of the hated MacKenzie? Did they think Morrison and he plotted together as secret agents of the Papacy, playing a deep game of obfuscation? It was all a network of deceit, rather than an association of the Godly.

Guthrie closed his Bible. 'Thank you aw for coming at such short notice, gentlemen. The killing of Johnston is an atrocious act. Just as God's work is near completion we are provoked by Antichrist. We must stand firm as we did at Drumclog. If God lets Satan slay us, we should nae run like cowards. God will shine his light upon the killer in his own guid time. Stand firm! Hold steady! The tyrant will be dispatched!'

'Thank you, Mr Guthrie.' Lammington's tone indicated he thought the minister had said enough. 'There's important business to attend to. Things are moving at a pace in the south, much faster than any of us anticipated. We need tae choose someone tae represent our interests in London at this critical juncture. Our views must be communicated tae the Prince of Orange.'

'You are the man to do so, Lammington,' said Guthrie. There were murmurs of agreement.

'I should be the one!' Grimston suddenly bellowed, rising to his feet. 'I've earned the right. I'm senior in years. I fought at Rullion Green and Drumclog. I've spent years in exile. I'm forthright in argument.'

'We need a man with diplomatic skills, nae one who will shout the roof doon,' replied Guthrie.

'I will do nae such thing!'

'You're well known for your temper, Grimston,' said Lammington, a slight smile on his lips.

'I should be the one to go. I've earned the right. I'm trusted by aw the brethren.' He pointed at Lammington. 'He's of... questionable moral character.'

'What are you accusing me of, sir?'

'I accuse you of cohorting with whores.'

'You had better watch that tongue of yours...'

'As we're divided, we must put it tae a vote,' intervened Guthrie. Scougall felt his uneasiness grow.

'All those in favour of Grimston representing us in London,' said Guthrie.

Scougall recalled the conversation on the Castle Hill and the image of his brains smeared on the rocks. He reluctantly raised his hand. He could not bear to look round to see if any others did likewise.

'I count only two votes. All those in favour of Lammington?'

The rest raised their hands. 'Carried in favour of Lammington.'

'He's a vile sinner!' roared Grimston. 'How can such a man represent the Godly? I want nae mair part in this… association of the Godless. I'll fight on myself!' He shouted as he stormed out the room.

Scougall caught Morrison's questioning look. He would have to explain why he had voted against Lammington. He felt the eyes of the others boring into him. Guillemot believed he had bought his vote. He had saved himself from Grimston, but made enemies of the rest. He wanted to be gone, but before he could make an excuse Lammington stood over him.

'We've a few questions for you, Mr Scougall, just as your friend MacKenzie has sought tae question us,' he said sharply.

'What do you make of Seaforth's brother?' Scougall saw he was now Lammington's enemy. He felt his face redden. 'I've heard he's a fine soldier but misguided in religion, sir.'

'I believe he's known to you?'

'I've met him once or twice. He's betrothed to MacKenzie's daughter.' Scougall immediately wished he had not mentioned Elizabeth.

'Where did you meet him?' asked Guthrie.

'At The Hawthorns – MacKenzie's house.'

'Did he talk of religion with you?'

'No, sir.'

'Did he try tae turn you frae the true faith?'

Scougall did not answer. He was to be smeared as an associate of Papists.

'Have you ever heard the Mass, Mr Scougall?'

He shook his head.

'Have you ever celebrated the Mass?'

He shook his head again.

'How close are you tae the Clerk of Session?'

'I'm his writer. I help him with cases.' Scougall was distraught.

He closed his eyes and prayed to God, asking Him to release him from his vows to such an unholy group.

'The MacKenzies are Erastian scum!' thundered Guthrie.

'They're vile hypocrites,' echoed Craig.

'MacKenzie is an honourable man,' Scougall whispered.

'Where does he stand at this juncture?' probed Lammington.

'I believe he takes no strong position.'

'But he's a kinsman of Rosehaugh and Seaforth.'

'He's no supporter of Bishop or Presbytery or Pope.'

Lammington's tone softened and he smiled. 'We're fortunate that you are his... friend, his associate. We must hunt down those that slayed Kingsfield. It's good that he's on their trail. Anything that resulted in Ruairidh MacKenzie being found would be viewed favourably by those close tae the Prince.'

'I'll do what I can,' said Scougall, a wave of regret washing through him. Politics was a dirty business which he wanted no part of it. But was that not hypocrisy? Did he not want bishops banished from the realm as much as the rest of them?

37

Turkish Baths

THE TENEMENT LOOKED ordinary enough from the outside. After passing through an unremarkable vestibule they went down a long passageway. Another door took them into a small chamber where a man sat behind a counter. He let them through another door into a huge room. Scougall had seen nothing like it before. It was the hottest place he had ever been in. Steam was rising from a floor of red tiles and pagan paintings decorated the walls. A few men sat on benches in a state of undress while others rested in bathing pools scattered about the place. Scougall could not believe such a place existed in the heart of Edinburgh – another immoral incursion like the introduction of Papist priests.

He followed MacKenzie towards a figure sitting alone, only realising it was Lord Glenbeath when he spoke. He did not recognise him without coat, wig, jacket and breeches.

'You may want to take off some garments, gentlemen,' Glenbeath laughed. He appeared little bothered by his nakedness, making no effort to cover his chest, which bore a striking resemblance to a woman's. He beckoned them to sit on the stone bench across from him.

MacKenzie removed his jacket, rolled up his sleeves and took off his wig. Scougall unfastened his jacket but left his periwig on. He felt sweat dripping down his back.

'I told you everything already,' Glenbeath began. 'I presume you're still looking for my brother's killer.' He spoke in a slightly mocking manner, not meeting their eyes.

'There are a few points I wish to clarify, my lord,' began MacKenzie. 'You've not been entirely honest about relations with him. We've learned you were not on good terms at the time of his death.'

'Brothers will argue; some will fight. Surely you're not holding to the view that I'd anything to do with his killing.'

'What caused your disagreement?' MacKenzie nudged Scougall, reminding him to take out his notebook and record what was said.

'I admire your persistence, just like good hunting dogs. If you must know, we disagreed on political matters. My father has painted a slightly false picture. I'm not like my brother, as you see. I enjoy food and wine and... I'm something of, how do they say in France, *le bon viveur*. I follow the Epicureans in philosophy. When I'm in the country, I hunt. When at court, I spend. When in Paris, I fornicate.' He said this with a lascivious smile. 'But I'm not devoid of political ambition. My brother was devoted to that side of life. I'm devoted to... life itself, in all its flavours, but I still have political views. They were seldom the same as his. My father took his side on such matters.'

'What did you argue about, my lord?'

Glenbeath was silent for a moment as he readjusted the towel wrapped around him. He stretched out his hairless legs towards Scougall. 'I must be careful what I say when so many of our countrymen are in such a frenzy. It's well known my brother supported the Prince of Orange. My father is more canny, although he'll be happy with developments. On the other hand, I'm loyal to the King. He did me great honour when I was at court in London. I saw much of him when he was Commissioner here in Edinburgh. Some might say he was placed on the throne by God.'

'Are you on good terms with Dundee?' asked MacKenzie.

Glenbeath hesitated. He looked down and swept an imaginary crumb from his towel. 'He's a loyal servant of the King and a... brave soldier. I've met him... a few times in society.'

'So you differed substantially on politics.'

'My brother held his views more strongly. He despised what he saw as my cynicism. He thought I took nothing seriously because of my devotion to pleasure. He grew angry when I questioned the wisdom of steering the family too close to the Presbyterian side. I thought we should maintain links with both parties, just in case the wind blew back towards King James, as it may still do. He cursed me. I cursed him back. But there was no violence between us, only silence. We didn't speak in the weeks before his death.'

'There was jealousy between you?'

'How do you mean, sir?'

'Everyone describes his eloquence in Parliament. You're not

gifted in that way.'

'You refer to my awkwardness, my strange posture, Mr MacKenzie. I was thrown from a horse as a boy. My spine was badly damaged. In my youth I could not stand straight like him. I'll admit I hated him. But I would never kill my own flesh and blood. How would I benefit from such an act? It was only a stupid argument. Within a few weeks we would've been on speaking terms again, if some Papist fool was not loose in the city.'

'Thank you for being so blunt, my lord... I've something to show you.' MacKenzie rummaged in his pocket. 'Do you recognise this crude piece of art?'

Scougall felt his skin crawl. As Glenbeath examined it carefully, a smile spread across his face. 'I hadn't put you down as a connoisseur of such pieces, MacKenzie. I thought you were the dull lawyer. I've seen many of these; most drawn better than this. I've a small collection myself which I'd be willing to show you sometime, if you're so inclined.'

'I'm not inclined, my lord. Can you buy these easily in Edinburgh?'

'You can buy them wherever there is money and men and most places have both, although I fear our country has more men than money. To build up a collection of quality you must purchase pieces in London or Paris or Italy. There you can find art of the highest quality.'

'Who do you buy from in Edinburgh?'

'There are a few dealers. The merchant William Smeall is an importer and George Cairnes and...'

'Andrew Quinn, perfumer, previously of Dublin,' added MacKenzie.

'Yes. I've bought a few pieces from him. He draws some himself.'

'How did you come to know him?'

Glenbeath pulled himself up on the bench, took another towel and wrapped it round his shoulders. 'I don't know. I must've met him in a tavern.'

'Was it through your brother?'

He was silent, looking perturbed for the first time, as he rubbed his fat thighs with the palms of his hands and continued to address the wall rather than looking them in the eyes.

'Quinn and your brother were known to each other,' Scougall found himself saying.

'Yes. I believe it was through my brother.'

'He was also a collector?' asked MacKenzie.

'No. He was influenced too much by our preachers. He worried about sin. I was introduced to Quinn one night.'

'Where?'

'I believe it was at Law's.'

'Law's gambling house.'

'That's correct, sir.'

'I asked this question before, my lord. I would be grateful if you would answer it this time. Who are the principal usurers in this city?'

'You don't give up, Mr MacKenzie. Let me think a little harder. There's a man called Smith who provides funds at short notice. But his rates are high.'

'Who else?'

'The Lamb has been active in recent months. That's what he's known as. His name is Baillie of Lammington. He's an exile returned from Holland.'

'Have you borrowed from him?'

'I have. It's much faster than securing a bond from a lawyer.'

'How much do you owe him?'

'That is between us, Mr MacKenzie. All I will say is that the sum is large.'

'Did Lammington lend to your brother?'

'I'm sorry for misleading you before. I didn't want to draw attention to my own indebtedness. Yes, he owed significant amounts to the Lamb.'

'How large was the debt?'

'I believe it was substantial.'

'But why would Lammington kill him?' Scougall could not help asking.

'Was it done to frighten you, my lord?' asked MacKenzie. Debt was corrosive, eating away at the fabric of society, he thought.

'I'll say this. It's made me more diligent in my repayments, but I've no idea if Lammington was responsible for his death. Now, you must excuse me, gentlemen.'

On leaving the baths, they passed straight to Quinn's shop in Niven's Wynd. Scougall was relieved when MacKenzie asked him to wait outside. Quinn was behind the counter preparing a perfume. When he raised his head, MacKenzie was reminded of his sister.

They shared the same pointed features. He introduced himself and said he was acting on behalf of Stirling.

'I don't know any of those concerned, but I'm sorry to hear of their demise. They were all stout Protestants.'

'I'm told you've recently come to Edinburgh. Tell me something of your history, sir.'

Quinn placed a cork in a tiny green bottle and returned it to a shelf behind the counter. 'I followed the trade of perfumer successfully in Dublin for over twenty years. I had a shop on Castle Street where I lived with my wife and sister. My wife was taken by plague a few years ago. Many fear another rebellion like '41 when we were slaughtered by the Papists. I knew a couple of Scottish merchants who imported my goods. They provided an introduction to the Privy Council so I could obtain a licence to trade in Edinburgh. I'm very grateful for all that the Scots have done for me.'

MacKenzie nodded in a friendly manner. 'Are you known to Pittendean or members of his family?'

'I'm not well known in Edinburgh yet, sir. But I hope to extend my list of clients.'

'Are you acquainted with the Earl's eldest son, Lord Glenbeath.'

'I'm not.'

'Have you ever borrowed money from a man called Lammington?'

'I've not, sir.'

MacKenzie placed the etching on the counter. 'Are you a purveyor of these?'

Quinn did not say anything. MacKenzie noticed cold calculation in his reptilian eyes.

'You were seen beside the city walls with Glenbeath. This was dropped by his lordship.'

Quinn smiled, gesturing with his hands, as if to say what a fool he had been. 'I offer another service to some gentlemen. The perfume trade is a fickle one. When times are good, people are happy to buy such trifles, but when business is soft demand falls suddenly. Such pieces sell whatever the weather. They might be described as illicit by some. They show men and women, or just women or men in various poses. Despite being frowned upon by the church, they are very popular. I believe there's nothing wrong with them.'

'You may not, Mr Quinn. But what of the association to which you belong?'

'I don't know what you mean.'

'Sodomy is a capital offence, sir.'

'I don't practise sodomy, Mr MacKenzie. The prints do not show sodomy.'

'They don't show it but they hint it's about to occur.'

'That's in the mind of the viewer. It's nothing to do with me,' he smiled.

'How did Glenbeath become a customer?' continued MacKenzie sternly.

'I attended a gambling den where I met a number of gentlemen who indicated they were interested in buying my goods. I provided a selection for Glenbeath.' Quinn leaned towards MacKenzie over the counter and dropped his voice. 'I beg that you say nothing about this to my sister, sir. She's of a... pious disposition. She knows nothing of my other business. It would be most upsetting for her.'

He raised the hatch and moved quickly to the door, locked it and turned roud the sign to indicate he was closed. MacKenzie feared he was about to be assaulted, but Quinn returned to the counter and dropped down behind it, reappearing with a metal box. He placed it on the counter and opened it with a small key. 'I buy these from France and the Low Countries. I draw a few myself.'

Scougall was waiting outside.

'Nothing is quite as it seems among the Presbyterians, Davie,' MacKenzie said, seeming to enjoy his discomfort. 'The word hypocrite is never far from my lips when such men are concerned.'

'Quinn may be a liar and a dishonourable tradesman but does that make him a murderer?' Scougall asked.

'He can't be excluded. He stands in public as a pious man.'

'I agree he is a hypocrite, but it's difficult to think of a reason why he would kill.'

38

Storming of the Palace

FOLK HAD FLOCKED to Edinburgh from Galloway and Dumfries and Ayrshire where the Presbyterians took their strength, areas which had always supported the Covenant. The tension rose day after day as thousands flooded into the city, swelling the mob night after night. The target was no longer the windows of suspected Papists, but Holyrood Palace itself, regarded as the centre of the King's power.

When Scougall closed his office at about four in the afternoon, there were already huge crowds, perhaps thousands, swarming around the High Street, chanting, shouting and singing psalms. It was as if the entire nation were crammed into one thoroughfare. Drums were beating through all the quarters of the town, summoning everyone to the street.

He locked his door carefully, hoping his office would not be ransacked, and returned to his lodgings, unsure if he should venture onto the streets later to observe events. MacKenzie warned him to remain in doors. As he sat with Mrs Baird over a capon and a cup of ale, the noise from outside kept getting louder. After eating, he retired to his chamber to dip into a book. He had only read a page or two when there was a banging on his door. Mrs Baird was screaming that she had heard from her neighbour Mrs Strachan that Papist soldiers were in the town. God help them, they would be slain in their beds!

He felt he had to venture out to find out the truth. Puting on his cloak, he pulled the hood over his head to avoid being recognised. As soon as he reached the High Street the shout went up that the Popish Chapel in the Abbey was to be pulled down.

With the greatest difficulty Scougall struggled through the vast crowd, edging his way down the High Street, keeping close to the tenements. It took him almost an hour to make his way to the foot of the Canongate where he took up position beside a stone pillar outside a shop which provided a view of the Palace gates.

Stamping his feet to keep warm, he stood listening to the chants and songs of the crowd. At last a serjeant from the Palace appeared at the gates. Scougall was close enough to hear him address the leaders of the rabble. 'Retreat or my troops will fire!' he screamed.

This threat only increased the ire of the crowd and the soldier was barracked violently as he retreated into the grounds. Suddenly there was a volley of shots. A group of soldiers had taken up position behind the gates.

There was mayhem as those at the front of the mob tried to get back up the Canongate. Scougall was shoved against the pillar so violently he could hardly breathe. He prayed he would not lose his footing, fearing he would be trampled to death.

When the smoke cleared a dozen bodies lay near the gates. Word spread back through the vast assembly that some of the protesters, including a number of children, were butchered, whipping up the anger of the people to fever pitch. Drums continued to beat, psalms were sung; the Papists more violently decried. Scougall remained where he was, fearful about what would happen next, but mesmerised by the frenzy.

At last the town company marched through the crowd. It was commanded by Captain Graham and at the front were a group of gentlemen including the Presbyterian leaders Sir James Montgomery, William Lockhart and Lord Mersington. Scougall spotted some of the association. Guthrie with sword in his hand; Grimston proclaiming his hatred with raised fist; Lammington back in the ranks. They were followed by the Lord Provost and the magistrates of the city in their robes of office. The rabble was armed with a variety of weapons, including old guns, pitch forks, knives and swords.

Scougall realised something significant had happened. The privy councillors had switched sides. They now stood with the mob.

Heralds and trumpeters in bright liveries approached the gates with a warrant ordering the soldiers to quit the Palace. Scougall heard the captain inside shout: 'The warrant's nae legal. It was nae made with full quorum of the Council.'

It was not clear which side fired first but all hell broke loose in front of the palace gates as weapons were disengaged on both sides. Scougall dropped instinctively to the ground and crawled behind the pillar as shots ricocheted off the tenements. The gentlemen and magistrates fled for cover, leaving Captain Graham with the trained bands and the mob behind him. It was a confusing scene. All was smoke and cries and screams.

After about ten minutes of chaos, someone shouted that Graham had taken his men round the back of the Palace through the Water Port and gained entry to the courtyard. The shout went up that the captain of the King's soldiers had fled. In despair his troops began to throw down their arms, encouraging the mob to surge forward. Those at the front were over the gates in seconds, opening them for the rest, who swarmed into the palace.

Scougall moved cautiously from his hiding place in their wake. He entered the courtyard where many of the soldiers were taken prisoner. A number who were lined up against a wall, begged piteously for quarter. It was a sickening sight to observe the mob's blood lust. God's creatures reduced to beasts, slaying with joy. Limbs were hacked off by youths as young as twelve in a frenzy of hatred. He had to avert his eyes in disgust.

The rabble flooded through the palace, pulling down all they could find in the private Chapel and demolishing everything in the Abbey Church which smacked of Popery, plundering the house of the Jesuits in an orgy of destruction, smashing the exquisite carvings of Gibbons, ransacking the furniture from church and palace; chairs, pews, tables, beds, cabinets, pictures, everything that could be hacked loose, was thrown onto a great pile in the courtyard and set on fire. When their work of destruction was done and all the apartments looted, they raided the Chancellor's wine cellars and made themselves as drunk on wine as they had been with zeal.

Scougall was sickened by it all and had a deep desire to be gone. He wandered off in the direction of Arthur's Seat, climbing the lower slopes to St Anthony's Well where he looked back at the huge bonfire in the Palace courtyard. He dropped to the ground in despair and lay on the damp grass watching the rioters like small insects against the flames. He could not understand why the Godly were destroying and killing. When it appeared the frenzy was abated he descended to wander through the devastation. The Palace of Holyrood, once the seat of Scottish kings, was ransacked. It was terrible to see it reduced to such a pitiful state. In the long gallery, portraits of kings stretching back generations were trampled on the ground. There were tears in his eyes as he reflected how King

James had stirred up the spirit of revolt in his people, subverted the constitution of the kingdom by allowing the Mass to be celebrated contrary to the laws of the realm. He had whipped up the people's anger and unleashed the mob like a storm. He was responsible for the atrocities. He did not deserve to be King. The people had risen up to overthrow a tyrant.

As he stood in the courtyard he was tapped on the shoulder. Lammington had a strange smile on his face. He had been drinking. 'It's a famous day, Mr Scougall. A famous day for Scotland. A famous day for Presbytery.'

Scougall did not have the heart to disagree.

'All those who side with the Papist will be cast asunder,' Lammington laughed. 'A glorious revolution is come tae this nation. It's oor time at last!' He glugged from a bottle and disappeared into the night.

Scougall walked home despondently through crowds of drunken marauders. Many were taking advantage of the anarchy to engage in wanton destruction. Shops were looted, storerooms ransacked, taverns raided. Every rogue took the opportunity to seize what was not his. The Godly brethren did not protect the inhabitants of the town. Some were no doubt drunk like Lammington, but the leaders had melted away, leaving the streets to the scum that had floated to the surface. A drunk took a swipe at him for no reason, swearing at him and calling him a servant of Antichrist. Pushing the man aside, he ran off up the High Street, not stopping until he was at his door. A terrified Mrs Baird was overjoyed to see him alive. He told her all that had happened as they sat in the kitchen, sharing a cup of the brandy which she kept for such desperate times.

'I'm an auld woman who's seen muckle in ma life back tae the days of the Covenant. I've never seen such hatred in the people, even during the prayer book riots in the '30s.'

Scougall remained awake for a long time in his chamber, looking out of his window onto the High Street below. He could see bodies lying unattended. The city was transformed into a scene from Hell. Was this part of God's design, preordained from the start of time? He could make no sense of it.

A short message from MacKenzie summoned him to the Tolbooth. Someone known to them was among the slain. As he plodded through the devastation, he saw that windows were smashed everywhere; goods pulled from shops lay strewn across the street.

Men were lying in corners, nursing wounds or in drunken slumbers. It was as if an army had passed through the city during the night, an army of the damned. MacKenzie was waiting at the door from where Stuart was carried to his execution.

'Is Elizabeth safe, sir?' Scougall blurted out.

'She's fine, Davie, so is Meg. Libberton's Wynd was thankfully unscathed. There was only a little damage done to the shop on the ground floor. This is your new world of Presbytery.' His words were not said in anger, but with resignation. 'Edinburgh was never treated like this, even during the Great Rebellion of 1638.'

'I didn't think it would be like this.' Scougall lacked any desire to argue about politics. He was sick of the whole business of revolution. They had lived in relative peace before. What waited for them now such evil was unleashed? 'Is it Guthrie?'

MacKenzie nodded. Scougall's first emotion was relief.

Stirling took them to a whitewashed chamber on the ground floor where two lines of bodies lay under winding sheets. 'Four of the association are dead. Six remain, including you, Davie,' he said.

Relief gave way to fear in Scougall's heart. The killings would continue until they were all slain. It was God's will that he should be murdered too! 'Should I leave for home, sir?' It was the first thought that came into his head.

'The killer will know you're a Musselburgh man, Davie.'

'It would be foolish, sir. I forgot myself. I would not leave you… or Elizabeth.'

Stirling told a guard to pull back one of the sheets. They looked down on Guthrie's battered corpse. His old face was smashed to pulp. The nose and ears were cut off, the eyes plucked from their sockets. But the countenance was still recognisable. His long grey whiskers descended to a loose hanging jaw.

'He was found in the courtyard of the palace,' said Stirling. 'No one saw anything in the chaos.'

'What will happen now?' asked Scougall.

'Twenty bodies are brought in from across the city. Others still lie in the streets. My guards have no authority any more. Most have fled themselves. How am I to investigate all these crimes?' Stirling seemed oddly calm, resigned to the situation. 'Rosehaugh's time is over. I'll fall with him. It's all come sooner than expected – freedom from the burden of office. I can retire, although considerably poorer than my wife hoped.'

'We still need your help, Archibald. It'll not aid the King, but we may save the lives of the rest of the club, including Davie's.'

'I'll do everything I can, you know that.' There was a hint of a smile on Stirling's face.

'An agreement is still possible, although I know many want rid of him. He's still the King… whatever he does,' added MacKenzie.

'It's perhaps time for another.'

Scougall was shocked that the words came from Stirling, a faithful servant of James Stewart. His reign was surely over if his own supporters were voicing such sentiments. But he felt no elation. He had seen the face of the Beast on the streets, watched men being hacked to pieces. He had learned that the Devil was in the hearts of those who wanted Presbytery as well as those who served Rome.

MacKenzie kneeled beside the body, opened the jacket and searched the pockets. He pulled out a letter. The handwriting was familiar. Scougall could see it was addressed to Rosehaugh.

Urging me to join the dance with my fellow creatures, the drums call me to action, pulling me with their rhythm, drawing me to the streets.

Lay aside thy lassitude. Tonight they burn with anger. They scream, chant and curse, condemning the reign of Antichrist. They declaim the Whore of Babylon. I join the throng. I am one with them. I exalt in their anger. I am engulfed in the current sweeping them to the palace of sin.

Like a tumultuous river made from paltry streams. They are no longer lost or afraid. They are a proud people again. I have made them so.

Oh land of the coward. Oh land of the hypocrite. Oh land of the vanquished. I feel your spirit. This is what I have waited for. This is what I have helped ignite.

Covenanted with God, oh holy land! Tonight the Papist will burn. I am the transforming one in the blackness of the night. I lead them to the palace of shame. The Papists will be dismembered, their limbs thrown to the dogs. They are nothing in the great river of being.

Storm the palace of the priests! I stand with you on the barricade. Those within must be sacrificed. A mighty fire will burn. A mighty conflagration to consume the old order.

All will be reborn, transmogrified through blood.

Scotland renewed! Oh mighty spirit of change, I beseech
you.
    Glorious will be thy revolution.

MacKenzie's eyes darted through the text picking out eight capital letters O...U...S...L...A...G...C...L He sighed deeply.

39

The Road to London

SCOUGALL WAS EXHAUSTED, his face deathly white, dark crescents beneath his eyes. He had not slept a wink since the discovery of the letter four days before, despite Stirling appointing a guard for his personal protection. The lugubrious fellow was standing outside his office door picking his nose.

He saw MacKenzie on the street outside. 'Have you heard the news, Davie?' he said as he entered.

'I've heard William is at St James's Palace and Whitehall full of Dutch guards,' said Scougall in an agitated state. 'The King's taken barge for Gravesend. He's abandoned his kingdom!'

'The House of Stewart does not furnish good kings,' replied MacKenzie. 'It's careless to lose a throne once, but for a father and son to do so is ridiculous!'

'I should be pleased by the news, sir. But I'm... beside myself with worry. I don't know what I should do. I can't stop shaking. I can't be guarded like this for the rest of my days.'

'We'll find him soon, Davie.' MacKenzie put his hand on his shoulder. 'Let's try to think of other business. Politics is fickle but commerce endureth. Tell me of your venture.'

Scougall's appetite for business was diminished by his state of anxiety. He said nothing as MacKenzie placed a small pile of silver coins on his desk. 'There's your hundred pounds sterling.'

Scougall counted them carefully into a leather bag, placing it in the kist at the back of the office. He wrote out a receipt before opening the subscription book for him to sign.

MacKenzie took the book carefully in his hands, staring at it intently. 'I should've thought, Davie!'

'What is it, sir?'

'This contains the hands of all the subscribers.'

'It does, sir.'

'It's worth checking.'

'Checking what?'

'The letter sent to Stuart, of course.'

Scougall had forgotten about it. 'Stirling has the original.'

'Then we must retrieve it.'

A couple of minutes later they were in Stirling's office.

'I'll leave it to your sharp eyes, Davie.'

Stirling was leaning back in his chair. 'Rosehaugh is incensed. The nobles and lairds are all on their way to London, or preparing to go, hoping for audiences with William himself. They'll offer proclamations of loyalty, so that whatever the new settlement brings, they'll not be forgotten in the scramble for office. It's expected by everyone except the King's most loyal supporters that power will soon be in the hands of his son-in-law.'

Scougall studied each signature in the book against the hand in the letter. There were about forty in total. He took his time, savouring a task which took his mind off the prospect of his own demise. The thirty-eighth name matched perfectly. He looked back and forward between the letter and the book half a dozen times to make sure. 'Archibald Craig is the author of the letter. It's as clear as day.'

'We've no time to lose,' said MacKenzie taking his hat.

They were followed down the High Street by the old guard who struggled to keep up, his sword swaying at his side. A coach and horses was waiting outside Pittendean's house in the Canongate. MacKenzie admired the exquisite gold gilding of the exterior and the six black horses. 'It must've cost a small fortune. Such fine craftsmanship doesn't exist in Scotland. Pittendean will make a speedy journey south, providing him with a significant advantage in the scramble for position.'

Scougall was not impressed.

As they entered the gates, Pittendean emerged from the door of the mansion, a diminutive figure in a long wig. Beside him was the stocky figure of Craig. They were deep in conversation.

'May I have a few words with your lordship,' MacKenzie asked politely as they stepped through the gates.

Pittendean looked bemused while Craig was clearly annoyed by the interruption.

'It's not convenient, MacKenzie. I must be in London as soon as possible. The road south hasn't been so busy since James the Sixth inherited the English crown, nor so full of scoundrels!'

'It's very important, my Lord.'

'If you'll sit with me inside, I'll give you a couple of minutes.'

MacKenzie climbed in after him while Craig remained on the street with Scougall. The guard stood a few yards back saying nothing. The coach door was open so they could hear the conversation within.

'My Lord,' MacKenzie began calmly enough, 'We've discovered something about your man.'

Pittendean leaned forward in his seat, suggesting that he was hard of hearing.

'We've identified Craig as the author of a letter.' MacKenzie raised his voice.

'What letter?'

'A letter to Alexander Stuart.'

'What are you getting at?'

'A letter pretending to be from the Jesuits. A letter encouraging Stuart to kill Kingsfield.'

'I believe Craig has little business with Jesuits,' scoffed Pittendean.

'The same man signed Craig's subscription to the company's shares in the Royal Coffee House.'

'Come, MacKenzie, he's accused from his handwriting! Many men have similar hands.'

'It cannot be a coincidence that Craig and the Superior General of the Society of Jesus have the same hand,' Scougall interjected from outside.

'The supposition is preposterous,' Craig replied angrily.

'That's not all,' MacKenzie continued. 'Craig is the cousin of a man called John Pringle.'

'I've never heard of him,' replied Pittendean.

'Pringle is also known as Cornelius Cathcart.'

'I've never heard of the fellow,' said Craig.

'Disguised as a priest, Cathcart was supposedly roughed up by the mob on the night Ruairidh MacKenzie was discovered in a Papist cell. However, the fellow was seen a few minutes later shaking hands with his captors and bidding them good night.'

'I'm afraid you've lost me, MacKenzie.'

'Cathcart was a spy. He was passing information back to the Presbyterians. He encouraged the gullible Stuart, no doubt by suggestion at first. The letter was a master-stroke, making the poor boy believe he had orders from the highest authorities in the Catholic Church.'

'What say you to all this Archibald Craig?' asked Pittendean leaning out of the coach.

Scougall was surprised that the Earl wore the same unperturbed, slightly weary expression.

'I've a cousin called Cathcart. He's a blacksmith in Cupar, my lord. He's no spy. As for the letter, it must be a copy by someone else, surely an attempt to make mischief.' Craig did not smile, however.

'All is explained, MacKenzie. It's just a little misunderstanding. Why on earth would Craig be involved in such a plot?'

'There's more, my lord. Craig also made a request of Davie.'

'What request?'

'That he should assassinate Rosehaugh, just as Stuart slew Kingsfield.'

'Mr Scougall misunderstood me,' interjected Craig. 'I was testing his loyalty to the cause. I didn't think he would take what I said, literally.'

'And you are a beneficiary of Kingsfield's death,' continued MacKenzie. 'A rival is removed from the scene. Kingsfield is not riding to London, but is six feet under the ground.'

'I'm not the only one. What of Atholl and Melville and Queensberry and a host of other nobles?'

'They didn't owe him so much money. You are indebted for 100,000 merks. His death brings breathing room, time for your lawyers to delay proceedings while you seek high office to alleviate your financial distress.'

'I must ask you to leave my coach, sir. You're accusing me of complicity in murder. It's ludicrous!'

'I'm accusing you of arranging Kingsfield's death. I'm accusing you of paying Cathcart to infiltrate Papist meetings. I'm accusing you of a conspiracy of a most evil kind.'

Pittendean looked on the point of saying more, but he sat back in the plush red leather seat and removed a small ivory snuff box from his pocket. Placing a quantity of tobacco on his hand, he sniffed loudly. 'I've never seen the like,' he said calmly. 'The mob is driven to such a fever I fear for my house. Remember I've lost a son, MacKenzie. I'm still in mourning. You were supposed to find his killer. Instead you accuse me of murder and make preposterous accusations against my man, while your chief and future son-in-law flee the city in disgrace... Rosehaugh will soon be out of office. The MacKenzies are finished and you've made an enemy of me!' For the first time there was anger in his voice.

'We have evidence linking you with Kingsfield's death.'

'Your suppositions are fantasy. You clutch at straws because you make no progress in finding my son's killer. I've heard enough. Join me within, Mr Craig. We need to prepare my address. Much is at stake in London. I ask you to reconsider things while I'm away. Stuart was a foolish Papist driven by fanatical delusions.'

As they watched the coach speeding off in a clatter of hooves down the Canongate, MacKenzie cursed violently in Gaelic. 'I fear the evidence will not stand up in court, Davie. Life may be difficult for us if he returns with a dukedom and a place in the government.'

When he was back in his office, Scougall wrote to his parents telling them he would not be home over the New Year holiday as events in Edinburgh made it impossible for him to travel. He knew this would be taken badly, especially by his mother who set great store on the family being together at that time of year. It grieved him that he would not enjoy her table. They were not strict puritan folk but liked to eat and drink well as long as there was not too much show. He feared that she might come to town herself to give him a piece of her mind, so he also penned a short note to his father, directing it to his place of work, telling him the serious nature of the occasion, and advising him that he must not allow her to travel to Edinburgh. He would return home as soon as he could. Nonetheless, a nagging doubt remained in his mind that she would not take a telling, for in the Scougall household there was only one true monarch and despite being Presbyterians, her rule was absolute.

40

Christmas Day in Edinburgh

MACKENZIE LOOKED DOWN on the High Street from his apartments in Libberton's Wynd. Another vast assembly was gathered beneath, the cacophony of sound reverberating through the sash window. He could see a huge construction beside the Mercat Cross, perhaps ten feet in height with a gruesome witch-like visage, a mitre on its head and a crozier in its hand, dressed in the crimson gowns of the Whore of Babylon. He shook his head. This was how the Presbyterians celebrated Christmas; this was their message of joy and rebirth. He could just hear the church bells ringing to celebrate the day above the roar of the crowd.

The effigy burned against the darkness of the early evening as an orgy of hatred rained down upon it. He hoped this would mark the high tide of the people's anger. It was surely not possible for the nation to protest more vigorously its opposition to the King or articulate more stridently its support for William of Orange.

In a matter of minutes it was melted to nothing. The Mass would be said no more in Reformed Scotland. The Papist was banished from the realm. But would the people be content?

Meg was at the door. A boy had a message from Stirling. MacKenzie read the note quickly. There was an important development. Maggie Lister had remembered the surname of the French girl who was with Black. She was called Christine Guillemot.

He wasted no time in summoning Scougall and heading for the wig shop, the tall guard following in their wake. Guillemot looked puzzled by their sudden appearance.

'How's your new piece, Mr Scougall? I see you don't wear it yet.'

Scougall nodded but did not say anything.

'I hear the persecution continues in France, sir,' began MacKenzie.

'It's difficult for me to think of my homeland without shedding tears, especially today,' sighed Guillemot. 'How long it will last, *je ne sais pas*. Louis wants every Protestant turned into a Papist.'

'Have you news of your family?'

Scougall wondered why MacKenzie was asking these questions given what they had just learned.

'I've a cousin in Mazamet converted to Papist who's still in the village. He keeps me abreast of news. There's nothing heard of her.'

MacKenzie straightened his back. Scougall recognised it as a mark of resolve and looked down at his shoes.

'I must apologise for asking, Monsieur Guillemot. I don't know if it's true. We have some intelligence.'

'What do you mean, Monsieur MacKenzie?'

'Maggie Lister has recalled the name of a young woman who was living in Baxter's Land a few weeks ago. She was called Christine Guillemot.'

The colour drained from Guillemot's face. 'Then you must take me to her, sir! How did you hear this?'

'She was employed by Maggie. She disappeared on the day Black was killed. We've just been told her surname.'

'Is this true… how can this be?… is this true, Mr Scougall?' Guillemot turned to him, his face pleading.

'It's what we've been told,' replied MacKenzie.

'In what manner was she employed?'

'Please sit down, Mr Guillemot. I know it's a shock.'

'How was she employed, sir?'

'She was employed… as whore.'

Scougall closed his eyes, not wanting to witness the impact of the blunt statement.

Guillemot howled incomprehensibly. Taking to his feet, his face entered a paroxysm of agony.

'We don't know if it's true,' MacKenzie continued. 'It might be an attempt to mislead us, but I had to tell you. I'm sorry for the pain it's caused.'

'My daughter reduced to whore!' Guillemot screamed. 'I must speak to Maggie Lister, now!'

'You should not do so in such a state. Stirling's men have searched Baxter's Land already. There's no sign of her. No one has ever heard of her. You must calm yourself, sir.'

'How am I to calm myself?' There was a small knife in his hand. 'Just try to stop me, just try!'

Guillemot lounged forward, suggesting he was willing to use the weapon, but he did not look proficient with it. There was a crazed look in his eyes as he fled the shop.

'He'll make a more vigorous search than we ever could. I've already sent a message to Maggie telling her not to let him into her house.'

Scougall was surprised to see MacKenzie looking pleased.

'We're making progress at last,' was all he said.

41

Revelations

MACKENZIE WAS EXAMINING the letters again in his study. He read each backwards, then forwards; he read each word out loud, then every second one, then every third; looking for some kind of pattern. He wondered if they were just a clever trick, perhaps they provided nothing else. His eyes darted from letter to letter, looking at particular phrases – nothing. He rose from his desk and wandered round the study observing his books. His eyes fixed on a copy of the Bible – the source of so much discord among humanity, he thought. Taking it down from the shelf, he placed it on his desk and began to flick through it. He came to the Book of Revelations, his eyes darting through the text, readingly randomly:

'Blessed is he that readeth, and they that hear the words of this prophecy... for the time is at hand... stood a Lamb as it had been slain, having seven horns and seven eyes... the wrath of the Lamb... a rod of iron... upon his heads the name of blasphemy... drink of the wine of the wrath of God... for all nations have drunk of the wine of the wrath of her fornication...'

The letters were clearly influenced by the book, but to what end?

There was a brisk knock on the door and Elizabeth entered. 'I must talk with you, Father.'

He turned his chair towards her as she took a seat beside the fire. 'You must tell me where Ruairidh's gone,' she said.

'I don't know, my dear. Seaforth wouldn't tell me. He said only he'd left the city.'

'I don't believe you. You must know something.'

'He wouldn't tell anyone. It's too dangerous for anyone to know.'

'I don't believe you, Father!' she said shrilly.

'He's maybe gone to the Highlands. He'll be safe in the west or in the islands.'

'When will he return to Edinburgh?'

'That will depend on what happens in London... how things develop there... you know as we say in Gaelic... *Is ioma car a tha'n saoghal a' cur dheth*. Many a turn the world takes.'

'What about our marriage?' she replied in English, ignoring his Gaelic.

MacKenzie rose to his feet and walked to the window. 'We mustn't be hasty... we must tread carefully... I don't know how we should proceed...'

'I will still marry him, whatever happens. I don't care about his religion, father... I care nothing about his past...'

'Things are complicated... we must look at the arrangements again... the financial details... tighten a few clauses... make full provision for your children... are they to be raised as Papists, for instance?' He realised he was sounding like a lawyer rather than a father.

When he raised his head he saw she was crying, holding her head in her hands. He wished with all his heart that his wife was alive to help him. She would know how to proceed. All he knew was that he could not risk losing her. He would have to be conciliatory. 'When things are calmer, I'll meet them. I'll travel to the Highlands, even to France if that's where they've gone. But the path might be difficult... for you both... if there's a change of government... if the Presbyterians are in the ascendancy, or if the King loses his throne. It'll be a trying time for those who were loyal to James. It will be a difficult time for the Clan MacKenzie.'

'It's what I want, Father. I'll do anything, go anywhere. I love him.'

MacKenzie took her hand and squeezed it gently. 'You must be patient. When it's safe I'm sure he'll return. In the meantime I'll keep in contact with Seaforth through my brothers in the north. We'll learn where they're bound.'

Meg's old head appeared at the door and she barked at him in Gaelic.

'Bring it here.' She handed him a note from Stirling.

He sought out Scougall immediately. When they arrived at Stirling's office, Lawtie was leaning over a table working on something. Stirling sat behind his desk.

'A bag's been found in the Nor Loch,' he said. 'Lawtie's

examining the contents.' He pointed to a long knife lying on the table. 'This was found inside it.'

Lawtie turned towards them, his eyes magnified through thick spectacles. He nodded curtly and returned to the task at hand.

'Why's he here?' asked MacKenzie in a whisper. He did not like the grasping little doctor who was only concerned with his fees.

'The contents of the bag... the contents are of an anatomical nature,' replied Stirling, beckoning them to have a closer look.

The sodden bag lay on the table like a black liver. MacKenzie removed the piece of material found in the bawdy-house from his pocket. It was a perfect match. 'The pieces of the jigsaw are coming together.'

Lawtie was poking at something on a china plate with a pair of tweezers.

'These belonged to Black?' asked MacKenzie.

The doctor nodded.

With horror Scougall realised he was looking at the remains of Black's genitals, shrivelled and festered by their time in the loch. Lawtie was trying to prise something out of one of the testicles. He made a number of attempts, cursing each time he failed to dislodge it. At last he held up a small piece of dark tissue, about a quarter of an inch long. Dropping it into a dish, he poured water over it. A small translucent crescent was revealed.

'What on earth is it?' asked Stirling.

'A piece of fingernail,' smiled MacKenzie.

'You're right, sir,' replied the doctor. 'It must've broken off during the attack. It was left embedded in the tissue.'

'May I congratulate you on the discovery, Lawtie,' said Stirling.

'I'm perhaps useful for something,' he laughed. 'Look carefully, gentleman. There's a hint of red varnish on it.'

'He was attacked by a woman, after all!' exclaimed Scougall.

'We seek a woman with red nail varnish,' said MacKenzie turning to Stirling. 'I believe you're well acquainted with such a woman, Archibald?'

'My God! Maggie's such a loving wench. I've never known her to raise her voice in anger.'

42

A Confession

*On the twelfth day of November in the year of God 1688
I killed Isaac Black, doctor, by strangulation within a
chamber in my house. Thereafter I did great dishonour to
his body, by removing his sexual organs with a sharp knife
and disposing of them in the water of the Nor Loch.*

*It was Dr Black's first visit to my house. He appeared
at about six o'clock in the evening saying my establishment
was recommended to him. As soon as I opened the door I
recognised the man who defiled me when I was a ten-year-
old child. He still carried a stick with an elephant's head
carved on the handle. I had never forgotten it.*

*I said nothing although anger rose within me like a
storm. I led him to the chamber, smiled at him, encouraging
him to relax. I helped him remove his wig and pulled off
his boots. There was no doubt in my heart. I offered to rub
his neck and shoulders. He was a little drunk which made it
easy for me.*

*I had him lie face down on the bed and took up position
at his side. I rubbed him softly. I stood up. For a few
moments I looked down on him before raising my skirts
and jumping on his back. I was surprised by my own
strength. It was as if I possessed unnatural power. As I
straddled him I thanked God for bringing him back to me
and providing me with the opportunity for revenge. I felt
power coursing through me. I was exultant. The cord was
round his neck in an instant. I thrust his head down into
the pillow and choked the life out of him, enjoying every
grunt and gasp he made.*

*I waited for a minute. I pulled again. I was lost to
myself. I did not know who I was but I knew I did right.*

I climbed off and checked his pulse. There was none. I looked down on him for a long time, hatred still burning through my veins. He was not an ugly man. He was tall and handsome, so why had he abused me? Why had he beaten me with his stick after he was done with me?

I turned him onto his front and removed his breeches and undergarments. I observed the member that had taken my virginity all those years before.

I left the room to retrieve a knife from the kitchen. I returned and stood beside the bed watching him one last time, my mind pulsing with memories of my debauch all those years before. I sliced off his organ as if it were a carrot or parsnip, cupping it in my palm. It was worth its weight in gold. I dropped it into a bag on the floor. Blood was seeping onto the sheets. I sliced off his balls, and threw them into the bag too.

When it was done, I did not know what to do. My revenge was complete. I felt empty, my anger dissipated. I heaved the body over onto its back. When I looked down on my dress which was covered in blood, I came back to my senses. I went to my chamber, took everything off and threw my clothes in a corner. I would burn them later. I put on another frock, washed my hands and face. I went back to the chamber and tidied the room. As I swept it, I listened to the drip drip drip of his blood on the floor.

I told Janet I had discovered a body and fabricated the story of a French whore. I do not regret what I have done. If I had the chance I would do it again. Black is in Hell where he belongs.

I did not kill Thirlsmuir, Guthrie or the boy Troon with the harelip. I wrote no letters to Rosehaugh as I have difficulty writing.

This confession was written by the notary public John Hastie under direction from me. I sign with my own hand having heard the words read back to me.

Margaret Lister, the Tolbooth of Edinburgh, 26 February 1689

43

A Walk in the Gloaming

SCOUGALL SPENT AN hour in his office attending to business, before meeting Morrison in the Royal Coffee House to discuss the affairs of the company. He was accompanied everywhere by the guard who sat at the adjacent table supping ale after ale, saying nothing.

'I've secured the services of Captain Rammage,' said Morrison enthusiastically. 'He's experienced in the Indies trade. I've begun to purchase goods for the voyage. I'm storing them in a chamber rented in Leith. We'll travel to London in the New Year; take the coach to Newcastle before catching a ship.'

A journey to London would allow him to escape Edinburgh for a few weeks. The killer might be caught by the time he returned.

He spent the afternoon at his desk working on an instrument, a task which brought him no satisfaction. In the gloaming he decided to wander over to the Parliament House for news of events in London. He was accompanied everywhere by Stirling's man who followed a few yards behind him with a loaded pistol in hand. There were more rumours that the King had fled, but they were not confirmed. The Presbyterians were in buoyant mood, but he could not share their exhaltation.

It was good to be out of his lodgings. He had spent too many hours cooped up like a bird in a cage. He walked aimlessly down Greyfriar's Wynd into the Cowgate, passing St Magdalene's Chapel. The demise of Guthrie and Johnston were overshadowed by other matters; the manner of their deaths concealed by Rosehaugh. The opinion on the street was that Johnston was killed in a brawl with another student; his decapitation was suppressed. Bribes were liberally distributed to the town guards. Guthrie's killing was painted as a tragic accident during the great riot when many lost their lives. In other words, it was as if the murders had not occurred. No one knew those slain belonged to the same Presbyterian group. No one referred to the killings in the taverns and coffee houses. Events in England were the sole obsession.

Scougall turned up Niven's Wynd, his mind drifting back to Agnes. He had still not broached the subject of marriage with Morrison, having lost confidence since the last letter was found. He could think of little else but his own demise.

He climbed slowly up the wynd, passing Hunter's storeroom where Thirlsmuir was found. He thought of the boy Troon who had disappeared. There was still no sign of him. He recalled Guillemot telling them that lanterns were to be installed soon. Niven's Wynd required them badly. He could hardly see where he was going in the shadows. He nervously looked behind every few paces. The guard was still there. He looked up as a murder of crows flew overhead.

It was almost dark by the time he reached Guillemot's shop at the head of the wynd. He recalled Helen Quinn's description of Maggie Lister looking in the window. The whore had been executed the day before, her life of sin brought to an end, although he felt pity for her, believing she was a good soul corrupted by Satan. He recalled his Tippendale wig which was still in its box in his press. He had not found the courage to wear it, nor his new shoes or suit. Everything was on hold.

He crossed the vennel to Quinn's shop. It was also shut. He took a deep breath. He could smell the perfumes emanating from within. He was becoming used to the smell, indeed began to like its sweetness. He closed his eyes and inhaled deeply. When he opened them, he thought he saw a figure inside the shop. Perhaps it was Quinn or his sister tidying up after the day's work. He looked round for the guard. There was no sign of him. Where was the fool? Probably off to urinate in a dark corner. That was all he seemed to do: drink and piss. Uneasiness spread through him. He looked around again for the fellow. He had disappeared into thin air. It was getting late. He must get home soon for his meal with Mrs Baird. He would complain about him the next time he saw Stirling. How could a guard spend his time drinking? He was not paid to do that.

After about ten minutes standing alone in the cold he decided to return to his lodgings himself. The foolish fellow would get a fright, but it was his own fault. He would take a shortcut through Jessop's Lane. It was a very narrow passageway, but would save him a couple of minutes. As he entered the shadows, something whistled through the air above his head.

44

Cabinet of Wonders

SCOUGALL'S HEAD WAS stooning when he came round. He could hardly breathe. Something was stuck in his mouth. It was a gag. His eyes blinked open. A thick metal chain was wound round him, pinning him to the floor. He was naked as a newborn bairn. Someone or something had removed his clothing, even his undergarments. Feelings of breathlessness and nausea gave way to terror as he realised he was incarcerated somewhere. He looked around as his eyes adjusted to the dim interior. There was only one source of light – a single candle on a dressing table. He had no idea where he was. He did not know how long he had been lying there.

The first thing that caught his eye was his own periwig on a wooden head on the table. There was a mirror against the wall and above it shelves reached up to the ceiling. On them was a collection of some kind, an assortment of leather goods. He wondered if he was in a craftsman's studio or workshop. The walls were covered in drawings. He craned his head round to get a better look. A disturbing image caught his attention; it looked like a huge pillar of interconnected bodies burning in the flames of Hell.

He looked back at the shelves. In a glass container, a round shape was suspended in translucent fluid. With revulsion he realised it was Johnston's head. Gradually the other pieces came into focus – an assortment of body parts – ears, tongues, legs, arms, hands, fingers, feet, toes, organs – all shrunken and desicated. He was in a shrine to the dead, the lair of Satan himself.

He struggled violently against the chain in an effort to escape. But with each movement it dug more deeply into him. He could only move his neck and hands without severe pain. In despair he began to pray, confessing his vanity and pride. He must have sinned gravely to be imprisoned in such a place, to face an excruciating death at the hands of the Devil. He begged God to save his life.

He thought of Agnes and his desire for marriage and his hopes in the trading venture and his mother and father, kind folk who loved him, and his twin sisters, annoying at times, but whom he loved dearly. He thought of the game of golf which he would miss above all earthly pursuits, recalling the wonderful feeling of a sweetly hit wood on a spring day. He thought of MacKenzie whom he admired above all men. He begged God he would hear the Gaelic tongue spoken by him again.

None of them would have any idea where he was, although Mrs Baird would know he had not returned for his evening meal. She would surely raise the alarm. Then there was Stirling's man, if he was still alive.

He did not know how long he lay in a state of horrified distraction, looking on his nakedness with shame, fearing his fate with an ache as deep as the coldest ocean. He was reduced to utter dejection, the weight of self-pity like a heavy stone upon him. He felt a presence in the chamber coalescing round him, enveloping him, overpowering him. Death was very close.

45

A Visit from Bessie Troon

'I'M SORRY TAE bother you, sir. But I've naebody else tae turn tae.'

'Come in, Bessie. Take a seat by the fire. Would you like some ale?' asked MacKenzie.

'No, sir. I'm fine. Thank you. I need tae speak with you. I'm sorry for the trouble.'

'It's no trouble, Mrs Troon.'

She was cowed by the thought of sitting in a gentleman's chamber but she must do something. 'I've nae seen my boy for twenty days now, sir. It's nae like him. He disappears sometimes for a day or twa, but never as lang as this. I fear something's happened tae him.'

'The town guards are still looking. He might show up.'

'He willnae, sir. I ken he's deid. They've killed him. I ken they have.'

'Who has?'

'There's a coven of witches in the city. They've taen him for Satan. I ken.'

'Why do you say that, Bessie?'

'The ministers tell us witches are aboot…' She began to cry. 'I'll never see him again. It braks ma heart.'

'Tell me about the last time you saw him. You must tell me everything.'

She gathered her thoughts. 'I'd just sold some gear tae Shields. Ye ken his booth by the Kirk. I had a wee bit money, so I gave Doad a few pennies, just a little. He thanked me and aff he goes tae spend it, nae doobt in a tavern, I dinnae ken, but he sauntered aff and that was the last time I saw him.'

'What gear were you selling, Mrs Troon?'

She looked down at the floor. 'I'll tell you, sir, but you must understand I've tae feed ma bairns. Doad took a couple of wigs frae

Guillemot's storeroom.'

'Did he have a key?'

'No, sir. The ither door, there's anither way in.'

'I thought it was bricked up.'

'It is, sir. But a small boy can squeeze through. He just took a couple. But he saw something. He telt me.'

'What did he see?' MacKenzie edged forward in his chair and stared at her intently.

'He saw something the night Thirlsmuir was killed. When the door tae the vennel opened, he hid behind the ither ane in the darkness. He couldna see everything as he peeked through a crack in the door, but he saw Thirlsmuir come in followed by a beast in a cloak. As soon as the key was turned Thirlsmuir was hit. He never saw it coming. He was dragged tae the fireplace. Dodd couldnae see much aifter that. He was so terrified, he slipped through the gap tae safety.'

'You said a beast, Mrs Troon.'

'It was a creature, sir, nae human, a witch. That's what he said. Thirlsmuir was slain by a witch.'

'What did the witch look like?'

'I dinnae ken, sir. Aw I ken is Satan walks among us. Satan is killing these folk, nae other! Doad was a guid lad, sir. I was saving a little for an apprenticeship so he might follow a trade and mak something of his life.'

'Is there anything else, Mrs Troon?'

'No, sir. I should've telt you before, but I feared we would hang for stealing.'

MacKenzie's mind was spinning. He went to his desk and looked down at the Bible still open at the Book of Revelations. He flicked through a few pages, then read: 'And when he had taken the book, the four beasts and four and twenty elders fell down before the Lamb, having every one of them harps, and golden vials full of odours, which are the prayers of saints.'

46

The Lair of Satan

THERE WERE NO windows to hint at what hour of day it was, only the single candle on the dresser which was burned down by about an hour, Scougall guessed, since he had come round. His eyes darted across the horrific drawings on the walls. Obscene images of destruction were everywhere: castrations, crucifixions, impalings. Fear engulfed him like a shawl.

Time lost meaning. Life was reduced to heartbeats. He kept trying to visualise the face of Christ on the Cross... the bristles of his beard, the tears on his dirty cheek, the sweat on his neck. He had died so that he might live. He must cling to that. But did all this show he was not one of the chosen, that he was not one of the Elect? If that was so, he was bound for damnation anyway, he always had been.

There was a sound outside the room. He did not know if he was in a cellar or the highest loft. But there was definitely a sound. He feared that the creature would be the Devil himself. Satan had preserved him for some vile purpose. He awaited torture infinitely worse than the Boot or Thumbscrew.

The sound was getting closer. He realised it was footsteps. Someone was climbing a stair far below. As they got louder he heard MacKenzie's voice speaking as if he was inside the room with him. His words were full of sympathy. 'Calm yourself, Davie. Observe everything carefully. This isn't the Devil but a man. All men have weaknesses. While there's life, there's hope. Use your wits, for God's sake!'

Someone or something was slowly climbing the stairs outside the chamber. For what seemed eternity, he listened to the footsteps getting closer. He imagined a high turnpike stair. He knew he was not in a cellar but a tenement.

When the door opened, he was surprised to see a woman enter.

At first, he was suffused with relief thinking she had come to his aid. He was to be saved after all. He looked up from his chains expectantly. But his hopes were dashed in an instant. Helen Quinn peered down at him. He knew from her expression she was not his saviour. She bore a look of anticipation as though she had come upon meat after a long fast.

'The time is at hand, Mr Scougall.' She spoke in a different voice from the one she had used in the shop. It was deeper and predatory, with no hint of an Irish accent, but the refined diction he associated with a laird's wife.

'You were delivered unto me,' she said as she sat on the stool in front of the dressing table. She observed herself in the mirror, tilting her head coyly to the side, fiddling with her hair. 'You were delivered unto me,' she repeated as she carefully removed her wig. Underneath, her scalp was clean shaven. Scougall had never seen the like on a woman before. The egg-like dome made a vivid impression. She took a cloth and began to wipe her face, removing the makeup that was thickly applied. He could not clearly see her face, only a dim reflection in the mirror. There was no sign of panic in her movements. She took her time, languidly drawing the cloth round her face, wiping it clean.

When she was done, she stood up to look at herself in the glass, admiringly, then in a flourish removed her gown over her head and let her petticoat and undergarments fall to the floor.

Scougall was shocked to see her standing naked before him. For the first time in his life he beheld a woman naked. She moved forward, enjoying her display, swaying as if a dancer on a stage, exhibiting her body to him. It was thin with no breasts. As she turned he saw that the skin over her abdomen and groin was disfigured, rising in rumples of scarred flesh. His fear disengaged rational thought as he tried to take in everything. He began to retch.

'Have you never beheld a eunuch before, Mr Scougall? I served the Sultan in his seraglio.'

Quinn went to the press and removed a garment, a vest or semmet, wrapping it round him. He moved closer to Scougall.

'Do you like my coat of many colours, sir? It's made of the finest leather. Touch it. Feel its soft texture.'

Scougall realised it was a human skin. His heart stopped working. It would not beat. It was stuck. At last there was a thump inside his chest. It began to pump again. There was a ghastly smile on Quinn's face. Round his neck was part of a face attached to the skin. There was a cleft in the palate. It was the boy Troon.

'Do you know how much time it takes to flay a body, Mr Scougall? But it's worth the effort, don't you think? A fashionable piece, indeed.'

Quinn removed the skin, folded it carefully and placed it back in the press. She took out a shirt, undergarments and breeches and put them on, placing another wig on her head. Andrew Quinn stood before him. 'I'm ready for you now, sir.' His voice had an Irish brogue again, but shifted to the higher lilting tone of Helen Quinn: 'Some perfume for your lady, sir?'

Scougall was confounded, unable to take everything in. He tried to say something through his gag.

Quinn dragged the stool to the middle of the room a couple of yards in front of him. Turning it round, he sat down, his legs spreadeagled. His voice changed to a refined Scottish one. Scougall tried to place the part of the country it was from. He was reminded of the gentry from north of the Forth, perhaps Fife or Angus.

'My work's almost done,' began Quinn. 'I returned to my native land after years of absence. I was born and bred in Scotland. I'm of noble birth, the eldest son of an ancient family. I'm no merchant or money-man like those in the association.

'My family believe I'm dead. They kept me chained like a beast in a turret, just as you are incarcerated. They said I was a creature covenanted with the Devil. But I was made by God like all his creatures. I escaped their clutches and wandered the world. I travelled to the Holy Land and beyond, to India and Sumatra. Near Madgascar our ship was taken by pirates. Many were crucified on board. I was a lucky one. Molten tar was poured over me and I was left for dead. I lay for days on the abandoned deck. Finally we were found by slavers. God preserved me for some reason. It was written in the book of life from the start of time. I was taken to the seraglio where I lived with the most beautiful creatures in the world. My manhood was destroyed... but I was still alive. I bided my time. I became the most trusted eunuch... I earned liberties and one day I escaped. Since then I've followed another trade. I've perfected my craft. It's a path only a few can follow.'

Quinn stood up with the candle in his hand to illuminate the walls. 'It's the trade of death, Mr Scougall. I do God's work. I smite the degenerate. I've killed in a multitude of ways. I've committed fratricide. I will end with patricide.'

He continued to speak calmly. 'Like all exiles I longed to return to my native land. I heard the cries of my people. I heard their souls calling me. They begged me to end the rule of Antichrist and I've brought them deliverance. I inflamed the crowd on the streets. I moved it towards fruition. Without the killings, none of it would have happened. I'm the spirit of revolution! I've made glorious revolution!'

Scougall felt an acute pain across his chest. His eyes darted round the room, looking for something that might help – anything. There was nothing else other than the press, the dresser, the shelves, the stool and Quinn.

'Each killing was a sacrifice which brought it closer. I dispatched Thirlsmuir with a blow to the head after the association, summoning him to St Magdalene's, where I asked him to accompany me to a quiet place where I could provide him with the money he desired. I'd taken the key from Guillemot's shop. I cut off his hand and hoisted him onto the spit, extinguishing the flames myself when he was done. Then fate intervened. Black was taken in a bawdyhouse, strangled in his bed as he waited for a whore. I stood in the chamber after it was done, astonished. God was on my side, aiding me. I slit Johnston's throat in a vennel beside the Weighing House, took his head off with a stroke of my sword. I shot Guthrie in the mayhem of the great riot. I plucked out his eyes with my thumbs, cut off his ears, nose and tongue. Behold my handiwork.' He held up the candle beside the shelves.

'Behold my cabinet of wonders! They are my holy relics. On the top shelf there's room for another piece, Mr Scougall.' He gave out a hellish laugh.

'I hear others calling me from across the sea in Ireland and France and America – I'll go wherever Antichrist must be fought. I'll bring them revolution too. He's made me this way. This is how I must serve Him.'

He began to rummage in a drawer under the dresser.

Scougall felt another sharp pain across his chest, like a dagger being stuck into him. He was having difficulties breathing.

Quinn took out a leather bag and placed it on the dresser. He removed a long metal implement, a rod about a foot in length with a sharp curved spike at the end.

Scougall tried to scream, anticipating the agony, but the gag was too tight. He tried frantically to move, but the chains only cut more deeply into him.

Quinn tested the weapon's sharpness against his finger. 'You'll suffer, Mr Scougall. You'll suffer, as I suffered. That's the way of things. I couldn't help what I was. I couldn't help what I did. It was in my nature from the start of time. They didn't know I was born to serve Him.'

Quinn moved towards him, a smile on his thin lips.

Scougall begged God to save him. He had not sinned. He was a loyal servant of Christ. He sought only to serve. He would do anything he asked of him. He prepared for death. The last thing he saw before he shut his eyes was a quizzical expression on Quinn's face. He felt the implement against his chest.

There was a noise beneath. Scougall opened his eyes. Quinn was standing over him listening intently. It sounded like a distant knocking. The knocking continued. There were faint voices, then muffled shouts.

Quinn looked disgruntled, as if at a meal interrupted by the call of an unexpected visitor. He waited, expecting the person to go away. It was surely only a late customer.

The voices stopped. Quinn turned towards him again, hungrily.

But they started again, louder this time, more urgent. There were shouts. The knocking became a banging. The door of the shop was being smashed down. Someone knew he was there! A glimmer of hope appeared.

Quinn held the blade inches above his chest, a look of indecision on his face.

In his mind Scougall pictured his own ribcage being ripped open, his heart pulled out. Quinn feasting on it.

There was a crash far below. The door was down. He could hear footsteps on the stairs, shouts of something familiar. It was his name. 'Davie!' They were shouting his name. He prepared to tackle Quinn somehow. He would do all he could, even head-butting him. It might give him a few seconds.

In an instant Quinn was gone from his side. Putting the tool down on the dresser, he left through the door, closing it after him.

Scougall thanked God. He looked up at the empty space on the shelf. Terrifying moments of silence followed. He could hear the blood pounding in his ears. There was a much louder crash. More shouts and screams, then another long silence. Suddenly, a gun went off, and then another shot, and another. More silence. The moments seemed to last for ever. He counted each beat of his heart, each second of his life. There were footsteps again on the stairs. Someone was climbing up to the room. He closed his eyes, praying it was not Quinn. There was another agonising silence, then murmuring outside. Finally, the door opened.

Stirling entered with a pistol in hand. He looked round the room in shock. Another taller figure was behind him. With joy, Scougall saw it was MacKenzie.

'Are we too late?' MacKenzie asked.

Stirling was at his side. 'He's still alive, but God knows what he's suffered.'

When MacKenzie removed the gag, Scougall tried to thank them. He wanted to shout out that God had answered his prayers. He was not condemned to Hell. It was decreed that he was to live. But all he could do was mumble incomprehensibly before collapsing into unconsciousness.

47

Recovery at Libberton's Wynd

FOR AN AWFUL moment when he woke he thought he was still in Quinn's chamber. But as he came round he saw he was lying in a soft bed under clean sheets in a bright room. When Elizabeth appeared with a tray at the door, he was overjoyed.

'You're in Libberton's Wynd, Davie. You've been out cold for a day and night.'

His body ached everywhere. The chains had badly bruised his arms, legs and torso. His skin was lacerated all over. But he had survived somehow.

Elizabeth sat on a stool beside the bed. She took a bowl and fed him chicken broth with a spoon. He was just able to raise his head.

'What has become of you, Mr Scougall?' she said as she tipped the soup into his mouth, concern in her voice. 'You must eat if you're to get your strength back.' She seemed to have forgiven him for not helping her.

'Is he caught?' Scougall said at last.

'Not yet. But he will be. Don't worry yourself. There are guards at the door.'

The last guard was a useless drunk, he thought. 'What happened to Quinn?'

'He escaped, although Stirling thinks he took a bullet in the leg. He's likely fled the city.'

'He'll have somewhere else, another lair. He could be anywhere, playing another role, male or female. He could be in the tenement next door. He might be one of the guards outside.'

'That's ridiculous. They are two large men, much bigger than him.'

He fell back into a fitful sleep. When he woke in the evening MacKenzie was at his side with a cup of ale and more food. He could just pull himself up in bed.

'What happened, sir?'

'Rest now, Davie. I'll tell you everything later.'

'I must know.'

MacKenzie put down his cup on the table beside the bed. *'Is fheàrr àgh na ealain.* Luck is better than skill. We were very lucky, Davie. Mrs Baird, the good old soul, raised the alarm as soon as you didn't return for dinner. She ran all the way up the High Street to tell me herself. I went straight to Morrison's lodgings, hoping you were there. They were not at home so I searched the usual haunts, returning to Mrs Baird's in case you had appeared. I then got Stirling to have his men search for you. That's when they found a body in Stein's midden with a slashed throat. I feared it was you, Davie. It was the guard.

'I was in a state of confusion. I wandered up the High Street, my mind spinning. I had excluded Morrison based on a critique of his character, in particular the hunger in his face at the company launch. He is driven by money rather than blood-lust. Craig was gone with his master to London. I didn't think Guillemot could be the killer because of the way he reacted to the news about his daughter. I'd already narrowed the field to Grimston, Lammington or Quinn. It was here that luck intervened. Without thinking, I found myself standing before Sarre's players in the Lawn Market. The harlequin stood above me on stage. The close association of 'Harlequin' and 'Helen Quinn' came to me. In a flash I remembered her words when she described her shop with *golden vials full of odours* – echoing Revelations 5:8. The letters were peppered with phrases from the same source. You were saved by a player, Davie! There was another hint a woman was involved. Bessie Troon's boy claimed he saw a witch in the storeroom attacking Thirlsmuir. I didn't realise Quinn and his sister were the same person, but it makes sense. There was an uncanny resemblance. The disguise provided Quinn with the perfect cover to pursue his murderous acts.

'Anyway, I fetched Stirling and we headed straight to the shop. He had no hesitation in ordering his men to break down the door. When we reached the fourth storey Quinn fired at us before jumping through a window. He landed on a roof below and dropped down into the vennel. Stirling and his men returned fire. A search has uncovered no sign of him yet. We found his secret chamber on the top floor.'

There were tears in Scougall's eyes as he recalled his captivity.

Slowly and with many breaks he told MacKenzie what had happened, describing Quinn's claim he was the eldest son of a noble family, his travels and incarceration in the seraglio.

'He said his first crime in Edinburgh was fratricide. What did he mean, sir?'

MacKenzie nodded knowingly. 'Pittendean told us his firstborn was taken from them. Quinn is perhaps… Thirlsmuir's brother! Pittendean's long lost son, returning to wreak havoc on the family that abandoned him.'

'What kind of creature is he?'

'He's a broken spirit, Davie.'

'He's surely the servant of the Devil – a vile demon!'

'A disease of the mind drives him to kill. For him murder is a compulsion. This is suggested by the trophies and bizarre drawings in the chamber. We found the parts of fifty different bodies. He passed from city to city, taking his collection with him, adding to it as he went. A pilgrim of slaughter.'

Over the next few days Scougall recovered his strength helped by Elizabeth's gentle nursing. Even old Meg revealed a tender side of her character he had not seen before. The old woman barely spoke a word of English, but her Gaelic laments helped him find slumber as she sat spinning her thread on the wheel in the corner.

On the fifth day after his captivity he was overjoyed to receive a visit from his parents. He did not share everything that had happened. He knew it would be too painful. MacKenzie only told them the killer had made an attempt on his life.

'I'll hae the beast maself. Gie him tae me!' Mrs Scougall screamed when she was told in MacKenzie's study. But when she looked upon her son, she broke down in tears. Taking the cloth from Elizabeth, she tended him as she had when he was a child with fever.

The presence of his parents comforted him. He knew they would defend him to the last drop of their blood. They had no hesitation sleeping in chairs by his bed at night until his spirits were revived. His father read chapters from the Bible, the words a balm to his battered spirit.

He hoped Agnes would come to visit him. But there was no word from her or Morrison. He was troubled by this, although he expected they had left town for a few days. He dearly wanted to see her, so he could introduce her to his family.

During his days of recuperation he spent much time in prayer, thanking God for his delivery from Satan. He saw he was guilty of the sin of pride, having sought a higher station for himself influenced by Morrison's flattery. God had punished him. The Devil had almost taken him. He felt contrite and begged forgiveness. When he was strong enough, he went down on his knees on the floor of the chamber, prostrating himself before his Maker, calling himself to account before his maker, thanking him from the core of his heart for saving him.

Meg folded down his sheets, fluffed up his pillow and brought him a bowl of soup or a hot drink. Elizabeth sat beside him, chatting over her needlework or reading a book to him. He wanted to ask her what had become of Ruairidh MacKenzie, whether she was still betrothed to him, whether she still loved him, if she knew where he was gone. But it was not his place. She was above him, out of reach.

After ten days, he was recovered enough to return to his lodgings. On the day of his departure, there was a commotion in the house. He could hear Meg crying. MacKenzie came up to his room to break the dreadful news. Elizabeth had left during the night to find Ruairidh. They did not know where she was gone. He feared the worst – they would be married against his wishes and live in exile. Scougall had never seen MacKenzie so despondent. The life was sucked out of him. He tried to find words of comfort, but all he could say was that he would do everything he could to help bring her back.

During his time at Libberton's Wynd it was confirmed that the King had passed over to France, where the Queen and child were gone already. James Stewart was an exile again. There was much debate in Scotland and England about what should happen. Some desired that the princess Mary be made queen in her own right as his daughter; others called for a Regency. The Tories wanted to invite James back upon conditions, while Republicans wished to give the Prince of Orange the powers of a Stadtholder and not a King. Everything would be decided by a Convention to be held in London at the end of the month.

48

Failure of a Bill

TWO WEEKS AFTER his ordeal Scougall felt strong enough to return to the office. As he walked down the High Street in the rain accompanied by two guards, he was surprised to see a small crowd gathered outside his door. Some of them were gesticulating in his direction.

As he got closer he heard shouts of 'There he is. There's the rogue.' At first he wondered if he misheard, thinking that they knew of his experience at the hands of Quinn and wanted to ask him about it.

A merchant who he knew by sight spoke angrily to him: 'A bill of exchange drawn on the company has failed in London, Mr Scougall. We want oor money back.'

Scougall was dumbfounded. 'I've been away for a couple of weeks. I know nothing about it, sir.'

'Feathering your ain nest!' shouted another.

'Open up and gie us back oor money,' said the first.

Scougall fumbled in his pocket for the key. His hand shook as he opened the door. About twenty irate investors pushed in behind him, filling the tiny office and knocking over his writing desk. There were only a few pounds left in the kist. An angry soldier pinned him against the wall by the neck. 'You ken whaur it is, ye greedy wee shite!' Thankfully, the guards intervened, breaking up the protestors and forcing them to leave.

'You'll get all your money back… I'll check with Mr Morrison. There's surely some mistake,' he shouted as the last one left.

When he was alone, he locked the door, leaving the guards outside. He turned his face to the wall and shed tears of self-pity. The world stood against him. He recalled Morrison's drinking and gambling and cursing and his request to borrow money against the subscriptions. He had reaped what he had sowed. He should have probed more deeply into his character, as MacKenzie had suggested. He had been terrorised by Quinn. Now he was humiliated by Morrison. But most of all he felt anger towards himself.

Sitting in The Periwig that afternoon, MacKenzie told him the details of the fraud. Morrison had transferred all the company's money to London using bills of exchange. But it had not paid for a ship or insurance. All of the funds simply disappeared. It was a confidence trick. Money was raised from investors in Scotland and transferred to a rotten merchant in London who could not be found. The tentacles of the fraud spread wider. Morrison had used some of the money to secure a supply of hair for Guillemot's wigs. They were stamped falsely with the mark of Tippendale and shipped to London to be sold as genuine ones. The margin of profit was huge. The export of hair was illegal by act of Privy Council. Guillemot had been caught transporting a batch out of the city and was incarcerated in the Tolbooth awaiting trial. He knew nothing of the whereabouts of Morrison.

'I'm sorry for your hundred pounds, sir. I promise I'll pay it back.'

'You should not take all the blame, Davie. Frauds are not uncommon in the world of business. We should all have delved more deeply into the history of George Morrison. Reputation is everything in finance.'

Scougall shook his head in disbelief. 'I must speak to Agnes.'

He rushed to their lodgings, followed by the guards, but found them deserted. There was nothing left to hint that she or her brother had ever lived there. All the furniture and cooking utensils were gone. The presses were empty. There was not a crumb left in the pantry.

As he was about to leave, a woman appeared. He recognised the wife of the landlord who lived in the floor above. She did not look pleased. 'They left without paying the rent. Are you David Scougall?' She handed him a letter.

My dearest Davie,
    I know you'll never forgive us for what we've done.
    You must believe me when I say I did have feelings for you as a kind and gentle man. I didn't mean to encourage thoughts of marriage in your heart. This was not part of our plan and makes our subterfuge appear all the more cruel. With all my heart you must believe me when I say this.
    George and I are gone to another land where we'll start

our lives again with money to make our arrival less miserable than our coming to Holland. We'll never see each other again. For this I'm very sad, as I was grown fond of you. I know you'll find another woman who is worthy of you and who'll make you a loyal and loving wife.

Agnes Morrison

Scougall felt wretched. Like a tormented schoolboy, he stormed out of the tenement making for the crags beside Arthur's Seat to throw himself of the precipitous cliffs. When he reached the top, he stood at the edge looking down on the city. He could just make out the bells of St Giles Kirk where he worshipped every Sabbath. He recalled the view of the spire from his office window. He thought of Jesus Christ who had died for him on the Cross and realised his family and friends would be devastated if he took his own life. He took a few steps back and felt his anger fall away. He thanked God for helping him reject the folly of self destruction. A few minutes later, he heard the cries of the guard who had followed him down the High Street. 'Mr Scougall! Mr Scougall!'

He stood panting for a while beside him. 'I'll nae get ma siller if you're deid, sir.'

It almost made Scougall laugh. 'I just came up here to think. Don't worry yersel, your siller is safe.'

He had never known a broken heart before and it pushed the hours spent as Quinn's captive out of his mind for a while. In the days following he was more miserable than he had ever been. Even the game of golf appeared a pointless pursuit.

At last, as he was wont to do, he turned to prayer. God spoke to him, telling him he was suffering as His Son had done on the Cross. When Scougall thought of the crucifixion, he recognised his own selfishness and was determined to make amends for his foolishness.

Now and then over the following days, his mind strayed to Elizabeth. He was moved by her kindness during his recovery and saw she was afflicted by her own torments. He hoped she was safe. Above all, he prayed that she was not wed.

49

Jacobite Rebellion

THEY STOOD OUTSIDE Scougall's office watching the long procession making its way down the High Street, a congress of the political nation of Scotland: dukes, earls, viscounts, baronets, knights, officers of state and burgesses plodding slowly towards the Parliament House behind St Giles Kirk, a Convention of Estates to decide who should be King and Queen.

MacKenzie and Scougall followed at the back and stood under the equestrian statue of King Charles II among a large crowd outside the doors of Parliament House. MacKenzie was relieved to see the people's passion was abated. He hoped they would determine the future of the realm by words rather than swords.

'Still no sign of him, sir?' Scougall asked timidly. He prayed every night for Quinn's capture. How could he ever live at ease with the thought he might return hanging over him?

MacKenzie shook his head. 'We'll get him, Davie. Even the Presbyterians are looking for him.'

Scougall noticed how the light was taken out of MacKenzie since Elizabeth had gone.

The doors suddenly burst open and there were cries of 'God save the King' and other proclamations of support for King James from a few Jacobites in the crowd. Scougall was surprised to see the diminutive figure of Viscount Dundee. He was welcomed by a few supporters and enveloped in the waiting throng, before heading down St Monan's Wynd in the direction of the Cowgate.

At the same time Scougall became aware of another commotion beside the doors and shouts of 'he's been stabbed!' An old man in a long wig was holding his neck and screaming in pain. He sank to the ground, blood spurting from a wound. 'Pittendean's stabbed!' someone shouted.

Scougall looked round in panic. It was then that he saw him. He was dressed like the other Cavaliers who accompanied Dundee in a large hat, flowing wig and velvet jacket. For a few moments terror paralysed him. He could not move or utter a word. Quinn turned in his direction. As he looked into his eyes a smile spread over his face. He nodded knowingly, before ducking down into the crowd.

'It's him! It's him! Quinn!' Scougall found his voice again. He was relieved to find MacKenzie and Stirling at his side. 'There he is!'

Quinn was making his way back up the High Street towards the castle.

MacKenzie shouted for the guards to get after him. They had to battle against the flow of the crowd. Few had seen what had happened to Pittendean and they were not interested in stopping Quinn. Scougall feared they were falling into a trap as they sped down the Bow, Quinn's lithe body darting this way and that about forty yards in front.

When they reached the Grass Market, Scougall kept catching sight of him, but losing him again. He was aware of a noise coming from the Cowgate, a deep rumbling sound. One guard was only a few yards behind Quinn, but the crowd was tightly packed and he could not grab him. Everyone was craning their necks to observe something to the left. With every fibre of his being Scougall fixed his eyes on the white feather sticking from the hat of his tormentor.

Quinn slipped through a gap in the crowd, darting across the street towards the south side of the Grass Market where steps led up to Heriot's Hospital. At that moment a troop of horse exploded onto the street, galloping at speed. Scougall lost sight of him in the melee. There were screams as onlookers tried to get out of the way. His eye was taken by the figure at the head of the dragoons. It was Dundee himself, his long wig billowing in the wind, a man of action done with argument who had chosen war. He would fight for King James until his last breath. Scougall saw this in an instant before his eyes sought Quinn among the horses. His nimble body dodged across the street… then he lost him again. The dragoons were gone through the West Port, abuse reigning down on them from the people. Taking up the rear was the ponderous figure of Glenbeath, looking uncomfortable on horseback.

A number of bodies lay on the street. Scougall prayed the creature who had almost claimed his life was one of them.

MacKenzie stood beside a pulverised corpse. 'He was trampled by the horses, Davie. The Harlequin's dead. His final act was patricide: the slaying of his father.'

Scougall looked down on the battered body. He would never forget the thin pointed face. He thanked God from the bottom of his heart.

Epilogue
Glorious Revolution

11 April 1689

'THE CLAIM OF RIGHT is a just document which will form the basis of a lasting settlement,' said Scougall. He took a sip of coffee before continuing: 'King James the Seventh invaded the fundamental constitution of the Kingdom, altering it from a legal limited monarchy to an arbitrary absolute power to the subversion of the Protestant religion. It has pleased God to make his Royal Highness William Prince of Orange, King of England, the glorious instrument of delivering us from Popery and arbitrary power.' He put the pamphlet down.

'I would follow Dundee to the Highlands if I was a younger man,' MacKenzie sighed.

Scougall continued to read quietly: 'The Convention has declared the Crown of Scotland vacant and resolved that William and Mary, King and Queen of England, France and Ireland, be declared King and Queen of Scotland. An oath of allegiance is to be taken by all Protestants.'

MacKenzie took his hat to leave. 'I must return to The Hawthorns, Davie. Elizabeth's been seen in the north. You said you'd go with me.'

Scougall nodded, uplifted by the news.

'We leave tomorrow morning,' added MacKenzie.

Scougall would have baulked at such a journey before, but he felt loyalty burning in his veins. He prayed every night that Elizabeth would not be wed to the Papist.

MacKenzie left to get his horse, while Scougall sauntered up the High Street. The thoroughfare was packed. The city was still splitting at the seams. At the Mercat Cross, the Duke of Hamilton was addressing the crowd. He was proclaiming William and Mary King and Queen of Scotland. There was great rejoicing at every word.

When the Duke had finished, Stirling appeared at Scougall's side. He was in a relaxed mood following his retirement from his position as Crown Officer. 'I've something to ask you, Davie. I'll be finished my history soon... perhaps in a few months. I'd like you to make a fair copy of the manuscript as a man skilled with the pen. I'll pay you, of course.'

'I'll have to look to how much business I have when the book's finished, sir.' Scougall was sure that it would not be completed for a long time.

After the crowds dispersed, he remained at the Cross, pondering everything that had happened. The people had risen up against a tyrant. Scotland had a Protestant King and Queen again. The bishops were still in place for now, but they would be gone soon. Some called it a glorious revolution; others, an unexpected one. The old King, or rather the deposed one, who was still called the King by the Jacobites, was in Ireland, preparing to take his kingdoms back by force of arms, supported by King Louis, arch-enemy of the Protestant cause. Dundee was raising the Highland clans to fight for him. Seaforth and his brother were expected to join him.

Lammington had returned to Edinburgh with a position in the government and a pension of four hundred pounds sterling a year. It was said his forfeiture would be rescinded soon. Grimston had received nothing and was much aggrieved. Glenbeath had joined the Pretender in Ireland, as the old King was called by some.

Scougall thought about his own journey since the previous summer. The memory of Agnes was still fresh in his mind. His heart was still broken, although less so each day. He feared that he would never savour the joys of the married state. The thought of re-entering negotiations with his mother and examining new candidates in Musselburgh was unappealing. Perhaps he would talk to MacKenzie about it during their journey to the Highlands.

Thoughts of his torture at the hands of Quinn lurked in the recesses of his mind, ready to haunt him when he was alone. In his dreams at night, he often returned to the hideous chamber. There he saw himself chained to the floor, a naked creature, perplexed and distraught, preparing to suffer in Hell. He would wake in a cold sweat and pray fervently. He came to see that this was the state of all sinners without God's grace.

As he walked back to his office, the sky was crystal blue beyond the spire of St Giles. It was almost spring. Bells were ringing across the city to celebrate the reign of the new monarchs. His old self would have rejoiced, but he had experienced too much pain. The old certainties were gone from his heart. In their place was something new – a feeling of doubt.

Testament of a Witch
Douglas Watt
ISBN 978-1-908373-21-2 PBK £7.99

I confess that I am a witch. I have sold myself body and soul unto Satan. My mother took me to the Blinkbonny Woods where we met other witches. I put a hand on the crown of my head and the other on the sole of my foot. I gave everything between unto him.

Scotland, late 17th century. A young woman is accused of witchcraft. Tortured with pins and sleep deprivation, she is using all of her strength to resist confessing...

During the Scottish witch-hunt around 1,000 men and women were executed for witchcraft before the frenzy died down.

When Edinburgh-based Advocate John MacKenzie and his assistant Davie Scougall investigate the suspicious death of a woman denounced as a witch, they find themselves in a village overwhelmed by superstition, resentment and puritanical religion. In a time of spiritual, political and social upheaval, will reason allow MacKenzie to reveal the true evil lurking in the town, before the witch-hunt claims yet another victim?

Death of a Chief
Douglas Watt
ISBN 978-1-906817-31-2 PBK £6.99

The year is 1686. Sir Lachlan MacLean, chief of a proud but poverty-stricken Highland clan, has met with a macabre death in his Edinburgh lodgings. With a history of bad debts, family quarrels, and some very shady associates, Sir Lachlan had many enemies. But while motives are not hard to find, evidence is another thing entirely. It falls to lawyer John MacKenzie and his scribe Davie Scougall to investigate the mystery surrounding the death of the chief, but among the endless possibilities, can Reason prevail in a time of witchcraft, superstition and religious turmoil?

This thrilling tale of suspense plays out against a wonderfully realised backdrop of pre-Enlightenment Scotland, a country on the brink of financial ruin, ruled from London, a country divided politically by religion and geography. The first in the series featuring investigative advocate John MacKenzie, Death of a Chief comes from a time long before police detectives existed.

The Price of Scotland
Douglas Watt
ISBN 978-1-906307-09-7 PBK £8.99

The catastrophic failure of the Company of Scotland to establish a colony at Darien in Central America is one of the best known episodes in late 17th century Scottish history. The effort resulted in significant loss of life and money, and was a key issue in the negotiations that led to the Union of 1707.

What led so many Scots to invest such a vast part of the nation's wealth in one company in 1696? Why did a relatively poor nation think it could take on the powers of the day in world trade?
What was 'The Price of Scotland'?

In this powerful and insightful study of the Company of Scotland, Douglas Watt offers a new perspective on the events that led to the creation of the United Kingdom.

The Killing Time: Fanaticism, Liberty and the Birth of Britain
David S. Ross
ISBN: 978-1-906817-04-6 HBK £16.99

In 1638 almost everyone was a Covenanter. Fifty years later, they were a 'Remnant', their great manifesto irrelevant and half-forgotten. In 1685 the government began a draconian campaign against them, which they called, not without reason, 'The Killing Time'. The government of Scotland made it legal for soldiers to summarily shoot civilians without any form of trial. Seventy-eight people were executed and the policy remains notorious. Yet the decades before and after were far more deserving of the name. In the struggle to define what Scotland stood for, thousands perished. One of the victims was nationhood.

Details of books published by Luath Press can be found at:
www.luath.co.uk

Luath Press Limited

committed to publishing well written books worth reading

LUATH PRESS takes its name from Robert Burns, whose little collie Luath (*Gael.*, swift or nimble) tripped up Jean Armour at a wedding and gave him the chance to speak to the woman who was to be his wife and the abiding love of his life. Burns called one of the 'Twa Dogs' Luath after Cuchullin's hunting dog in Ossian's *Fingal*. Luath Press was established in 1981 in the heart of Burns country, and is now based a few steps up the road from Burns' first lodgings on Edinburgh's Royal Mile. Luath offers you distinctive writing with a hint of unexpected pleasures. Most bookshops in the UK, the US, Canada, Australia, New Zealand and parts of Europe, either carry our books in stock or can order them for you. To order direct from us, please send a £sterling cheque, postal order, international money order or your credit card details (number, address of cardholder and expiry date) to us at the address below. Please add post and packing as follows: UK – £1.00 per delivery address; overseas surface mail – £2.50 per delivery address; overseas airmail – £3.50 for the first book to each delivery address, plus £1.00 for each additional book by airmail to the same address. If your order is a gift, we will happily enclose your card or message at no extra charge.

Luath Press Limited
543/2 Castlehill
The Royal Mile
Edinburgh EH1 2ND
Scotland
Telephone: +44 (0)131 225 4326 (24 hours)
email: sales@luath. co.uk
Website: www. luath.co.uk